FEA
IN TH
LAKES

BOOKS BY GRAHAM SMITH

Death in the Lakes
A Body in the Lakes

FEAR
IN THE
LAKES

GRAHAM
SMITH

bookouture

Published by Bookouture in 2019

An imprint of StoryFire Ltd.

Carmelite House
50 Victoria Embankment
London EC4Y 0DZ

www.bookouture.com

ISBN: 978-1-83888-024-8
eBook ISBN: 978-1-83888-023-1

For Daniel. A young man who is a constant source of pride.

CHAPTER ONE

Laura Sinclair fed her key into the cottage door and wondered what shape she'd find her husband in. James had a while-the-cat's-away mentality and she fully expected that he'd have taken his chance to have a decent drinking session while she'd been off visiting her sister in Manchester. The whiff of stale beer that assaulted her nose confirmed her theory.

It had been great to see her sister, but she was glad to be home, not least because her two-year-old niece had spent every waking moment throwing high-pitched tantrums. With the bad weather that was forecast, she'd left first thing, but the drive back from Manchester had still been challenging, and Laura had feared on several occasions while passing over Shap that the billowing snow would close the M6 as it had been known to do.

'James? I'm home, where are you?'

Laura listened but heard nothing. Regardless of how much drink James had consumed the night before, he should have been up and moving around by now. After all, he was due to start work in an hour. His car was on the drive so he was sure to be here.

James's morning routine usually consisted of catching up on recorded TV shows or listening to the radio while he read.

She dumped her bag in the living room, took note of the four open beer cans on the coffee table and strained her ears.

Nothing.

'You'd better not still be in bed, you lazy sod.'

Laura's ire with James was softened by the realisation that if he was still in bed, he'd have to spend the rest of the day at work battling what was sure to be a monstrous hangover.

With the kettle filled and set to boil, Laura marched through to the bedroom, making as much noise as she could. The lazy beggar would have to get up soon and she had no qualms about disturbing his sleep.

The bedroom door squeaked as it always did. No matter how many times she'd asked him to oil the hinges, he'd never bothered to do the job as it wasn't him who got woken up each night.

A part of her suspected he liked that he woke her up when returning from work. He always wanted to chat about his night and then snuggle into her as he fell into his customary deep slumber.

Laura enjoyed the intimacy as well, although she wished James would come to bed before midnight just once in a while. She got that he needed time to unwind after his shift at the Fox and Hounds, but once woken, it often took her an hour or more to get back to sleep.

The further the bedroom door opened, the stronger the stench of stale alcohol became.

'Come on, James. Get up you drunken—'

Laura's recriminations devolved into a scream that became an audible fireball that burned through the cottage.

James was lying on the floor at the far side of their bed. His body misshapen and bruised. At first glance it looked as if he'd been in a car that had tumbled hundreds of feet down a ravine.

Laura wiped the tears from her eyes as she sped across the room and put a finger to James's throat.

He was cool to the touch.

'Please. Please God.'

Laura's fingers pressed down on the part of her husband's throat where she thought one of the main arteries was.

Her fingertips trembled when she felt no pulse.

Desperate, she moved them and forced herself to be calm.

When proof came that her worst nightmare wasn't a reality, it was so faint that it was almost unrecognisable. She pressed a fraction harder, fearful the pressure from her fingers would halt the flow of blood altogether.

There it was again.

A pulse.

It was fainter than a ghost at a thousand paces, but it was there. Confirmation of life. Proof of existence and, best of all, a giver of hope.

Now that she was sure James was still alive, Laura reared back up from her crouched position and retrieved her phone from the rear pocket of her skinny jeans.

Laura got connected to the emergency services and requested an ambulance. It was as she was gabbling to the call handler that the full horror of James's injuries hit her.

The woman on the other end of the line was calm, but she was asking what was wrong with James and that forced Laura to focus on James's shattered limbs.

She looked at how his lower legs had been smashed, his hands and forearms pulped, and his bare chest and face had been distorted beneath a series of what appeared to be angry red welts. Try as she might, she couldn't find the words to describe the damage wrought to her husband. 'Please. Just come quick. His body… it's been broken.'

CHAPTER TWO

DC Beth Young climbed out of her car and fed a few coins into the ticket machine. Not knowing how long she'd be at the hospital, she gambled on four hours, and once the ticket was stuck to her windscreen, she set off for the mechanised revolving door at the main entrance to Cumberland Infirmary.

The call from her boss, DI Zoe O'Dowd, had interrupted her Sunday afternoon with her boyfriend, Ethan, but he'd been due to start work at seven, so it wasn't the greatest disruption. O'Dowd's call had been short on details and long on intrigue. A woman had come home and had found her husband lying in a broken heap.

Beth's first thought was that the man had been playing away and had been attacked by another woman's jealous husband or boyfriend. She knew it was a cynical way to think, but as serious as James Sinclair's injuries might be, Cumbria wasn't exactly a hotbed of gangland beatings, even less so the sleepy village of Talkin, in the northeast corner of the county.

Such was Talkin's anonymity, she'd had to google the village to find out where it was. It lay three miles outside the market town of Brampton, and although its Wikipedia entry taught her about the soil conditions and how the village got its name, it didn't tell her about the village itself. Google listed a pub and a dog groomer as local businesses, but there was nothing else to be gleaned without hours of research.

As Beth marched through the atrium of the hospital, which had the look and feel of an airport, she spied O'Dowd jabbing a stubby finger at the buttons of a vending machine.

'Ma'am.'

O'Dowd plucked the packet of mints from the vending machine's dispense tray and tore at the packet. A faint whiff of cigarette smoke emanated from her mouth when she turned to Beth and gave a nodded greeting.

'What's the panic on this one, ma'am? Sounds like he just got a hell of a kicking. I bet that it'll turn out that he was sleeping around and got caught. My money is that either his wife found out and got someone to do it, or his lover's partner is the person behind it.'

'Awww, Beth, a few months in FMIT and you're turning into a right cynical sod.' O'Dowd's smile showed uneven teeth. 'I'm so proud.'

'Give over.' Beth waved a hand at O'Dowd's comment. She was pleased to be on the Force Major Investigation Team, as they got all the most interesting cases, but she didn't agree with O'Dowd's claim about her cynicism. 'Seriously, what's all the panic on this one that couldn't wait until tomorrow?'

The smile fell from O'Dowd's lips. 'You haven't seen the list of injuries Sinclair has. The beating he took doesn't look like the work of a jealous husband or boyfriend. His legs were broken from the knees right down to the toes. I'm not talking about one single break, I'm talking about a series of breaks a half inch apart.' O'Dowd lowered her voice as a man with a toddler carrying a huge congratulatory balloon passed by. 'His arms had the same treatment to the elbows, and his hip bones have been shattered, as have his ribs, jaw and cheekbones. How he's still alive is a mystery to me.'

'Jeez. Sorry, ma'am, I had no idea the beating was so severe. How is he? Will he make it?'

'He's in a medical coma and apparently the next twenty-four hours are critical, but that's a stock answer if ever I've heard one.' O'Dowd popped another mint in her mouth. 'What are your thoughts now you're clued up?'

Beth took the time it took them to make their way to the ICU before she gave her answer. She wanted to organise her thoughts into a semblance of order. O'Dowd had grown used to her trait of blurting out random words as she processed ideas and went to speak, but there were times when she still felt embarrassed by the habit.

'Come on then, Beth, let's have it. What does that sideways-thinking brain of yours have to offer?'

Beth had learned to ignore the DI's comments about her thought processes. She was well aware that her brain sometimes operated a bit differently to other people's. Her love of puzzles and riddles was what she credited it with, but on a deeper level, she was aware it was more to do with the way her brain was wired than anything she did.

'I called Control on the way here, as I'm sure you did, but for the record, James Sinclair has no police file. He's thirty-nine and he's not once come to our attention before today. No parking tickets, disturbances with neighbours, not even a call to us about something he's seen or wanted to complain about.' Beth saw O'Dowd nod agreement. 'That suggests he's a good citizen. However, the injuries you say he's picked up aren't synonymous with a normal punch-up.'

'The injuries I say?' O'Dowd's tone had grown as cold as the December weather outside. 'Just what do you mean by that? Do you think I'm mistaken? Or worse, exaggerating?'

'Neither, it's a figure of speech, ma'am. I haven't seen the victim myself and I don't know if you have, or if you're taking the word of a doctor. And if you are taking the word of a doctor, what's their experience with regards to the kind of injuries that Sinclair has?'

'Okay, okay. You're not taking anyone's word for anything unless you know their credentials.' Another mint passed the uneven teeth. Beth knew the DI was again trying and failing to give up smoking and that guzzling mints was her way of replicating the hand to mouth movements. 'Carry on and do your best to get to the point without making me feel like a complete imbecile.'

'The injuries are the key point for me. They speak more of a punishment beating or, dare I say it? Torture.'

'You dare. Why do you think we're here?'

Beth let the implied rebuke pass over her head. 'So, we've got an unknown attacker or attackers who're interested in someone who's never come to our attention before today. The obvious steps are to look into his life and see what crawls out from under the stones.' She looked at O'Dowd. 'I'm guessing that we're still going to have to run with the infidelity idea in case it's just a brutal retribution that's been dished out?' A nod of affirmation. 'But we're also going to see what else he's been up to. Someone his age not being on our system for even the tiniest thing isn't usual, which suggests to me that he's either the perfect citizen, or he's taken great pains to not bring himself to our attention. The latter makes me wonder who'd do that. Compared to Sinclair, my father is a lawless thug as he's been caught for speeding three times, and has been done for a bald tyre at least once. Ergo, maybe Sinclair keeps his public face clean while getting his hands dirty behind the scenes.'

'Agreed.' O'Dowd's face took on a softer expression. 'Although I would have said he was too good to be true and left it at that. I didn't need to see all of your workings out.'

Beth spied Sinclair's name on a handwritten piece of card poked into the slot on the door of an ICU ward.

Outside the window of the ward a woman in her thirties was weeping into the embrace of a tall, older man.

CHAPTER THREE

There was little doubt the woman was Sinclair's wife, but they had to make sure she was. So while O'Dowd verified who the woman was and made the introductions, Beth took the opportunity to steal a look at Sinclair.

His body was largely hidden beneath the bed's sheets and there was an array of machines connected to him with leads and tubes. A series of beeps was coming from one of the machines with a regular monotony that suggested Sinclair's current state was indeed stable.

Beth tuned back to the conversation between O'Dowd and Sinclair's family.

'I'm John. Laura's father.'

John's accent was the flat drawl of Carlisle and, while he looked shocked by events and appeared obviously worried about his son-in-law and daughter, he still exuded an air of calmness.

His presence was an unexpected bonus. Not only would he be there for Laura, they'd get his take on Sinclair. Good fathers were protective of daughters, and Beth had a feeling this was a man who would have been likely to have made enquiries of the man who'd married his little girl.

Perhaps it was because he reminded Beth of her own father. Through comments made by friends of the family, she'd learned that he'd made what he considered discreet enquiries about Ethan. When she'd taken Ethan round for Sunday dinner last week, to introduce him to her parents, her father had been his usual friendly self, although she noted that one or two of his questions showed knowledge that she hadn't given him.

It was part of life and, although she valued and wanted her parents' approval, she was enough of her own woman to not require it. But the sentiment behind her father's research was touching even if the way he'd gone about it was outdated.

With luck, John would know of a chink in Sinclair's facade that would lead them to the person or persons who'd attacked him.

O'Dowd led them to the ward's relatives' room and, finding it empty, gestured that they should sit.

To Beth, Laura appeared to be on the point of an emotional breakdown, but her father's guiding arm settled her into a seat and then curled round her shoulders in a way that was both protective and comforting.

Beneath the tear-stained face, Beth could see a prettiness to Laura Sinclair in spite of her evident worry about her husband.

O'Dowd cleared her throat with a phlegmy rattle. 'Mrs Sinclair, Laura, do you have any idea who may have attacked your husband?'

'No.' The single word was stretched into a wail that was backed up by a vigorous shaking of Laura's head. 'James doesn't have any enemies. He keeps himself to himself.'

'So, he's no enemies, then? Surely he's fallen out with someone at some time?'

Laura gave a mighty sniff and used the knuckles of her fore-fingers to massage the tears from her eyes. 'He hasn't. He doesn't like confrontation. Even when someone cuts him up in the car, he never reacts with an angry gesture or a beep of the horn.'

Beth wanted to share a glance with O'Dowd, as this news reinforced Sinclair's saintly lack of criminal record, but she resisted the temptation. The last thing she wanted to do was let either Laura or John see what points interested them with regards to Sinclair.

Rather than let O'Dowd hog the conversation, Beth tried a question of her own.

'At the Fox and Hounds in Brampton. He's the head chef in the kitchen there.' There was pride in Laura's voice as she described her husband's professional life.

O'Dowd's foot pressing against her ankle was unnecessary. Beth knew that commercial kitchens were a pressurised environment where tempers were wont to fray. As the head chef, Sinclair would be the one in control and therefore most likely the one to offend others when complaining about standards not being met.

It was all relative, of course. Depending on the size of the kitchen at the Fox and Hounds, Sinclair could be anything from a sole cook with a fancy title, or a proper head chef with a team of commis and sous chefs beneath him. This was a piece of information that would be easy to learn and, while it could be gathered with a phone call, Beth knew that a face-to-face visit with his employers and colleagues would establish a far more complete picture.

For half an hour they probed and prodded Laura until she could tell them nothing more about her husband.

The picture they got of James Sinclair was that he was a private man. To Beth he sounded obsessive about his privacy. He wasn't on social media and whenever he saw someone about to take a picture he'd turn his head away so his face didn't show.

His past was shrouded as well. He was a Londoner by birth but he'd moved to Cumbria as a teenager when his parents had died in a car crash. Sinclair had no siblings and both his parents were only children as well. At the age of eighteen he'd been not just orphaned, but left without a single family member to help him complete the journey to adulthood.

Whenever Laura had questioned him about his early years in London, he'd squeezed her hand and told her he didn't want to talk about it.

According to his wife, Sinclair had never looked at another woman, nor had he ever accused her of looking at other men.

Like so many other aspects of his existence, his personal life was kept private and he had avoided any possible areas of confrontation.

Laura rose saying she needed the loo.

O'Dowd lumbered to her feet. 'Me too.'

Beth caught the meaning of the sideways nod the DI gave towards the father. O'Dowd was on the same page as her regarding a father's protectiveness.

'Can I be blunt, John?' Beth knew she wouldn't have long to speak to Laura's father. O'Dowd would stall Laura as long as possible, but the woman needed her father's support.

'You want to know what I really think of James now Laura's out of the room?'

Beth smiled at him and nodded. 'You got me.'

'I'm sorry, but I can't add too much to what you've already heard from Laura.'

'You say you can't add too much, that tells me that you feel you can add something?'

'It's nothing concrete. Just a feeling. Look, I love my daughter with all my heart. But I'm also a realist and I know her for who she is, and she can be difficult at times. Argumentative for the sake of it, if I'm honest. With every other boyfriend she's had, she'd end up back at our bit in tears over some argument or other. That's never once happened since she met James. It's like they never argue, and knowing her, that just always seemed quite unlikely. Like all fiery people, she needs someone who stands up to her. Whether James does that in private or not, I don't know. He is a gentle soul. All I can say is, I don't know if it's the truth when she says they never argue.'

John grimaced, went to speak and then closed his mouth.

'What is it?' Beth spoke in a subdued tone.

'What if it happened to James because someone wanted to hurt Laura? She's very driven and isn't afraid to tread on people's toes to get what she wants.' He spread his hands wide. 'If she found out it was her fault he's ended up in this state, she'd be devastated. For all she's fiery, she's also very passionate and I know she loves James to pieces.'

Beth took a moment to think of John's contradictory statements. Her first thought was that John's wondering about Laura arguing with her husband was negated by his later admission. Opposites did attract and while James might be a calming influence on Laura's fierier nature, she would have had to have seriously wronged someone for them to have left her husband with such atrocious injuries.

Her second thought was that Sinclair seemed too good to be true and therefore must have a darker side to his personality. The fact he had told his wife so little about his childhood and teenage years made her curious as to his past. Was it possible that he'd had a rough childhood and had blocked out that part of his life? Or maybe James had done something terrible and had run away to Cumbria to escape justice?

Whichever way she looked at things, she grew more and more convinced that it wouldn't be easy to learn who'd attacked James. With him in a medically-induced coma, no known enemies, and his past a mystery, even to his wife, there wasn't much to go on.

Beth looked at John again. 'Is there anything else about James that concerns you? Does he gamble? Is he a heavy drinker?'

'He likes a drink, but our Laura hasn't ever complained about him drinking too much.' His eyes fixed on a spot in the ceiling as he thought. 'I can't say I've ever seen him drunk, and as for the gambling, neither he nor Laura have mentioned it.' His eyes snapped back and locked on to Beth's. 'Actually, I've just remembered something. We were all on holiday in Tenerife a couple of years ago. Laura and her mum wanted to go to the casino, so we all went.'

'Did he gamble there?'

'No.' A shake of the head. 'Quite the opposite, he watched as we all played roulette and had a few games of blackjack but he never joined in. He never complained, and he was laughing and joking with us, it was just that he didn't gamble.'

'Really? Oh well, that rules that out then.'

Beth wasn't telling John the full truth. A one-off holiday-visit to a casino wasn't exactly going to be a massively expensive experience provided he didn't get carried away. James had gone along and just watched. As much as she knew it was playing into O'Dowd's impression of her picking up the team's cynicism, it crossed her mind that James had deliberately not gambled at the casino because he didn't want a possible gambling addiction to be exposed.

O'Dowd and Laura returned and took their seats, Laura leaning exhaustedly against her father as she fought to maintain her composure.

Beth caught O'Dowd's glance and followed her eyes to the door. The DI was asking if she was finished with her questions and was ready to leave. The nod she replied with was as tiny as she could make it.

As they walked along the corridor on their way out, O'Dowd snagged the attention of a doctor and after flashing her warrant card, asked how bad Sinclair's injuries were.

'Terrible. To be honest, I've never seen such a series of bad breaks. Whether the bones will heal anything like they should is unknown at the moment.' The doctor grimaced and glanced along to where Laura and her father were sitting before lowering his voice. 'Being truthful, if he survives, it'll be a miracle if we don't have to amputate his arms and legs.'

The doctor's last sentence burned at Beth. Whomever had attacked Sinclair *had* to be caught. What if they attacked someone else in the same brutal way? And even if the perpetrator never harmed another soul—everything about the attack spoke of a personal vendetta against Sinclair—they deserved serious jail time for what they'd done to him.

With Sinclair being such an inoffensive type, there weren't many suspects to look at, but with luck, a deeper look into his life would give them a trail they could follow.

CHAPTER FOUR

Beth followed O'Dowd along the path and waited as the DI introduced herself to the sole CSI technician who'd been sent to inspect the Sinclairs' house. The frustrated expression he wore told of the futility of his search.

James's assault was a serious matter, but as he'd survived the attack, there was a limit to how many resources could be allocated to investigate the crime scene.

O'Dowd foot tapped with impatience as she stood in front of the CSI technician. 'Have you found anything?'

'About five billion hairs that could belong to the victim, his wife or his attacker. Other than that, sweet FA.' He gave a dispirited shrug. 'We'll test the ones with root bulbs on, but when you think about how little else I've found, I wouldn't get your hopes up of our attacker having left any trace evidence. I've bagged up the vic's mobile and iPad ready for you to take to Digital Forensics.'

Beth followed O'Dowd's scowl with a grateful nod and trailed after the DI. Once they got inside the cottage she glanced in the lounge, and then set off to find the bedroom. Beth's nose crinkled rabbit-style as she made her way along the hallway. The stench of stale alcohol hung in the air and it got worse as she made her way into the bedroom where James had been discovered.

Upon entering the bedroom, Beth took in the scene in front of her. The room was tastefully decorated in pastel colours and showed a mix of both masculine and feminine touches. One bedside table had a neat pile of books, whereas the other bedside table was littered with women's magazines. A thick duvet had been hauled onto the floor, and when she made her way to the far side of the bed, she saw a few drops of blood.

That was another thing which puzzled her. James's injuries were horrific, but there was very little blood at the scene. Considering the extent of the damage to his limbs, Beth felt that there should have been a lot more blood than the half dozen drops staining the oatmeal carpet.

Soft footsteps and a hint of tobacco competing with the stale beer told her O'Dowd had joined her.

'What's that brain of yours coming up with, Beth?'

Beth kept her smile internal.

'There's not enough blood for his injuries. His hands, feet, forearms and lower legs were shattered yet there's hardly any blood. And that's before you add in the fact that every exposed bone on his torso and face was broken.'

'I know what you mean. You'd think with all those wounds, there would have been a lot of blood.'

'Not just blood, ma'am. Pain. He'd have been in screaming agony with those injuries, yet none of the neighbours called it in.' Beth pointed at the blood on the carpet. 'Do you think he was taken away, beaten, and then brought back?'

'I doubt it. This cottage looks as if it's been around for donkey's.' O'Dowd gave a nod at the window. 'Look how thick the walls are, two foot at least. Plus it's detached. That means no shared walls.'

'I see your point, but I still think he'd have been screaming at the top of his voice. Can we do a test?'

Beth shivered as she walked round to the back of the cottage, her torch picking out the flagged path. The December air was laden with a cold wind and snow was forecast to fall later in the night. She knocked on the window to let O'Dowd know she was ready and focussed all her attention onto her ears.

She could hear O'Dowd's scream. It wasn't terribly loud, but it was unmistakeable. She walked away from the bedroom window until she was at the fence closest to the window. O'Dowd's scream was only just audible. In the neighbour's house, behind another layer of double glazing and thick walls, there was little chance of James's screams being heard.

Beth knocked on the window and gave O'Dowd a thumb's down as she returned to the house.

As she passed the row of bins a thought made her pause. She lifted the recycling bin's lid and shone her torch inside. The bin was empty save for a few magazines that coated the bottom. A check of the other bins revealed they too were empty.

The thoughts she was having were puckering her forehead. To give them further examination she went into the kitchen, looked in the bin and then found a glass.

In the lounge she used her gloved hands to tip each of the four beer cans into the glass. None of them offered up more than a tiny dribble. When she was done, there was less than a tablespoon of flat beer in the bottom of the glass.

O'Dowd walked into the room, a look of consternation on her face. 'Jesus, Beth. Don't tell me you're so desperate for a drink that you're collecting his dregs.'

Beth hoped the glare she fired at O'Dowd conveyed every one of the swear words she would have used had she spoken.

'Come on then. If you're not going to drink it, explain what you're doing.'

'I take it you've smelled the stale beer in here?' A nod from O'Dowd. 'The whole house reeks of it. Do you think this thimble-ful,' Beth swirled the glass at O'Dowd, 'is enough to stink out the whole house, because I don't. In fact, I don't think James drinking four cans is enough to create such a stench. I don't know if you've noticed, but there's a plug-in air freshener in here, the hallway and the bedroom. The house still reeks of booze though. I've checked the bins: there are no more empties, just these four cans.'

'What are you getting at?' O'Dowd rubbed the back of a gloved hand under her chin.

'Four cans aren't enough to cause the smell. Perhaps if one had been half full it could account for it, but they were all finished. Therefore I think he must have been drinking elsewhere, come home with a gutful already inside him and had these four cans before going to bed. That would account for the stink. The duvet being on the floor and him being attacked by the side of the bed suggests to me that he was in bed when he was attacked.'

O'Dowd nodded. 'That makes sense.'

'Unless the victim was unconscious with drink, he'd surely have fought back. Yes, he might have been pissed, but he'd still have given it a go. Other than the duvet being on the floor, there's no signs of a struggle, ergo, there wasn't one. His attacker may well have used his first blow to incapacitate Sinclair, but that doesn't tally with what happened after that. To me, his injuries speak of a punishment beating or someone being tortured. If you're punishing someone, or trying to get information from them, it's better if they're aware of what you're doing.'

O'Dowd tilted her head and gave Beth a look that was half appraisal and half astonishment. 'You don't miss much, do you? So what else do you have?'

'I took a look in his wallet. There are a few credit-card receipts for the pub across the road that are all dated either yesterday or the early hours of today. They're all for the same amount: £7.60. I'll be honest, I'm not that familiar with the price of a pint, but I'd guess that £7.60 would be a reasonable amount for two drinks.'

'So he was in a round with someone. That makes sense. How many receipts were in there?'

'Five, which means he's had five drinks for certain, but more probably a minimum of nine if his mate was standing his round.'

O'Dowd pulled a face. 'Nine pints and then four cans. He'd have been paralytic.'

'Probably. The first receipt is timed just after nine and the last one is at one thirty this morning. Four and a half hours to drink nine pints is one every half hour, or just under an hour if his mate wasn't buying.'

'So there was a lock-in at the pub then. We definitely need to have a word with the landlord. And tell me, why do you keep suggesting he'd be buying all the beer? Surely his mate would have stood his round?'

'You know what blokes are like when it comes to repaying favours with beer. Just last week Ethan and I took his mate out for a few pints as he'd come round and fixed my washing machine. It cost us forty quid on drinks but it was a damn sight cheaper than calling an engineer out.'

'Fair enough. You thought of anything else?'

'Just one thing, ma'am, and I'm not sure it's appropriate or even relevant. It may just be my own curiosity that needs satisfying.'

'What is it?'

'Sinclair's injuries. I'd like to know how they were inflicted; there might, just might, be a clue that'll give us a lead. I think we need to get in a specialist in working out how people have been hurt.'

'Where are we going to get such a specialist?' O'Dowd's eyes narrowed. 'You mean Hewson, don't you?'

Beth gave a nod as her answer. Dr Hewson was Cumbria's leading forensic pathologist and someone she trusted and respected. Twinkle-eyed and filled with a sense of devilment, he was exceptional at his job and she'd never failed to learn from conversations with him.

Hewson and O'Dowd had a somewhat frosty relationship, but Beth had learned that behind the barbs they threw at each other, they both respected the other's professional ability.

As much as she wanted to have Hewson examine Sinclair, she wasn't sure if there would be protocols against forensic pathologists seeing live patients. There was also the family to think of. If they learned the police had brought in a forensic pathologist there was no telling what their reaction would be.

It was at times like this that she was thankful for the chain of command, as it meant that O'Dowd would be the one to make this decision.

CHAPTER FIVE

Her father had gone off in search of a sandwich and some tea, but there was no way Laura was going to leave the ward. James was still the same, and when she'd asked the doctors and nurses looking after him how he was, they'd all given her the same stock phrase.

'Critical but stable' was an oxymoron if she'd ever heard one. The critical part indicated just how serious his condition was whereas stable offered that most destructive of emotions: hope.

If he was stable, then he wasn't getting any worse. That had to be a good thing. Yet the good thing was counterbalanced by the knowledge that if the stability was to change, it could go the wrong way and, as he was critical, it wouldn't take much for him to succumb to his injuries.

The idea of losing James was unthinkable; she didn't know how she'd cope without him. He was far more to her than an other or a better half, he was the person who completed her. James was her soulmate; he still made her heart skip when he smiled at her. A good conversationalist, he knew a lot about a variety of different subjects and he always offered wise counsel when she brought her work problems home.

When she snuggled up to him and felt his arms enfold her, she was safe from the world and all its tribulations. More than that, she was content, not just when she was in his arms or even his company, but with her life. She was happier than she'd ever thought possible and he was the reason for that happiness.

The feelings of angry frustration she'd carried from her teenage years had seeped away by the time James had proposed and while she still felt annoyance at times, James's calm outlook on life and his love for her had eroded her need for constant confrontation.

The questions the police had put to her were ones she kept going back to. Some had been easy to answer and some had been impossible.

James had told her how his parents died in a house fire. But he'd not told her anything of his life up to that point. He'd not talked of his parents or his school friends. She knew of no siblings and there'd never been a proper conversation about his transition from London to Cumbria.

The more questions the police had asked her, the more she realised there was an awful lot she didn't know about her husband.

As she sat on the chair outside the ICU, she vowed that if James pulled through, she'd get him talking about his childhood and his family. The void in her knowledge wasn't just frustrating, it could be deadly. She knew nothing of James's medical history. He'd never been seriously ill since they'd met, therefore there had been no need for them to have a conversation about conditions that had affected members of his family.

After her horror at what had happened to James, and her worry that he'd die from his injuries, her primary emotion was fury. How dare someone attack a kind, gentle and lovable man like James in this way? How dare they leave him in such a state? If he survived, his injuries were bound to be life-changing in one way or another. There would certainly be months of rehabilitation to go through. That would be a small price to pay if he survived. She'd be there for him. Championing every little triumph and helping him to face each new challenge that was put in front of him.

But the thing that most worried Laura was the reason for the attack. Whichever way she looked at it, she couldn't find a reason for someone to hurt James so badly. Compared to most men he was a mouse. It wasn't that he was a doormat, he would just state his opinion in a way that was respectful to the person he was arguing with. He picked his words with care and made sure his tone was level and non-aggressive. This trait meant grievances were discussed with civility rather than anger or bad language. In all the time she'd known him, she'd never heard him raise his voice in anger.

It shamed her that a month before their wedding she'd tried to provoke him into an argument to see what he was like when properly riled. She had insulted him with criticisms and jibes that grew ever crueller. James had taken everything she said without commenting and waited until she'd blown herself out. When she was sobbing in a chair, he'd taken her hands in his, looked into her eyes and told her that he loved her, but as much as it would break his heart, he'd walk away if that was what she wanted.

Laura had gripped his fingers tight and begged him not to leave. He'd listened as she'd apologised and when she explained what she'd done, he'd just shrugged and said that he didn't see the point in getting angry and shouting as it never resolved anything.

From that moment on, Laura had done everything she could to mimic his outlook and she knew that she'd grown as a person thanks to his influence.

James was her everything, and she'd do whatever she could to protect him and to assist the police in finding out who'd left her husband in that terrible state.

The first thing on Laura's agenda was making sure James got proper care and treatment in the hospital. Her work as a legal secretary to Cumbria's leading medical-negligence solicitor had taught her a lot about hospital procedure and she was using her mobile to email herself constant updates as to James's condition and the care he was receiving.

Laura wanted all the details on record. Her boss would review it for her and if they had any hint of a case, she'd wipe the floor with the hospital. Money wouldn't bring James back if he died, but if he survived it would help make his life more comfortable until he was back to full fitness.

As she straightened in her chair, Laura threw her head back until it bounced off the padded headrest.

She shouldn't be thinking this way.

James wouldn't die. Wouldn't leave her.

He was always positive in the face of adversity. She must be too.

The squeak of footsteps on the polished floor warned of her father's return. Laura's mother had died two years ago which meant her father was the only close relative available to be with her. She'd told her sister to stay in Manchester, as she had a young child to look after, plus Laura didn't want to have to deal with her niece's tantrums.

Laura stiffened her jaw and prepared for more of her father's flailing attempts to offer support. He meant well, she knew that. But unless he could tell her that James had made a full and miraculous recovery, he had nothing to say that she wanted to hear.

CHAPTER SIX

It wasn't hard to figure out how the Coachman Inn in Talkin – where James Sinclair had been drinking the night before – got its name. It was the kind of small country inn which had once been a stopping point for horse-drawn coaches, but now had little more traffic than locals drinking a Sunday pint. When Beth cast her eyes around, she saw various different rooms connected by archways.

Most of the rooms were dimly lit, but the bar was bathed in the glow of artificial light. There was a whiff of vinegar in the air and a number of the tables were set ready for the next day's meals.

Two couples were sitting at opposite ends of the main bar. One couple were in their fifties and were leaning back in a relaxed fashion that spoke of comfortable amiability borne of long association. The other couple were in their late teens. His hand was on her thigh and there was a charge of excitement in their eyes.

O'Dowd approached the bar. 'You the landlord?'

'Yeah that's me.' The landlord was a scrawny man who was little more than five foot three. He had a genial air and was untroubled by O'Dowd's gruff manner. 'How can I help you, ladies? What is it you're after, a drink, a room? I'm sorry but the kitchen closed an hour ago.'

O'Dowd's warrant card was thrust under his nose. 'We'd like to talk to you about last night.'

The landlord's shoulders drooped as he tried and failed to keep an unconcerned expression on his face.

'What is it you'd like to know?'

'James Sinclair was brutally assaulted in his home in the early hours of this morning. We have proof he was in here last night. We want to know if he fell out with anyone, if there's someone he doesn't get on with.'

'Shall we?' The landlord gestured towards one of the dimly lit rooms.

'Here is fine by me, Mr…?'

'Quigley, but everyone calls me Dougie.'

'So, Mr Quigley, want to tell me about last night?'

Quigley grimaced and tossed a glance at the older couple. 'There was a bit of a scuffle last night. James was goaded by one of the other locals, Charles Drewitt. James didn't react until he was pushed. I didn't see exactly what happened, but James had Charles backed up against a wall with his arm across his throat in a flash. Couple of other locals pulled them apart and I put the pair of them out.'

Beth pounced on the revelation before O'Dowd. 'What happened when they got outside? Did they keep on fighting?'

'I didn't throw them out at the same time. I sent James first. He'd never normally say boo to a goose, so I figured he'd go home. If I'd thrown Charles out first, he'd have just waited for James.' Quigley gave a shrug. 'It was handbags stuff really. Nobody actually threw a punch and, given the way he was goading James, Charles deserved what he got.'

'You said no punches were thrown, so what was it Charles got?'

'Just that he was humiliated when James pinned him to the wall. See, he's got at least six inches and maybe four stone on James. Yet James was quicker and stronger than he was.'

'What time did this all take place?'

'Around closing time.'

'And what's closing time for you?' Beth tossed a tight smile at Quigley. 'Before you answer that question, I'd like to point out that the proof we have that James was here last night is a number of credit-card receipts.'

Quigley's eyes closed for a few seconds and when they opened he flicked his gaze between Beth and O'Dowd. 'Okay, fair enough. We had a wee bit of a lock-in.' He gave a grimace Beth wasn't convinced was genuine. 'Bloody typical. The one time I have a lock-in, this happens. How is James anyway? Will he be all right?'

Beth's estimation of Quigley was changing by the second. While he might not be the worst person she'd ever questioned, there was a definite shiftiness to him, and his attempt to claim the lock-in was a one-off wasn't the slightest bit convincing. The way he'd changed the subject by asking after James was a red flag for her, as the question should have been asked a lot sooner. What pushed her buttons was the way his eyes were fixed on the scar on her cheek. It was as if that was all he could see of her.

'Tell me, Mr Quigley, where does this Charles Drewitt live?' O'Dowd had her notebook out. 'And did you serve him after you put James Sinclair out?'

Quigley straightened his back in indignation. 'Of course not. He'd started trouble, so I didn't give him any more booze. Even took his pint and put it down the sink.'

'You never told me where he lived. And while you're at it, I want to know the names of everyone who was in here when it kicked off and where they live.'

Beth tuned out as O'Dowd extracted the information from the landlord. The last half hour reminded her of her days in uniform when she'd dealt with the aftermath of one pub fight after another. It was a sad fact, but there was always a percentage of people who drank more than they should and spoiled things for everyone. Her cheek was a constant reminder of what could happen when anger settled on top of alcohol.

O'Dowd turned away from the bar and lifted an eyebrow at her. Beth gave her head a shake. At this moment in time, she couldn't think of any further questions. She knew they'd come to her after she left, but that was okay. It was five to eleven, and as bad as Sinclair's injuries were, the scuffle at the pub didn't seem serious enough to warrant knocking on doors at this late hour.

It was odds on O'Dowd would send her back tomorrow to speak to everyone though. That suited her as she'd get some thinking time to assess what she'd already learned. There was one thing she was sure of, Quigley wasn't telling them anything close to the whole truth. For now she didn't have anything more than a gut feeling and instinct telling her this, but once she'd had a chance to assimilate all the information, she'd either be able to figure out what he was holding back, or a way to get that information out of him.

The interviews with the other patrons of the Coachman Inn would be very enlightening, and Beth was looking forward to learning what had prompted a mild-mannered man to get involved in a drunken fight.

CHAPTER SEVEN

Beth slid beneath the duvet and made sure it was tucked around her body. Once she was neatly cocooned she rolled onto her left side and wriggled into a position that let her make notes as she ran through her thoughts on the day.

Her first notes were on the extent of the injuries Sinclair had received. The beating he'd taken seemed far worse than could be expected over an argument in the pub or for getting caught with someone's wife or girlfriend. If the latter of these two scenarios was the case, then she might have expected his groin would have been attacked.

That part of his body had escaped punishment though, with the nearest injury being on his hip bones. The more she thought about it, the more she focussed on the fact that Sinclair's attacker had concentrated his efforts on bones rather than the soft-tissue areas of the body.

When she traced the human body in her mind, every part of it which had bone near the surface had been smashed on Sinclair with two exceptions: his skull wasn't harmed and neither was his backbone.

There must be a reason for those areas being untouched and the only one she could think of was that the attacker had wanted to send a message. He'd had the power to kill Sinclair by breaking the bones of his skull, or to leave him in a paraplegic state by smashing his vertebrae. The attacker having done neither made her think Sinclair was being taught a lesson or used as a warning to others.

Killing Sinclair would have been easy, yet the killer had chosen not to do that. The more she puzzled on it, the more her thoughts were leading her in another direction.

Sinclair would have been in agony as his bones were systematically broken. He was sure to have been begging for mercy, pleading for his attacker to stop. To Beth's mind he would have done or said anything for his ordeal to be over.

Her fingers gave repeated clicks as she pursued her latest thought.

Beth was thinking about the possibility that Sinclair had been tortured. As a mild-mannered chef who spent his life avoiding confrontation, she couldn't begin to think what information he might have that would have resulted in him being tortured to share it.

Her earlier thoughts about Sinclair being a secret gambler returned as she pursued the theory that he'd had a punishment beating for failure to pay a gambling debt.

There was also the possibility that his more abrasive wife had upset someone to the extent that they'd exacted their revenge by crippling her husband.

Frustrated by the myriad of possible reasons for the attack on Sinclair, Beth turned her attention to the events in the pub. While it was possible that Charles Drewitt had drunkenly decided to punish Sinclair for humiliating him in the pub, it was a stretch to think he'd gone quite so far.

All the same, she was convinced that Dougie Quigley had been economical with the truth and that he was covering something up.

She knew from experience that little villages like Talkin were the kind of communities where everyone knew everyone's business. In the absence of a village shop, the Coachman Inn would be the place where Talkin's residents met to exchange news and gossip.

When you peered beneath the surface of any community, there were almost always secret affairs, money troubles and deep-seated resentments that festered and caused twisted perceptions. These were the facts she wanted to get from Quigley. As the landlord of the Coachman Inn, he'd hear all the titbits of gossip. He'd know who was sleeping around and who was at war with their neighbours.

With a less confrontational approach than O'Dowd's, she hoped to get him to open up to her. Perhaps getting him to talk would present them with a decent suspect.

CHAPTER EIGHT

Beth strode along the sterile corridors of the pathology lab. They'd been given clearance for Dr Hewson to see Sinclair and assess his injuries, and as she had the best relationship with the pathologist, O'Dowd had nominated her as the person to meet with him.

'Good morning, DC Protégé.' Hewson's eyes twinkled beneath the unruly mop of curly grey hair. 'While I'm flattered that you want my opinion on Mr Sinclair's injuries, I'm also extremely busy today and have a court appearance to prepare for as well.'

The pathologist's habit of calling her DC Protégé was borne of their first meeting shortly after she'd joined the FMIT. He'd assumed that O'Dowd would take Beth under her wing, and in the months since her becoming part of the team, he'd been proven right in his assumption. O'Dowd was a tough boss to work for, but she was fair and would defend her team with the same ferocity as a lioness protecting her cubs. Beth felt honoured she was getting O'Dowd's experience passed down to her, but she doubted Hewson would see it the same way due to his fractious relationship with the DI.

'I appreciate you making time in your schedule to help us out.'

Beth had learned the best way to deal with Hewson was to be direct and businesslike, as, while he was generally good-natured, he had an ornery side. However, she was well aware how much Hewson loved to solve the puzzles his job presented him with. Whether it was a medical mystery, or there was foul play to investigate, he took a vicarious thrill from extracting answers from those unfortunate enough to find themselves on his dissecting table.

Hewson pulled on his white coat and affixed a name badge to the pocket. 'I have to say, DC Protégé, this is most irregular, albeit intriguing.'

As they made their way to the ICU, Hewson ran through what he'd learned from Sinclair's medical notes. Because he talked in formal medical terms, Beth only understood a fraction of what he said. This didn't worry her though, as she knew that once he'd had a look at Sinclair himself, Hewson would share his thoughts in layman's terms.

Laura Sinclair was sitting outside the ICU ward and she looked terrible. Her hair was a mess and the bags under her reddened eyes told Beth that she'd had little or no sleep. It was understandable, in fact, expected. Had she looked any other way, Beth's suspicions would have been raised.

Beth watched as Laura recognised her and lurched to her feet. 'Have you got him? Please, tell me that you know who attacked my husband. Tell me that you've arrested him and that he'll spend the rest of his life in jail.'

'I'm sorry, but we're still investigating the case. We're doing our very best.'

'Are you kidding? You're passing me off with platitudes? I want that bastard caught and caught soon.'

'So does she, Laura. She's doing her best. Let's leave her to do her job.' John pushed his way between Beth and his daughter and thrust a cardboard coffee cup into Laura's hand.

Laura leaned past her father and took a look at Hewson. Beth saw her eyes go to his hospital ID.

'Hang on. He's a fucking forensic pathologist. What's he doing seeing James? Oh my god. Is this your way of telling me he's died?' Laura's head twisted and she looked into the room where a doctor was standing over James. Her shoulders slumped a little as she realised that the machines were still keeping her husband alive. 'Well, what are you doing here, Dr… Hewson, is it?'

'Mrs Sinclair, I know this must be a worrying time for you, and yes, as a forensic pathologist I shouldn't be anywhere near your husband as I'm not the kind of doctor he needs. However, due to the nature of my job, I have been asked to consult with the police regarding your husband's injuries and what may have caused them.'

'Oh.' Laura raised the coffee until the escaping steam wafted towards her face. 'I just thought—'

'I thought it too. It's okay. James hasn't died. Come on, darling.' John took Laura's arm and led her back to the chair she'd just vacated.

As Hewson went to begin his examination, Beth wandered off to a place where she was out of Laura's eyeline. The way Hewson had dealt with Laura was a reminder that behind the twinkling eyes and sometimes haughty manner, a compassionate doctor still remained.

While she waited for him to return, Beth went back over her morning; after her usual run, just the two miles today as she wanted to make an early start and the dark, sleety conditions made the route treacherous, she'd got into the office by seven and had started compiling a spreadsheet for the case.

O'Dowd had arrived at eight followed by DC Paul Unthank and DS Frank Thompson. With the whole of FMIT assembled, O'Dowd had set her team off on different courses. Beth to the hospital; and Unthank to dig into James and Laura Sinclair's lives, with special attention to be paid to their finances. Meanwhile, Thompson had been given the task of getting the details of the people on the list Quigley had given O'Dowd, and then he was to meet Beth at the Fox and Hounds where James Sinclair worked.

The DI was to stay in the office and coordinate their efforts while also liaising with the higher-ups.

Beth was on her second bottle of water and granola bar when Hewson left Sinclair's room. His face was grave and there was pity in his eyes as he nodded at Laura and her father.

As he walked towards the stairs, Beth fell in beside him and asked for his thoughts.

Hewson gave his head a slight shake. 'Wait until we get to my office, please.'

Beth wanted to get the information from Hewson as soon as she could, but respected the doctor enough not to push the issue. If he was waiting until they were back in the privacy of his office to give his report, then he would have a good reason.

When they'd got to his office and were both seated he rested his head in his hands and took a moment to compose himself. It took a full three minutes before he looked up at her.

'On my table, I've had people who died of terrible diseases, been burned alive, crushed and killed in a thousand other ways. I've treated the bodies of one hundred and forty-nine murder victims. It's not a boast when I say that I have seen just about every way one human being can harm another.' Hewson's torso and arms shook with a contained fury. 'But never, in my thirty-year career in pathology, have I seen anything quite like James Sinclair's injuries.'

Beth nodded. She didn't want to speak, to break Hewson's flow. This was his moment and his territory. He might be shaking with anger and his voice may be stretched to breaking point, but she was here to mine his expertise, and she could tell that he had to get to the point where he was ready to talk in his own way.

A fist unclenched and rubbed at his face. 'I'm sorry. That wasn't terribly professional of me.'

'There's no shame in being human. You reacted to a series of horrible injuries in a way that shows you're not some unfeeling sod. So far as I'm concerned, you've just gone up in my estimation.'

'Thank you.' Hewson fixed her with an appraising look. 'I've said it before, but I'll say it again, your name may be Young, but you have a wise head on your shoulders and a good way of dealing with people. You'll go far.'

Beth flushed and flapped a hand at his compliments. 'Away with you.' She held his eye. 'Are you ready to tell me your thoughts?'

Hewson's nod was followed by a slight pause. 'The person who attacked James Sinclair was methodical in his brutality. I counted fifty-five separate injuries to each leg and thirty-seven to his arms. His ribs have forty-two individual breaks. There are fourteen attacks on his face and three to each of his hips. It was a systematic destruction of any bone that wasn't protected by a thick layer of muscle. Every injury broke a bone. If that isn't bad enough, there is a pattern to it. A symmetry. I didn't do any measurements to confirm, but from what I could see, the bones on the left-hand side of his body have been broken in the exact same place as the ones on his right side.'

'Wow.' Beth felt her stomach lurch as she took in the numbers. 'That's well over two hundred broken bones.'

Sadness filled Hewson's voice. 'Those bones aren't broken. They're shattered, smashed into tiny pieces. I saw the X-rays of his legs; the tibias and fibulas looked like someone had laid out a trail of coarse gravel. His patellae were the same as were the bones in his arms.' A shake of the head. 'I've seen people who've been hit by trains, or jumped off a motorway bridge and gone under a lorry whose bones were in better shape than his.'

'Okay.' Beth stretched the word out as she gathered her thoughts and tried not to envision Sinclair's broken body. 'Do you have any idea how his bones could have been broken so systematically? So thoroughly?'

'Without doing a full examination I can't be sure, but I'd lean towards a blunt instrument which had something of an edge to it. Kind of like a very blunt axe, but there is little damage to his skin considering the extent of the breaks. There is a welt where every break is.'

Beth closed her eyes as she considered what the doctor was saying and its implications with regards to the investigation. 'What's his prognosis? Will they be able to fix his bones?'

Hewson's head gave a gentle shake. 'The other doctor who was in there with me is an orthopaedic surgeon. Like me, he's never seen such destruction. If the patient stabilises, they're realistically going to have to amputate both legs above the knee and his arms above the elbow. His ribs, face and hips can be operated on, but his arms and legs are beyond salvation.' Hewson gave a scowled grimace. 'At the moment they're fighting to keep him alive. His body has had an immense amount of trauma and there's no telling whether he'll have blood clots, a strained heart or some other condition which may be the final straw. For his sake, I hope he makes it, but if he does survive, his life will have changed for ever.'

'The poor, poor man.' Beth thought of Laura. 'And his wife. If he pulls through, it won't just be his life that'll change, will it?'

Hewson didn't answer, but that was okay, the question had been rhetorical anyway.

As she walked back to her car, Beth couldn't shake her thoughts away from Sinclair's condition. Not the specific injuries, but rather their effect. If he survived, he'd face years of rehabilitation learning to master his prosthetic limbs. He'd be in constant pain. He'd find himself reliant on others. There was also the psychological effect to add in. There were bound to be fits of depression and trauma-related stress for him to deal with. Reports had him as a personable man who caused and took no offence, but to adapt to his new reality would take an immeasurable mental strength.

When Beth put herself into Sinclair's position, she couldn't begin to imagine how she'd cope. A part of her was thinking it might be preferable to succumb to the injuries, when she stopped walking and stood where she was. Her voice was filled with anger as she berated herself. 'You're being ridiculous. Millions of people all over the world live with disability. This isn't even happening to you. And anyway, you survived what happened to your face, now stop wasting time thinking of stuff that isn't happening to you, and start thinking about how to catch the bastard who did that to James Sinclair.'

'Mummy, that lady said a bad word.'

When Beth looked to where the voice had come from she saw a young boy pointing her way.

'Sorry.'

The glare Beth got from the boy's mother told her the apology didn't begin to earn her forgiveness.

Beth climbed into her car and took a moment to settle her thoughts. She'd been on this case for less than twenty-four hours and already she was rattled to the point where she was having to give herself a talking to. On a deeper level she knew her wandering thoughts were a symptom of her horror at how brutally Sinclair had been assaulted, but to Beth that was an excuse not a reason. Flights of fancy, however unfanciful, had no place in her brain. Her job was to solve horrific crimes, not fall apart when she encountered them.

She twisted the ignition key and set off for the Fox and Hounds, her mind already forming questions to fire at the people who'd worked with James Sinclair.

CHAPTER NINE

DS Frank Thompson was waiting for Beth when she pulled in to the car park of the Fox and Hounds. He had a vacant look on his face. There was a paper bag in his hand and he was munching on what looked like a sausage roll. Flakes of pastry decorated the front of his coat like overgrown dandruff.

Since his wife had died from the bout of pneumonia that she hadn't be able to fight due to suffering from early-onset Alzheimer's, he'd struggled to deal with his grief. Instead of his usual smart appearance, he'd let himself go. His clothes were rumpled, there was an ever-present whiff of alcohol about him and his eyes were always bloodshot in the mornings.

As tragic as his circumstances were, Beth knew he needed to pull himself together. If not for his own sake, and for the team, then for his teenage daughters. They'd lost a mother and now they had a father who seemed to be disintegrating more with each passing week.

'What did Hewson say?' To Beth, Thompson's question showed perhaps a little more interest than his bored tone suggested. Inside the heartbroken DS, a conscientious officer and a good man still existed.

Beth ran through the major points of her conversation with Hewson and saw her own reaction mirrored in Thompson's face.

'Poor bugger.' He looked towards the pub. 'C'mon then, let's get on with it.'

Beth led the way and entered the Fox and Hounds.

Unlike its whitewashed exterior, the inside of the pub was decked out in a contemporary style with good lighting and a relaxed but classy feel to it. A couple of waiting staff were setting tables for lunchtime service. Rather than the usual uniform of skinny jeans and a logoed polo shirt worn by bar and waiting staff in country pubs and hotels, they wore smart black trousers and crisp white shirts.

When one of them approached, Beth noticed a tiny hole in his nose that would house a ring when he wasn't working. 'Hi there. Welcome to the Fox and Hounds. Table for two, is it?'

Thompson told Missing Nose Ring who they were and that they'd like to speak to the manager, or owner.

While they waited Beth lifted a menu from the nearest table and opened it for a look.

'If you're having something to eat,' Thompson pointed at the menu in Beth's hands, 'I'm gonna have a pint.'

Beth knew Thompson was serious. Alcohol had become his crutch and she'd begun to suspect that he was sneaking a drink when he should be working. 'I'm not hungry. I just wanted to have a look, see what level of chef Sinclair is.'

Thompson's only answer was a half-hearted scowl.

Beth turned her attention to the menu and scanned not just the dishes, but the pricing structure.

After perusing the menu, Beth realised that the Fox and Hounds was a cut above the usual town pub. The prices were twice what she was used to paying for a meal and there was a pretentiousness to the menu that spoke of fine dining rather than a plateful of food. If Sinclair was the head chef here, he must be very good at what he did.

Beth heard the clack of heels approaching and turned to look at the woman striding their way.

'Sorry for keeping you. My head chef hasn't turned up for the second day running and I can't even get hold of him, so we're a bit run off our feet, I'm afraid.'

Beth made sure to speak before Thompson did. Wound up in his own grief as he was, he'd lost the few morsels of tact he once possessed. 'If you're referring to James Sinclair, then I'm afraid I have some bad news for you.'

The woman's face blanched and a hand flew up to her mouth. 'He's not dead, is he?' A flap of the mouth-covering hand. 'No, he can't be, you wouldn't come to tell me he's dead. Is he in trouble?'

'He's alive, but he's been the victim of a brutal attack. It will be a long time before he's able to come back to work.' Beth wanted to add 'if ever' to her sentence, but she knew it wasn't her place to pass such judgement.

'Oh my god. What happened? Will he be okay?'

'He was attacked in his home. He's in hospital now, and his wife is with him.'

'He's in hospital? How serious is it?'

'The doctors say he's critical but stable.' Beth gestured to the nearest table. 'I know this is a shock for you and that you'll have to go and sort things in your business, but we have a few questions we'd like to put to you.'

Twenty minutes after sitting down at the table Beth was plipping the locks on her car. The owner of the Fox and Hounds had been polite and had answered all of their questions without any hint of guile, but her answers hadn't given them any help at all.

According to his boss, James Sinclair was hard-working and low-maintenance. He led his team well, preferring to inspire them rather than terrorise them. Beth hadn't been able to hide her smile when the woman had blamed foul-mouthed TV chefs for making the majority of chefs hard to deal with, but she'd understood the woman's point.

The only pertinent thing she'd gleaned from the conversation had been Sinclair's desire to maintain his privacy. He wasn't shy but he'd turned down any publicity opportunities they'd had and had sent others in his stead when the Fox and Hounds had been nominated for awards.

To Beth it seemed like his role in the kitchen was ideal for his nature. He got to do what he loved without compromising his desire to live an anonymous life. In the kitchen he could stay behind the scenes, let his culinary skills be his way of communicating with the public while keeping his private life separate.

Meanwhile, the longer they'd been in sight of the bar, the more Thompson had cast glances towards the beer pumps. Beth hadn't commented on it, but it was clear to her that he was desperate for a drink and her presence was the only reason he wasn't having one.

Thompson obviously needed help to overcome his grief, but Beth didn't know if he'd accept it. O'Dowd was the closest to him, but to involve the DI would mean telling her how Thompson had been. Also, he hadn't actually done anything wrong and for Beth to go running to O'Dowd might be seen as being akin to grassing him up. This wasn't something she wanted to do, as the DI might then feel she had to follow procedure and involve HR, or worse, the Professional Standards Department.

On a professional level, Beth knew it wasn't down to her to manage Thompson. The counterpoint to this was that the way he was disintegrating, sooner or later Thompson was going to overstep the mark and, as a close colleague, she wanted to help him overcome his grief in a way that didn't involve self-destruction.

CHAPTER TEN

Dougie Quigley was wiping down the tables when Beth and Thompson entered. Beth saw his face twist into a scowl before he remembered himself and produced a more welcoming expression.

Beth made the introductions and fixed Quigley with a stare. 'We've a few follow-up questions for you.'

'Ask away.' Quigley spread his hands wide as if he'd nothing to hide, although Beth could hear in his voice that he was dreading what the questions would be.

'You told us last night that James Sinclair got into a bit of argy-bargy with a Charles Drewitt.' Beth made a self-deprecating gesture as she wanted Quigley to underestimate her. 'It was silly of me not to ask it, but what was Drewitt saying?'

'Oh, that. Charles was complaining about a meal he'd had at the Fox and Hounds. He told James that his meals were overpriced for what you get. Said he'd had to stop for chips on the way home because he was still hungry.'

'And what was James's reaction to this?'

'He apologised, as I remember it. And said that perhaps Charles would be better off avoiding the Fox and Hounds in future as it obviously wasn't a cheap-as-chips place.'

'That seems fair enough.' Beth cast her eyes around the room before returning her gaze to him. 'Tell me, Mr Quigley, did you think Mr Drewitt was spoiling for a fight?'

Quigley shifted from foot to foot. 'I thought he was just mouthing off a bit. It's a free country and people are allowed to express their opinions.'

'I'd agree, except it ended in a scuffle. What happened after Sinclair apologised?'

'Charles went back to his game of darts.'

Beth noticed Thompson was ignoring Quigley and staring at the bottles of whisky as if they were the only thing in his world. He was standing at the top of the slippery slope of alcoholism and reaching for a set of skis.

'So how did the scuffle happen if Mr Drewitt walked away?'

Again, Quigley shuffled his feet before speaking. 'He came back for another pop at James. James got up to leave and Charles pushed him.' Quigley tried to give an unconcerned shrug, but it was nothing more than a hapless gesture. 'You know the rest.'

'I do. That's a perfect reconstruction of events. Thank you for that. Who was James drinking with?'

'Him and Nicky Johnson were in a round, but he was chatting with most folk.'

Beth gave a short nod. 'What's he like, this Nicky Johnson?'

'A decent lad. Does something with computers but I'm not sure what.'

'According to Mr Sinclair's credit-card receipts, this all happened after one thirty in the morning. Those credit-card receipts suggest that he'd drunk quite a lot. At that time of the morning, I'd hazard a guess that Mr Drewitt had also been drinking for quite some time. Tell me, Mr Quigley, you obviously witnessed what went on. At what point did you realise that trouble was brewing and why didn't you intervene to prevent the inevitable scuffle? After all, as the licensee you were already breaking the law by serving outside licensed hours, so you'd surely not want there to be any trouble.'

To Beth, Quigley couldn't have looked guiltier if he was wearing a striped jumper, eye mask and was carrying a bag marked 'SWAG'.

Thompson tapped a finger on the bar. 'DC Young asked you a question. Perhaps you'd care to answer it?'

Quigley huffed out a sigh. 'You can see the size of me.' He gestured at himself to further emphasise his point. 'Charles is twice my size. No way was he going to pay any attention to what I said.'

Beth nodded. 'No offence, but I can see your point. Except that last night you told us that you put Mr Sinclair and then Mr Drewitt out. So, would you care to tell us what really happened, or do we need to arrest you for obstruction?'

'I'll tell you. But believe me, what happened isn't my fault.' Quigley poured himself a whisky and leaned on the bar with one hand wrapped around his glass.

Beth made rapid notes, as Thompson went back to eyeing the whisky. She didn't like what she was hearing, but she knew it would give them several leads to follow.

CHAPTER ELEVEN

Beth sat in the passenger seat of Thompson's car and willed the heater to get up to temperature a lot faster. There were flakes of snow in the air, and while it added to the picture-postcard effect of the quaint village of Talkin, the cold was insidious in its attempt to numb her fingers and toes.

She put a call into Control and requested the known histories of all the names on the list she'd created when Quigley had told the truth about Saturday night's events.

Thompson raised an eyebrow as he looked at her. 'What do you make of it then?'

'Sounds like all that being nice, mild and private was a front for what James Sinclair was really thinking.' Beth tucked her hands under her armpits. 'It also sounds like the majority of pub fights I've ever dealt with. Punches get traded and when the fight gets broken up threats are made and one of the fighters mouths off a lot more than the other. What surprised me more than anything else, is the way Sinclair apparently rounded on all the other patrons in the pub. I mean, look at what he said and think of the damage it'll do to the local community.'

Beth's mind was specifically on the things Sinclair had announced in the pub and the doubts he had cast on the parentage of Drewitt's daughter. When you added in the accusations of wife-swapping he'd levelled at another table's occupants and the way he'd outed one local man as being gay, it meant there were a multitude of possible suspects for the attack.

All things considered, it was a miracle the fight hadn't ended up in a mass brawl. As it was, if Quigley was to be believed, it had taken the non-combatants half an hour to make sure that the fight was broken up and those intent on throwing punches were sent home.

Thompson drummed his fingers on the steering wheel, oblivious to the low temperature. 'I wouldn't worry about the community too much. Villages are tough places, the suspicions about the farmer's daughter would have come out eventually, and there's no way you're telling me that no one thought that guy was gay. Oh, and for the record, the wife-swapping, there's tales of that happening in every village and tales is what it usually turns out to be.'

'So you think nothing else will happen because of his rant?'

'Well there's the beating he took, that's happened, and I dare say there might be a divorce or a move away on the cards, but on the whole, villages are self-healing in such matters. Those affected might stay away from the pub for a few weeks, keep their head down and sort their issues out, but then life in the village will just go back to what it was.'

Beth accepted Thompson's version of events as she knew that he lived in a village of a similar size to Talkin and had done so for twenty years. As a townie herself, she knew there was a lot she didn't understand about village life.

She didn't consider herself to be a private person, but she didn't like the way that in a village very little was kept truly private. Everyone seemed to know each other's business and there was always a busybody or two who made it their business to pry into lives for the sole purpose of collecting gossip they could spread.

Her own police-owned house was situated in a quiet cul-de-sac in Penrith, and while she exchanged everyday pleasantries with her neighbours and attended the odd barbecue or festive party, there wasn't much contact. Beyond their names and what they did for a living, she knew little of her neighbours' lives, and that's how she liked it.

Beth moved her feet closer to the heater vent. 'So where do we start, the wife-swappers, the suspect parentage, or the guy who got outed?'

'Whichever one lives the nearest will do for me.'

There was no need for Beth to check her notes. She knew the nearest person was Alan Fisher. He was the man who'd apparently been outed as homosexual, though whether there was any truth in it remained to be seen. A more pressing question was what had caused Sinclair to step so far out of character? It could just be that he was drunker than usual and his normal inhibitions were lowered. Perhaps Drewitt's comments had cut deep, or the years of turning the other cheek had caused a lot of unspoken resentment to be bottled up and his rant hadn't been so much about the people he was mentioning, but rather an explosion of pent up fury that aimed itself at the targets he could see.

Before climbing out into the cold, she wanted to mine Thompson's experience of village life. 'You live in a village, is it normal for the pub to have a lock-in?'

'Christ yeah. Happens all the time in places like this. There's not the manpower to keep an eye everywhere and things rarely get out of hand.'

Beth gave him a look that needed no interpreting. 'So, it's a blind-eye job, is it?'

'If you like.' Thompson gave a shrug. 'Back in the day, I worked with an old inspector who told tales of how it was in the sixties and seventies. They'd know which pubs were having a lock-in, knock on the back door and go in for a couple of pints. I'm not saying it was right, but there was less chance of anything kicking off with a couple of coppers in.'

'So what happened if there was a shout? If they were needed elsewhere?' Beth was incredulous. She knew things were different in the old days, but publicly drinking on duty?

'They went to it.' Thompson shrugged again. 'I'm not saying it was right, it was just the way it was, so don't go judging what happened in the past by modern standards.'

Rather than argue with Thompson when he was irate as well as distracted by his grief, Beth reached for the door handle. 'C'mon then, let's go see this Alan Fisher guy. See what he has to say about Saturday night.'

CHAPTER TWELVE

The rap of Thompson's knuckles on the door was harder than it needed to be. Beth's old sergeant had always advocated a firm and powerful knock, but Thompson's effort was only a half-step below a full-blooded punch.

Beth could hear footsteps approach, but they lacked the urgency of Thompson's summons. When the door creaked open they came face-to-face with a good-looking man in his forties. He was dressed well and his shirt covered his torso in a way that showed off a toned physique. His face was clean-shaven and there was obvious care and attention taken with his grooming.

Thompson's warrant card was thrust forward. 'You Alan Fisher?'

'Yeah, that's me.' He pulled the door wide open. 'I suppose you better come in.'

To Beth, Fisher wasn't showing any of the usual signs of worry or shiftiness that normally accompanied a police visit. People with something to hide couldn't help but display signs of nerves. They'd lick their lips or babble to fill silences, yet Fisher wasn't doing any of that.

As she followed Thompson through Fisher's cottage she was taken aback at the lack of doors. The doorways were there, as were painted door casings and the architraves, but there were no doors in any of the doorways.

When they entered the kitchen and Fisher gestured for them to take a seat at the table, Beth saw that all the cupboards had a series of pictures on their doors. The images weren't the usual family snaps or reminders to get milk, bread or some other product when next at the shops, they were of pots and pans, cleaning products and canned goods. Plates, cups and mugs were all depicted, as were tea towels, cutlery and biscuits. The fridge had an array of images all showing what was inside.

Beth didn't understand it, but she accepted it for the time being. She cast a look at Thompson but his features were as blank as any she'd ever seen; his eyes were set straight ahead, but it was like they were unseeing. He looked numb, or like he was miles away.

Rather than wait for Thompson to snap out of his funk, Beth went ahead with the questioning. 'Mr Fisher, your name was given to us in connection with a case we're investigating.'

'I'm guessing that it's to do with James Sinclair? By all accounts he got a right kicking from someone.'

'Your guess is right.' Beth went for broke. 'We know there was a fracas at the Coachman Inn. That Mr Sinclair got into a fight and then slagged off just about everyone he could see; yourself included. According to our sources, he outed you as being gay.'

'Shhh.' Fisher's finger jumped to his lips. When he spoke again, it was in a whisper. 'Please, keep your voice down.'

Beth dropped her voice to the same volume as Fisher's. 'Okay. Now, about what James Sinclair said.'

'Yes, of course I'm gay. In fact, I have a very nice boyfriend who lives in Brampton. For the most part, I don't care what James said. He was pissed and all he wanted to do was lash out.'

'Then why are we suddenly whispering?'

'In case my father hears us.'

Beth managed not to raise an eyebrow at Fisher's desire for his father not to overhear them. Fisher was a grown man, so surely he wasn't keeping his sexuality from his father.

'Dad's got Alzheimer's and every time he learns I'm gay, it's like he's hearing it for the first time. He'll rant and rave about it until he forgets why he's angry. Then he'll remember and start all over again. He's in his seventies and his opinions on the subject are outdated to say the least.'

'So you weren't bothered about what Mr Sinclair said, or why he said it?'

'Why would I be? It's a pretty open secret. It's just easier if Dad doesn't keep finding out I'm gay. He doesn't understand it and it hurts him. That makes him say things that hurt me. James was pissed and he was mouthing off about everyone. To be honest, I'd have been more surprised if he hadn't included me. It was like a whole different side to him.'

'What about the way Mr Sinclair announced it to the whole pub? Surely someone in there will have an opinion?'

A shrug. 'Most of them know anyway. The last time Dad found out, he went berserk. He followed me out to my car and shouted abuse at me for the whole village to hear. For the most part folk were supportive and understanding. A couple of old biddies turned their noses up at me for a few months, but that was the end of it.'

'Fair enough. Do you have an alibi for the early hours of Sunday morning?'

'Will an argument with my sister do?'

'I beg your pardon?'

'When I got in I banged the front door behind me. My sister had come to stay so I could get some respite and go out for a drink. Because there are no internal doors, the bang woke her. She wasn't very pleased, and because I was pissed I opened a bottle of wine. She gave up twining at me in the end and got a glass for herself. I think it was about four when we passed out.'

Beth went through the formality of getting the sister's name and address so she could check the alibi even though she expected it to come to nothing. All of her instincts were telling her that Fisher wasn't Sinclair's attacker. He was too calm; his story made logical sense.

When she thought about the way the house was, she realised the pictures on all the cupboards were memory aids for Fisher's father. The missing doors were odd, but the whole house was minimalistic and it may have just been a stylistic thing.

The longer she was in the cottage though, the more Beth was aware of Thompson's catatonic presence. He was breathing raggedly and his eyes were flicking around the kitchen, but he'd made no attempt to join the conversation and looked for all the world as if he hadn't heard a single word. Fisher had given him a few odd looks, but had refrained from commenting.

Beth touched Thompson's arm as she rose to leave. He didn't move. Even his eyes remained still. She knew that he was struggling to get over his wife's death and that hearing Fisher senior had Alzheimer's must have brought back memories of his wife; but it looked as if he'd totally shut down.

'C'mon, sir. Time to go.' Again there was no response. Beth took hold of his arm. Gave it a shake. When she spoke she made sure her voice was soft but loud enough to snap him out of his stupor. 'Frank. Let's go.'

He rose and walked to the door like an automaton. As Beth followed she halted at the door and put one final question to Fisher.

'Who do I think did it?' A scratch of his smooth chin. 'I don't think anyone local would have followed him home and kicked the shit out of him. Half of what he said was bile and the other stuff has been rumours for years. If it was anyone he ranted about, I'd say Dougie Quigley got the worst of it. His wife went tonto when she heard he was shagging the brewery rep. It took three people to pull her off him and she made all kinds of threats about him never seeing his kids again. James was also shouting about the scams Dougie was up to when he worked for him.'

'Really?' Beth was liking this new development. She didn't trust the pub's landlord one bit.

*

She looked over her shoulder to see where Thompson was and saw him walking towards the pub. The first flurries of the forecasted snow were starting to fall, but it wasn't yet settling.

Beth crossed her fingers and hoped he'd stop at his car.

With a goodbye tossed over her shoulder, Beth broke into a run; she knew she had to stop Thompson before he got into the pub, if that was his aim. After what Fisher had just told her, Dougie Quigley had been promoted to chief suspect. If an on-duty policeman was drinking on his premises, it'd raise all kinds of complications with the investigation and would likely end in a suspension for Thompson.

As she dashed along the road, Beth's feet slid on the snow that was starting to cover the ground. Ahead of her she could see Thompson reach his car. With luck he'd climb inside and wait for her to arrive.

Beth didn't see the indicators flash, which told her that he hadn't unlocked it, so she put on an extra burst of speed to try and catch him before he bought a drink.

CHAPTER THIRTEEN

It was too late by the time Beth got into the pub. Quigley was putting a glass of what looked like whisky on the bar and Thompson's hand was reaching towards it.

'FRANK!'

Thompson didn't bother to look round. He dropped a twenty on the bar, lifted the glass and drained it.

'Another. And a pint of bitter.'

Beth marched forward and pulled at Thompson's arm until he was facing her. 'That's enough.'

Thompson didn't move. Didn't speak. When Beth looked at his face she saw that his eyes were filled with unimaginable grief.

'Come on.' Beth took hold of his wrist, gave a gentle tug. 'Let's sit over here.'

Thompson turned back to the bar. Used his free hand to lift the whisky glass to his lips and once it was drained, he curled his fingers round the pint.

Beth managed to guide Thompson to a corner table in one of the little rooms. Rather than urge him to speak at once, she let him have a moment to collect his thoughts. Beth needed to do the same herself. The situation had turned to shit with Thompson drinking while on duty, but she had the first glimmer of an idea as to how she might rescue it.

The idea was a stretch at best, and would rely on O'Dowd reading between the lines. She also had to make sure that Quigley heard her. He was already watching them with interest. There was an air of triumph about him, and she didn't care for the way he was revelling in the way Thompson was knocking back the whisky.

Before the situation deteriorated any further, Beth put her plan into action. She crossed over to the bar and waved her phone in front of her as if she was trying to find a place where she got a signal. She wanted Quigley to hear her conversation but not Thompson.

O'Dowd picked up on the second ring.

Beth made sure her voice was light and airy, as if the call was a catch-up rather than a distress flare.

'Hi, ma'am, it's just me checking in. I've spoken to a couple of people and I think I have an idea who attacked James Sinclair. One of them really reminded me of Julie. DS Thompson said the same, but you know how he felt about her. You do remember Julie, don't you? I'm at the Coachman Inn now; DS Thompson's shift has finished, but I'm still on the case. You know what DS Thompson's like, he's off in a world of his own with his reminiscing.'

When O'Dowd replied her voice was a weird mix of concern and unvented fury. 'Do you mean Frank's Julie?' A pause. 'Shit. Are you saying that you've encountered someone with Alzheimer's and it's tipped him over the edge?'

'That's right, ma'am. I'm with him now, but as *I'm* still on duty, I'm not drinking.'

'Do you need me there?'

'It might be an idea if you came. I'm planning on making an arrest later today and I'd like you here beforehand to help me coordinate it.' Beth caught Quigley's eye, pointed at him and gave a thumbs up.

Quigley's smile told her he believed he was in the clear.

'Give me half an hour and I'll be there.'

Beth ended the call and tried not to feel dismayed. Half an hour was good going from Carleton Hall to Talkin. Especially considering the snow that was now falling. All the same, she'd have to babysit Thompson for that time and he seemed hell-bent on drinking himself into oblivion. Not only that, she'd have to endure Quigley and his staring at her scar.

She could tell the Coachman Inn's owner was still a bit worried and she didn't want him to get suspicious when she stayed in the pub. As a way to ease his doubts about her presence, she ordered a couple of bowls of soup from him.

Getting some food into Thompson would be a good idea, and the idea of a bowl of hot soup instead of a sandwich for lunch held a lot of appeal considering the weather.

Beth took a seat beside Thompson where she could see the whole room. Thankfully, the weather was keeping the bar empty, which meant they could talk without being overheard. She knew she had to engage with Thompson on some level, drag him back from whatever abyss his mind was staring into; her problem was that she didn't want to inadvertently give him the nudge which plunged him headlong.

'I don't think Fisher is our man, do you?' Beth kept her voice low.

She didn't expect a response, so she was surprised when she got a grunt.

As much as she wanted to remind Thompson of what Fisher had said about the allegations Sinclair had made against the barman, she didn't dare in case he tried to arrest Quigley right there and then. With him having drunk alcohol he'd purchased from Quigley before making the arrest, even the most incompetent lawyer would have Quigley's arrest quashed within minutes.

'Who should we go see next? The wife-swappers or the farmer Sinclair had the argy-bargy with?' Beth hoped talking about the case would distract Thompson from his thoughts.

'See who you want. I don't care.' Thompson lifted his glass and gulped down half a pint. 'Don't give a shit.'

'What's upset you?' Beth was sure it was to do with Fisher senior's Alzheimer's but all her instincts were telling her the answer had to come from Thompson.

'Fisher. He's faking it.'

'What, the case?'

'Stuff the case. The coping. To you he probably looked as if he was coping. He maybe thinks that he is, but he isn't. Alzheimer's is a cruel disease. It eats away at people, steals them from their family one step at a time. At first it's a little memory loss. Then when that gets worse, there's anger when they realise they're being mollycoddled and treated like a child. More anger when they realise something's wrong but they can't understand what. They're snappy and ratty.' Thompson paused to empty his glass which he then jiggled in the direction of Quigley. 'It's not their fault, it's the disease taking them. Fisher is terrified because he knows how little of reality his father is comprehending now, let alone remembering. The pictures on the cupboards. They're memory aids. I had them for my Julie.'

'And the doors? Is that to do with the disease too?'

A nod. 'Yeah. I took all the doors in the house down too. Julie grew terrified to open them because she couldn't remember what was behind them. She couldn't tell me what she thought they might hide, but she went into hysterics too many times.' The smile he attempted to give was the saddest thing Beth had ever seen. 'You know what it's like when you go into a room for something, but when you get there you can't remember what you want? Try imagining what it's like to not remember what's behind the doors in your own home.'

Beth sat in silence and did as instructed.

After a suitable period for reflection had passed, she laid a hand on Thompson's arm. 'I'm sorry, I know you've been through a living hell, but until today, I've never really understood.'

'I've lived with it for years. Seen it first-hand and I don't understand it. All I know is my Julie has gone and she's never coming back.' He slumped forward, his chin on his chest and his forehead an inch above the empty pint glass. 'She promised to love, honour and cherish me; in the end, she didn't know who I was. I miss her, Beth. Miss her every day. Every night. You know what's worse?

Early-onset Alzheimer's isn't full-on hereditary, but if you have parents who have it, you stand a greater chance of contracting it. My girls could well get it. Can you imagine that? Two sweet and innocent girls who've just lost their mother now have this potential death sentence hanging over them.' Somehow Thompson's face and voice grew even more anguished. 'I haven't been able to tell them about the hereditary aspect. I've tried to find the words a thousand times because they need to know, deserve to know, but the words, they just won't come for me. Every time I go to tell them, I lose my bottle. They watched their mother deteriorate before their eyes. One had a million questions and the other didn't say a thing. Neither was right in their approach and neither was wrong. They just coped in different ways. God knows how they'll cope when I tell them they have a higher chance of contracting it.'

Beth felt nothing but pity for Thompson. His world had been ripped apart by a disease that attacked the essence of a person's being as well as their body. He'd had to watch as his wife slipped inexorably away from him. For a man used to having a measure of control, it must have been terrible to be powerless to save her. That his daughters may one day contract the disease was too scary to even contemplate.

Quigley brought over the two soups along with Thompson's latest pint. As she cut her roll open, Beth was pleased to see Thompson reach for his spoon rather than his glass. The soup was a hearty vegetable broth that was delicious, and from the first spoonful, Beth could feel its warmth spreading through her body.

O'Dowd strode in as they were finishing off their soup. Her face a mixture of concern and anger. Beth saw the DI's mouth tighten when she saw the half-full pint glass beside Thompson.

'That good?'

There was enough of an edge to O'Dowd's tone to make Thompson's head snap up from his latest reverie. The left side of his top lip curled upwards as he reached for the pint, a look of uncaring defiance in his eyes. 'Bloody lovely.'

This wasn't what Beth had wanted; Thompson wasn't fit to have a confrontation, his mental state too fragile. She gave a shake of her head to O'Dowd.

'C'mon then, Frank, let's go for a smoke.'

Beth watched as Thompson lifted his jacket and went to follow O'Dowd. She was about to rise when O'Dowd's hand signalled that she should stay where she was.

For the want of something to do, Beth cleared their table, putting the dishes and Thompson's empties on the bar. Upon returning to her seat, she pulled out her notes and wondered what else she could be doing to further the investigation.

All the people implicated in Sinclair's drunken rant would have to be spoken to, but according to Fisher's account, Quigley was the one who had the most to lose.

She checked her phone to see if Control had emailed her the details she'd requested, but there was nothing new from them.

O'Dowd marched back into the bar, and took the seat Thompson had just vacated. The anger on her face replaced with consternation.

'Right then, Beth. That's sorted. Now, you mentioned that you had an arrest in mind, want to explain?'

Beth watched O'Dowd's face as she filled her in on what they'd learned. What she saw appearing was a smug maliciousness she'd not seen in her boss before.

'Ooooh, Beth. You've no idea what a difference you've just made to my day. Nicking that slimy bastard will be fun.'

At that moment, Quigley walked out from behind the bar and approached their table. 'DI O'Dowd, can I get you anything?'

Beth followed O'Dowd's lead and rose to her feet. 'Dougie Quigley, I'm arresting you on suspicion of…'

CHAPTER FOURTEEN

Plucked from his own territory and deposited in an interview room, Dougie Quigley looked a lot less confident than he had while standing behind the bar of the Coachman Inn.

Durranhill Station at Carlisle was the closest to Talkin, so that's where they were. Built after the 2005 floods had decimated the original station on Warwick Street, the frontage of Durranhill Station always reminded Beth of the back end of a football ground or sports stadium.

O'Dowd had brought Unthank with her to the Coachman Inn and once she'd had a smoke with Thompson, she'd had Unthank take him home.

Beth had been told that the manner of Thompson's collapse was to be kept within FMIT and she agreed with the DI's decision. Thompson needed help and compassion rather than censure.

A duty solicitor had been appointed. He was one Beth was unfamiliar with, but judging by the rumpled mess of his clothes and the greasiness of his hair, he wasn't likely to be the most fearsome opponent she'd faced in an interview room. With the formalities recited for the benefit of the recording equipment, Beth took the lead with the questions.

'Mr Quigley, last night when you told us about the fight in your pub, you only told us part of the story. This morning you told us some more details. As we followed the lines of enquiry brought forward by your statement, we learned that once again, you'd been economical with the truth. Tell us, give us one good reason, why we should believe a word you say. Can you do that?'

'No comment.'

Beth had expected nothing less of Quigley. He was facing a whole different problem than he had been when they'd discovered the lock-in. His mind would be whirling and he'd be trying to give himself time to think. Like it or not, he wasn't going to get that time.

'How about the things Mr Sinclair is alleged to have said about you? The affair with the rep from the brewery? The fact that when he used to work for you, you were always looking for ways to cook the books? Or maybe you'd like to discuss what he said about you putting supermarket brands into premium-brand bottles?'

'No. Comment.'

'Damnit!' O'Dowd's shouted exclamation made them all jump, even Beth who'd been expecting it. 'He's said no comment twice now, DC Young. The second time he even separated the two words into separate sentences. He's obviously innocent. We'll have to let him go. He may even be guilty, but he's seen enough crime dramas on the TV to know how to behave.'

'I hardly think sarcasm is appropriate, Inspector.'

'Welllll.' O'Dowd waved a dismissive hand at Quigley. 'We've already got enough to nick him for: withholding information pertaining to an investigation, serving alcohol outside licensing hours, and that's before we even start looking. The Licensing Board will no doubt revoke his licence to sell alcohol. When we inform Customs and Excise of the allegations about his practices, there's no doubt in my mind they will go through his stock with a fine-tooth comb. You know the score, testing a sample of every bottle to make sure it's what it says on the label.' Her chin jutted at Quigley. 'What do you think of that? Think it might be wise to stop prating about lying to us and tell us the truth so that some of the shit you've landed in may be allowed to seep away?'

'Sorry to contradict you, ma'am, but you're forgetting the allegation that Mr Quigley was trying to dodge paying taxes. HMRC are likely to want their fair crack at him as well.' Beth had worked with O'Dowd long enough to know when to jump in and when to keep her mouth shut.

'Thanks for reminding me.' A look at the solicitor, then Quigley. 'What's it to be then, Dougie Boy, are you going to grasp the one chance you've got to lessen the shitstorm you're in, or are you going to be a tough guy and fall on your sword rather than tell us what the hell is going on?'

'I'd like to have a chance to speak to my client alone now if I may.'

Beth ignored the solicitor and locked eyes with Quigley. It was most likely the first time his eyes hadn't fixed on her scarred cheek. 'You'd probably like that break, wouldn't you? See, I've been in countless interviews, sat across from much tougher, and much smarter people than you. I've also sat across from blubbering wrecks who couldn't string a coherent sentence together. Trust me, your solicitor only wants that break so he can advise you. His advice will be along two different lines. If you're innocent of all the allegations and we've been fed a pack of lies, you should tough it out and be proven to be beyond reproach. We're human and make mistakes; however, if you're not squeaky clean, he'll advise you to sing like a hen party in a karaoke bar. After all, it's not like you're mixed up in organised crime or anything, the only person you may implicate is yourself, but when all's said and done, we'll learn about it anyway. Like it or not, everything about your business and finances is about to get examined with a microscope. The only hope you have of receiving any clemency, is to be cooperative.'

'What is it going to be, then?' O'Dowd leaned back in her chair, arms folded underneath her bust. 'You going to grab a lifeline, or press the detonator?'

The look in Quigley's eyes was pure malice, but when he spoke it was clear he'd made his choice. 'It's not what you think. The barney got out of hand. James was throwing accusations around like they were confetti. Just about everyone in the room copped it. I was trying to calm him down and usher him out. I guess, because I was in his face a bit, he started having a go at me. What he said about the brewery rep was true though, and my wife heard it and left me right away. She's taken my boys and has made it patently clear that she's going to take me to the cleaners. I daren't even phone her and try and win her back in case she does something stupid.' His hands shook as he laid them on the table. 'She always was highly strung.'

'And the other allegations?'

'I was only trying to keep the business afloat. You've no idea how hard it is to make a living in a place like Talkin.' A shrug that intimated he was blameless for his actions. 'Lots of other pubs do it.'

'Right.' Beth picked up a pen and hovered the nib over the notepad in front of her. 'You're going to spell out, in great detail, everything that happened, or was said, once James Sinclair started getting harassed by Charles Drewitt.'

CHAPTER FIFTEEN

Beth fed everything they'd learned from Quigley onto the spreadsheet she'd created for the case. Some detectives scribbled facts down on various pieces of paper, or used a single sheet with notes arranged in a haphazard fashion, in the hope the lack of conformity would spark random thoughts which would make unforeseen links. For Beth though, it was all about uniformity, of having the facts in neat ordered rows and columns. On simpler cases, sometimes the act of inputting the details was enough to help her memorise the facts and reach a solution. On the more complicated investigations, she would print off the spreadsheets and Sellotape them to a wall of their office so she could get an overview and cross reference known facts without scrolling back and forth.

Everything Quigley had said was an embellishment on the bare facts they'd been given earlier. Rather than mouthing off a bit and storming out, Sinclair had said his piece as he was being physically restrained from trading blows with Charles Drewitt.

Quigley's original statement taken on Sunday night suggested that everyone had sat in shock at Sinclair's outburst, but the truth of the matter had been rather different. Charles Drewitt had made repeated attempts to get at Sinclair, but had been held back by his friends. The older couples Sinclair alleged had been engaging in wife-swapping had protested and one of the women in question had managed to get close enough to Sinclair to slap his face.

For Beth, confronting Sinclair and slapping his face was as much an admission of guilt as outrage at the accusation. Quigley had backed up Fisher's claim that it was common knowledge, it was just that people didn't discuss it much as it all happened years ago. The real question was, were any of the people Sinclair ranted about furious enough at him to have attacked him in such a brutal way? That, above everything else, was what they had to discover.

Quigley had agreed that all the village knew Alan Fisher was gay and that, bar one or two of the older residents, nobody was bothered. They generally understood why he'd kept quiet about it at home and felt for him with what was happening with his father.

The most interesting part of Quigley's interview had been the elbow to the jaw that Sinclair had delivered to his mate, Nicky Johnson, when he'd stepped in to break up the fight. He'd caught Johnson hard enough to send him crashing back into a wall. Johnson had tried to get at Sinclair to return the blow, but Quigley had manged to keep them separate.

Johnson was definitely worth looking at, along with Charles Drewitt, the farmer, and the man accused of being the father of said farmer's daughter.

'What's our next move, ma'am? Do we go back to Talkin and start interviewing people?'

O'Dowd looked up from her desk and directed her eyes to the cheap clock that hung on the wall. As Beth had been doing her spreadsheet, she had heard the DI on the telephone, letting all the various agencies know of the allegations that had been made against Quigley. She'd downplayed each one and left it to each agency to make its own decision as to whether or not to investigate.

'We go home and see our families. There's no overtime budget for this one, and I'm not driving those narrow roads to Talkin in the middle of a snowstorm again if it can wait until morning.'

As much as she wanted to keep going with the investigation, Beth hadn't been looking forward to a trip back to Talkin either. There were only a couple of miles of the narrow roads O'Dowd had mentioned, but the village was far enough off the beaten track for there to be little chance of the roads ever seeing a snowplough.

Not only did the roads wind and wend their way past obstacles, they followed the contours of the land meaning there were steep inclines mixed in with sharp corners. To attempt to travel along them at night in a snowstorm could easily end in disaster.

To sate her desire to progress the case, Beth decided to spend another hour with her spreadsheet and then head home. With luck she'd be able to spot something that would give them a focal point for the next day.

CHAPTER SIXTEEN

Sandi White didn't normally drink on a week night, but after the day she'd had, she knew she'd need the alcohol to relax. Today had been a rough day at the law firm where she worked as a receptionist-cum-secretary. Just when she'd thought the day couldn't get any worse, she'd laddered her tights and had had to endure the rude ways of a local property developer who was their best client.

Sandi walked through the falling snow and made her way up the path to her little house, taking care with every step to make sure her heels had traction on the slick flagstones.

Her home on the fringes of Keswick wasn't much, an ex-council two-up two-down, but it was hers, or would be once the mortgage was paid off.

She put her bag on the kitchen counter and pulled out one of the ready meals she'd picked up on the way home. A minute later it was rotating in the microwave, its cellophane cover the innocent victim of a vicious stabbing.

Tonight would be spent eating a ready meal, drinking a bottle of wine and catching up on the soaps.

Sandi was tempted to message Kevin. He used to be such a good listener and had always known what to say. But Kevin was married now. Married to a woman who she'd never met. Could never meet. A woman she hated just for the fact she was with Kevin and Sandi wasn't. He'd made it quite clear that his wife could never know their secret. That she'd never learn about his past.

This meant Sandi had had to live on scraps. Occasional messages that were little more than the kind of letters her gran used to send with Christmas cards.

The other option was to call her current boyfriend, Leo, but his wasn't the kind of company she needed tonight. It was Kevin she wanted. Kevin she needed. However, it had been years since they'd last had a meaningful communication and as much as she loved Kevin, she was still angry with him for the cold way he'd rejected her all those years ago.

CHAPTER SEVENTEEN

Beth lifted a forkful of lasagne to her mouth and bent her mind to the latest puzzle she was trying to crack. She'd always enjoyed puzzles and riddles, and was always working on one in the background of her mind.

As well as challenging her brain to think on a lateral level, she loved to test her mental agility as she battled against those who set the puzzles.

It had been a spur-of-the-moment decision to drive to The Drover's Rest at Langwathby; in fact, had she not seen the gritter heading this way, there's no way she would have risked the five-mile journey.

But this was the place where she had recently found her quarry: the man with the kisses tattooed onto his neck. She'd been having a couple of drinks with Ethan a few months ago, when in the man had walked, and the way the barman had asked if he wanted 'the usual' had been a godsend, as it confirmed familiarity.

And now Beth found herself coming here as often as she could. She didn't really have a plan, but thought perhaps she could get friendly with Neck Kisses. Learn his real name and, most of all, find out who he'd been fighting with, so that man could stand trial for his actions that had left her for ever scarred. Because the man she thought of as Neck Kisses might not have been the one to thrust the bottle in her face, but he had started the fight with the man who'd held the bottle. She'd not seen him around for a few weeks, but that didn't mean he wasn't going to show up again.

Beth cleared the last of her lasagne from the plate and laid her knife and fork together just as the solution to her riddle became apparent. Now she'd worked it out, she realised how simple it was. The best puzzles were always that way, mind-numbing until you cracked them and then obvious when you knew the solution.

While the snow hadn't yet reached Penrith, Beth knew it was on its way and she didn't want to get caught in it. The road may have been gritted, but it was an exposed twisty route which was tricky enough to navigate at night without factoring in a snowstorm.

She was paying her bill when the door squeaked its usual warning of a new patron. Instinct made her head turn.

It was him.

Neck Kisses.

He was wrapped up in a hi-vis jacket and woolly hat. A tattered scarf was wrapped round his throat, but Beth no longer needed to see the tattoo to recognise her quarry.

As she handed her bank card to the barman, Beth ordered herself another glass of lemonade. She'd chance the drive home; she'd been waiting five years for this opportunity and wasn't going to let it pass her by because of a little snow.

Beth's stomach churned as she lifted herself onto a bar stool. What should she say to him? How should she start the conversation? Should she flirt with him? No, the last thing she wanted to do was really lead him on. She'd have to play it cool. Make sure he got just enough encouragement to join the chase.

She took a glance at his left hand. It was bare, but that didn't mean a lot. He looked as if he worked with his hands, so it was possible that he was married and didn't wear his ring for fear of losing it.

'Bloody hell. It's colder than a witch's left tit out there. Gie's a pint, will ya?' His voice as he addressed the barman was the drawl of Cumbria's most eastern reaches. His tone as earthy as his words.

Beth was about to share an agreeing word or two, but the barman beat her to it along with a mild admonishment about Neck Kisses' language. The barman's accompanying nod towards Beth drew her to Neck Kisses' attention.

He turned to look at her. A mumbled apology falling from his mouth as he checked her out.

Beth flapped a self-conscious hand. 'Don't worry about it.'

Neck Kisses kept facing her. His eyes flitting between her face and the room behind her.

As much as she looked for a sign of recognition, Beth saw none. Not even the slightest widening of the eyes.

'Sorry, love. Been working with a bunch of eejits all day and I kinda forget meself when there's a lady about.'

Beth reasoned he must like the look of her to have made a better apology. That was a plus, but now she had to play it right. Do enough to ensnare, but not so much that he thought it was too easy.

'Like I said. Don't worry about it.' She backed her words up with a tiny smile. 'Where you been working then?'

'Up on a farm, out the back of Skirwith. Right arse-end... Sorry, middle of nowhere.'

Beth knew Skirwith was one of the little hamlets that were dotted about on the Pennines, but she didn't know any more about the place than that.

'Sounds awful. Is that what you are then? A farmer?'

'Me, a farmer? Nah, I'm a drystane dyker.'

'Really? I didn't know they still built them. Didn't they, like, stop getting built years ago?' Beth didn't like presenting herself as an airhead, but she was determined to hide her intelligence from Neck Kisses. The last thing she wanted was him realising that she may be up to something. It was interesting to her to learn that people still built the drystane dykes that were such a feature of the Lakeland Fells. Constructed of stones that were interlocked rather than bound by mortar, they marked out fields and offered shelter to sheep when the weather turned bad.

Neck Kisses pulled a face. 'To be honest, it's more repairs these days. Some dic… divot will put his car through a wall and folk like me put the wall back up. Now and then, I'll put one up as a garden wall, but them jobs is few and far between.'

Beth liked the way Neck Kisses was tempering his language. It meant he was interested.

'Must be blooming freezing in weather like this.'

'You're not wrong.' His mouth twisted into a half pout. 'Gonna get a couple of pints, then home for summat to eat and a hot bath.' Again the half pout. 'That is, unless I get better offer. You know, a beautiful lady to chat to.'

'You mean you haven't got one at home?'

'Not at all. Wouldn't be chatting to you if I did, would I?'

Beth heard the unspoken message in his words. He wasn't only telling her he was single, he was letting her know he was faithful. Her estimation of Neck Kisses went up a few notches. Not for his apparent faithfulness, that could well be a lie. What she rated was the intelligent way he'd put it to her.

'Well, if I see one, I'll be sure to send them your way.' Beth levered herself off the bar stool and walked to the coatrack where she'd hung her jacket.

'You're leaving? And there I was, enjoying chatting to a beautiful stranger.'

'I'm meeting friends in half an hour. Otherwise…' Beth let the sentence dangle. This was his chance to ask her out.

'So you're happy to be the beautiful stranger I talk to, but tonight isn't good?'

He was sounding her out. Seeing if his interest in her was returned.

'You could say that.' Beth let a smile touch her lips as she zipped up her jacket. 'Or you could ask when I'm free.'

'How does Wednesday sound? Meet here for a drink and a chat? Say around eight?'

Beth cast her eyes to the ceiling as if thinking. 'Wednesday's good. I'll see you then…'

'Richie.' He picked up on her cue. 'And you are?'

'Lisa.' It was a half-truth. Lisa, as was Beth, was a shortened form of Elisabeth, which was her official, if never used, name.

CHAPTER EIGHTEEN

Laura let her father remove the undrunk coffee from her hands and place it on a table. The day had got worse by the hour. James had made no sign of regaining consciousness—she'd heard the doctors tell her they were keeping him in a medically-induced coma, but that meant nothing. He was her James and he'd always come back to her.

She'd loved him from their first meeting. The spark was very much still there for her. She felt giddy when he looked her way and smiled; a goodbye kiss from him still melted her heart and set her about missing him before he'd even left.

James would come back to her. He would. He was *her* James and he'd promised to never leave her. James always kept his promises. Always. Without fail.

He'd come back.

Except, when he came back, he'd be different. Not in her eyes. His physical being would never change for Laura. But he *would* be different.

The doctors had told her about the amputations they would need to do. Had explained that his only chance of walking again was to have prosthetic legs.

They hadn't mentioned his arms. Would they have to be amputated too? Sure, he would get prosthetics, but however good they were, they'd never properly replace his hands. How would he be if he couldn't cook? Laura knew fine well that, after her, cooking was his life. If he lost his hands, he'd never be able to work in a kitchen again.

More than the actual injuries, being forced to give up a job he loved would break him. She didn't want him to be broken. She just wanted him back. Dear, sweet, kind, funny James. Her husband. Her soulmate.

Laura reached across the table to where her father had placed the takeout coffee.

It was cold to the touch. *Had she really let another coffee go cold?*

It didn't matter. She wasn't going to drink it anyway.

Most of the coffee slopped onto the floor of the relatives' room as she coiled her arm back to launch the cup.

'Bastards. Fucking bastards. Why do they have to take his legs off?' The cup flew over her father's shoulder as he moved to envelop her in a hug. It bounced off the wall, spinning when it hit the floor. 'Why, Dad? Why?'

Laura felt her father's strong arms wrap themselves around her. He was saying meaningless platitudes in her ear. Didn't he get it? They were going to cut off James's legs. His. Fucking. Legs.

A hug wouldn't fix that. No amount of hugs would.

She wriggled to be free. His grip tightened.

'Laura!'

That was his angry voice. The one he only ever used when she was out of line.

So what?

'Let me go, Dad. I have to be there for him. Be with him.'

'Laura.'

That voice again. He could stuff his opinions where the sun didn't shine.

She reared her head back. Wanted to see his face as she told him to let go of her.

Laura felt herself go limp when she looked into her father's eyes and saw her own pain looking back at her. In a flash she knew her anger was borne of helplessness and that he shared it.

Her father was a good man.

One of the best of men.

His eyes were filled with sorrow. She knew him. Knew how he thought. He'd be desperate to salve her pain. Make all the hurt and worry go away. But he couldn't. He was human and it was his humanity making his eyes glisten and tightening his mouth. Laura could see it was killing him to not be able to solve this for her.

She put her head on his shoulder and returned his bear hug.

It was him who broke the silence. Not the hold, just the silence. 'You calmed down?'

Laura nodded into his neck.

'This is going to be tough, darling. The toughest thing you've ever done. I know you can do it. I'll be at your side every step of the way. You can cope. It's shit. Totally, effing shit, but you'll cope. You're strong. James will come back to you. But he's going to need you. Going to need strength you don't know you possess. I'm your dad. I know you've got that strength. And you know what I am, don't you?'

The childhood mantra tripped off her lips. 'Always right... unless Mam says different.'

The door to the waiting room opened and revealed a doctor with a grave expression on his face.

'Mrs Sinclair? Can I talk to you for a few minutes, please?'

CHAPTER NINETEEN

*I sip at the pint of lager and cast an eye around the room.
The Boilermaker's is a typical dive where the menu offers
either crisps or nuts.*

*It's my second pint and will be the last I have tonight.
As a matter of course, I've found a seat where the room can
be surveyed and there can be no ambushes. As always, I'm
paying attention to those around me. A man left five minutes
ago and a woman three minutes after him. Two other men
have come in together, but they are already looking around
with unease, so I pay them no heed. They are fish out of
water in a bar like this and will present no threat.*

*Today has been an interesting day: after an hour going
through a number of martial-arts training routines, I've
visited three separate suppliers with a view to making a pur-
chase for a new piece I've been commissioned to create.*

*It hadn't been easy driving back from the Honister slate
mine. The first three miles had largely been down a steep gradient and the wintry conditions had made the drive more than a
little treacherous. On more than one occasion the only solution
to halt a slide had been to stop braking and apply just enough
power for the front wheels to pull the van back on course.*

*The scenery had been shrouded by the low clouds for the
most part, but now and again a gust of wind had revealed the
jagged outcrops of the fells which flanked the Honister Pass.*

All in all though, the day has been a success as I've secured a block of stone for the commissioned project.

Honister slate is an interesting medium; its very composition means it will be susceptible to fracturing if the wrong approach is taken. Each cut, every strike of the mallet will have to be applied with the greatest of care. Yet, when the piece is complete, it will be unique, a testament to my skill.

I finish the pint, put the empty glass on the bar and say goodnight to the disinterested barman.

Twenty paces from The Boilermaker's, I hear footsteps and cast a look backwards. What I see isn't a surprise: the two hulking lumps who had been playing darts are now walking along the pavement. What's with local hard men always thinking I'm their enemy?

I had of course recognised their type at once. Low-level, and low-intellect, thugs who'd be the type to provide muscle for small-time crooks. They might work the doors on a weekend night so they can deal some drugs, but there is no doubt in my mind they are at the bottom of the crime pyramid.

Their agenda is something I neither know nor care about. They'll either make their move or they won't.

I keep a measured walk, neither speeding up nor slowing down. My hands hang loose, but ready to spring into action.

Strong hands grasp my arms just as I'm passing the mouth of an alleyway. It was where I'd expected the attack to happen. These two are so predictable.

My back gets slammed into a wall and they crowd forward.

It's like they're trying to intimidate me. But as if someone like me could ever be afraid of guys like them? One of the thugs has bad breath, the other a squint.

'Yours is a new face in The Boilermaker's.' The voice is full of supposed menace, but to my ear, the Cumbrian accent makes the words as intimidating as a death threat from Bambi.

'That's nice of you to notice.'

Bad Breath leans forward until his nose is an inch from mine; his breath the most fearsome thing about him. 'We don't like the way you were looking at us. You think we're some kind of scum. We're not.'

'Boo hoo.' I return his stare. 'What are you going to do about it?'

'We're going to teach you a lesson you won't forget.'

The corniness of the threat makes me smile. The irony of Squint and Bad Breath dishing out a brutal lesson to prove they aren't scum is lost on them.

'You don't know who I am, do you?' I have to fight the urge to smile as I ask him the question.

Squint shakes his head, so I look him in the eye to see if there is any recognition when I tell him my name.

'I'm the Sculptor.'

CHAPTER TWENTY

The dusting of frozen snow crunched beneath Beth's feet as she ran her usual route. The conditions weren't conducive to an attempt at beating her personal best, so she ran without competitiveness.

She got a few odd looks as she made her way along Penrith's streets, but she didn't care. The daily run kept her fit, gave her a cardiovascular workout and, best of all, let Beth tour her beloved Penrith.

From the narrow roads of the town centre, to the housing estates on the outer reaches, Penrith was as much a part of her as blood, skin, bone and muscle. Even the protein factory with its tendency to emit gag-inducing smells was part of the mix.

Other than her training days, she'd always lived in Penrith and could never see herself living anywhere else. Whatever her future with Ethan may hold, she had no plans to leave the town of her birth and childhood.

As she ran, the events of the previous day were turning over in her mind. There were the revelations about the fight, and the meeting/date she'd arranged with Neck Kisses. She couldn't yet think of him as Richie. Maybe that would come with time, and maybe it wouldn't.

Thompson's collapse was uppermost in her mind. She'd kept in touch with O'Dowd, who'd gone round to see him the previous evening. The DS had officially been given time off for compassionate reasons after Julie had died, but O'Dowd had managed to wangle him another fortnight, albeit only on half pay.

The different aspects to the Sinclair case were playing on her mind. As much as there were several suspects for the attack from the fracas in the pub, the brutality of it spoke of a different agenda. It was a disproportionate level of violence for a few ill-chosen words, or a punch or two being thrown.

There was also the symmetrical nature of Sinclair's injuries; it beggared belief that a person who'd been drinking until the early hours of the morning would have the necessary motor skills to inflict such a series of precise injuries.

The lack of obvious forensic evidence also didn't give any support to the theory it was one of the pub's patrons. To Beth's mind, there was no way a drunk person could have got into the house, committed such a brutal, yet precise attack, and not left any trace of their presence. It did though beg the question of whether there may have been someone in the Coachman who wasn't drinking. They should have checked with Quigley, but they'd assumed everyone had been drinking to excess.

This line of thinking triggered another thought about an overlooked question. Perhaps it had been the horror of Sinclair's injuries, or the state of his wife's mind, but she'd never asked Mrs Sinclair if the house had been locked when she returned home.

She made a mental note to get the answers to both questions as soon as possible.

The one thing she couldn't get past was Sinclair being involved in a fight. For such an allegedly mild-mannered man, it seemed out of character. It was possible that he'd been backed into a corner by the situation, but Beth didn't think that was necessarily the case. Her thoughts were that the drink Sinclair had consumed had destroyed his usual restraint, and when confrontation had come his way, all the years he'd turned the other cheek and bottled up his anger had caused him to react in a way that was out of proportion to events.

Beth was a half mile from home with the run having warmed all of her limbs, although her hands and feet were numb from the cold, and her lungs burned after gulping in the cold morning air. These were minor discomforts she was happy to endure.

Beth found herself thinking life was good. She had a job she loved, a boyfriend she adored and after years of trying to find the man responsible for her scarred face, she'd not only done so, but had learned at least his Christian name, and had arranged to meet him.

The music she had playing on her iPod was one of her favourite mixes to play when running. It was a mix of eighties hair rock. All thrashing guitars and upbeat lyrics it spurred her on and drove her forward.

Beth crossed Roper Street and hooked a left along the pavement. The sudden change of direction was a mistake, as her standing foot slipped on the snow layering the pavement.

She went down hard, her Lycra leggings offering no protection against the pavement's snow-topped pebbles.

Apart from a skinned palm and a sore knee, she wasn't badly hurt, but the pain in her knee saw her limp home rather than run the rest of the way.

She cursed every painful step as she made her way back. When she rounded the corner and entered the cul-de-sac where she lived, she was surprised to see Ethan's car parked in front of her own.

He was standing beside the car in his paramedic uniform. His breath misting in the cold morning air. When he saw her limping along the road, he jogged towards her.

'Are you okay?'

'Yeah fine. Slipped and skinned myself that's all. What are you doing here?'

'I had to come and see you, I've just had the most amazing shift.' Ethan looped an arm round her back and planted a kiss on her cheek. 'We got a shout that was in Cliburn. A pregnant woman had gone into labour.'

Beth could see where this was going from the way Ethan was beaming, but she let him tell his story without interruptions.

'So when we get there, the house is a half mile along this lane. The snow is drifting everywhere, and we're sliding all over the place even with the winter tyres on the ambulance. We get the woman loaded into the ambulance and we're heading back along the lane, unfortunately there's a dip in the lane and we can't get up the other side. By now the woman's screaming at each of the contractions and calling her husband all kinds of names. Two hours after we got there, she gave birth to a little boy. It's the first time I've done that, but oh my god, Beth, it was beautiful. You've no idea what a privilege it was to be there. The baby's first cry was something I'll never forget.'

He hugged her tight squeezing her body against his. When he released her, Beth could see the pride in his voice reflected in his face. She was thrilled that he'd had such a wonderful experience to counteract some of the bad ones he'd faced at work.

'I bet you won't. I'm so proud of you.'

'Give over, I was just doing my job.'

Beth tapped her watch. 'On that note, I have to be getting to Carleton Hall.'

As heartening as Ethan's news was, she had a vicious attacker to apprehend and very few clues as to his identity.

CHAPTER TWENTY-ONE

Beth switched off the power ballads as she drew into the car park of the Coachman Inn. The drive to Talkin had been treacherous to say the least. She'd felt her little car slipping and sliding on the snow-covered country roads and at one point she'd been sure she would leave the road and plunge her car into a ditch. Somehow she'd regained control, but the experience had shaken her.

On the road up she'd called Laura Sinclair to check if she had returned home to a locked or unlocked house.

O'Dowd hadn't given her a chance to check HOLMES. She'd only just had enough time to listen to O'Dowd's briefing before she was shooed out of the office.

On the drive over, she'd passed a sign for Talkin Tarn at a narrow road end. She'd learned, through researching Talkin, the tarn was a popular place for people walking their dogs or just taking a stroll. The sixty-five acre tarn was glacial in origin and fed by underground streams. It played home to a tearoom and was used for water sports during warmer weather.

Due to a road being used as a boundary, half of the village of Talkin was in the 'North Pennines Area of Outstanding Beauty'; the other half of the village, that was just a picturesque collection of houses in Cumbria.

The snow on the roofs added to the beauty of Talkin and there was a definite Christmas-card vibe going on with the light snow that was falling.

When Beth exited her car she found herself in front of a large man who had a ruddy face and a squareness about him that suggested he could have been made from Lego.

'You the DC?' His accent was as Scottish as Beth had ever heard.

'Yes I am.' Beth looked the man in the eye. 'I take it that you're DS McKay. DI O'Dowd said you'd be filling in for DS Thompson.'

'Aye. So tell me, DC, what took you so long to get here? The early bird catches the worm an' a' that.'

Beth noticed that he'd never bothered to ask her name. That he'd not given her the slightest hint of respect as a fellow officer. She might be a DC to his DS, but she was a permanent member of the FMIT whereas he was a temporary replacement. As tempted as she was to point all this out to McKay, she kept her mouth shut. He seemed the type who'd either make her life miserable for having the temerity to answer back, or worse, go running to O'Dowd or the Professional Standards Department with tales of insubordination. Her career was too important to Beth for her to risk a black mark just because a DS was acting like a prat.

As the only other vehicle in the pub's car park was an aging 4x4, Beth took a punt. 'My la'al car is only two-wheel drive, sir. Maybes when I make sergeant I'll be able to afford a 4x4 like you.'

Beth had made a point of pronouncing little as la'al in the Cumbrian fashion as an act of rebellion. Depending on how long McKay had worked in Cumbria would dictate how au fait he was with the local dialect. It was a small and petty thing to do, but it was her way of testing the DS while also keeping him in his place. He'd either be translating the Cumbrian terms into the English he knew, or he'd have to make guesses as to what the meanings were. Best-case scenario was that he'd be forced to ask.

The only reply McKay gave her was a grunt.

'So then, sir, I take it you've gone over the case notes. Where do you want to start?'

Again Beth's words were chosen to put the DS on the spot, find out if he'd bothered to bring himself up to speed, or had just arrived with the plan of winging it until he had a grasp of things.

'First off, we speak to the guy Sinclair elbowed. Then the guy who's allegedly the real father of Drewitt's bairn and then we finish off with Drewitt.'

'Fair enough. Nicky Johnson lives at Yew Tree Cottage.'

'Thank you, detective. I can read a report.'

Beth did everything she could to hide her anger at McKay's crass treatment of her as they walked along to Yew Tree Cottage. Her knee was throbbing and the plaster she'd put on the hand she'd scraped refused to stay in place. She really should have let Ethan put a bandage on it as he'd wanted to.

Nicky Johnson's cottage was fronted by local stone and a sliver of pavement. There was no room for anything else and, from the look of it, Beth suspected that Yew Tree Cottage was hundreds of years old.

When the door opened it revealed a young man with a beard that was all wisp and no substance. His eyes were bleary and he was dressed in loose joggers and a baggy T-shirt. Not that the T-shirt was too big for him, more that he was too small for it.

To say he was slight would be an understatement. Beth knew her father would have said he'd seen more meat on a butcher's pencil, yet that didn't begin to describe Johnson.

His was the emaciated look of someone who was on the point of malnourishment. Beth would have suspected drug abuse, but druggies who got themselves this thin didn't go to the pub on a Saturday night. Therefore Johnson was either in possession of a high metabolism, had an illness of some kind or he was on the breadline and couldn't afford to eat on a regular basis. Again, the latter part of this idea was disputed by his presence in the pub.

Beth trailed the two men into the cottage and found a large-screen TV with a video game on pause. On the TV a battleship's guns were blazing towards the holograph of an aeroplane at the bottom and centre of the screen.

The furniture was all decent quality and there was a neat pile of video games on a stylish coffee table.

McKay forged ahead with his questions. Each one belched out as if a shell from the battleship on the TV screen.

Beth couldn't help but notice the way Johnson deflected them all with ease.

With McKay taking centre stage and not letting Beth get a word in edgeways, she listened to Johnson's answers and made her own judgements. To look at, Johnson had the appearance of someone who'd be flattened by a sudden gust of wind, but she'd learned never to take things at face value. For all they knew, he could be a black belt at karate or some other martial art.

He had no alibi for the hours after the fight, having come home and crashed out, as he didn't have a partner who could vouch for his presence.

It was when McKay asked about Johnson's work that things got interesting. Johnson made his money as a vlogging gamer.

Like the Neanderthal he seemed to be, McKay clearly had no idea what vlogging was, and his incredulity that Johnson made a living by uploading videos of himself talking about video games to the internet was beautiful to watch. Johnson's income came from sponsorship by the games distributers and in-video advertising.

Beth had friends who were hooked on fashion or lifestyle vlogs, but whenever she'd looked at them, there hadn't been many which held her interest for more than a minute or two. She'd dug out a vlog or two that concentrated on puzzles and riddles, but rather than get puzzles to take away and work on, the answers were always given, and after watching them, Beth had been left with the underlying feeling that most of them wouldn't have presented the challenge she was looking for.

As the interrogation went on, Beth leaned forward, ignoring the protest from her injured knee, and picked up the pile of games on the table. She looked at each title in turn, both front and back, and learned enough to give her theory a foundation if nothing else.

McKay was pushing Johnson on his reaction to getting elbowed by Sinclair but the young gamer was passing it off as alcohol-fuelled bravery.

'I mean, come on, you can see the size of me, I'd get battered if I took him on. My reaction was a spur-of-the-moment thing in drink.'

'What makes you think you'd get a silver medal? Was Sinclair a hard man or something?'

'James, a hard man?' Johnson's head shook. 'Never known him to ever show even the slightest anger before Saturday. Be honest, I'm amazed at the way he kicked off. We had a few pints and a laugh together as we've done many a time before. I don't know why he kicked off, but it's definitely not like him.'

McKay kept pushing, but the answers kept coming back the same. Johnson had neither an alibi nor a grudge about what had happened. The elbow he'd caught had been a stray one aimed at someone else and his reaction had been alcohol-fuelled.

As they were walking from the cottage towards the home of the builder accused of fathering Drewitt's child, Beth's phone rang. She looked at the screen and felt a buzz of hope when she saw it was O'Dowd. With luck the DI would be calling to separate her from the obnoxious McKay.

The DI's first five words were enough to send a chill down Beth's spine that had nothing to do with the weather conditions.

CHAPTER TWENTY-TWO

Laura clutched her father's hand in hers and tried not to wring it. The counsellor sitting opposite her was well meaning, but she had no patience for the man's platitudes.

At this moment in time, all she could focus on was the news that James's condition had changed. He wasn't out of the woods, but the sensors monitoring his broken body had indicated that his heartbeat was strengthening. The doctors were now using the term 'cautious but optimistic' to describe how they felt regarding his condition. It had been music to her ears, the news she'd been praying for.

Then the realisation had hit her. Now that James's heart was strengthening, the doctors would be planning his care and rehabilitation. The first step of which was the double amputation.

The psychologist in his tweed jacket with the leather elbow patches couldn't know what she was going through. The coping mechanisms he was suggesting were a load of bullshit.

How could she take him seriously when he had one of those stupid over-sculpted beards? To Laura's mind, any man who could waste time on that amount of facial trimming had nothing better to do with their life.

The underlying feeling Laura had was that this was all too soon. James wasn't yet strong enough for the operation that would take his legs, therefore she didn't see why the psychologist had been brought in now when all he was doing was prattling on about how James would feel when he came out of his coma and learned of his amputations.

The psychologist didn't know James. He'd never lain on a blanket and looked up at the stars with James, shared hopes and dreams with him. He didn't know his favourite films, the music he liked or the kind of books he read. Most of all, he didn't know James's personality, the quiet acceptance he met life's challenges with, the passion he felt about cooking food from scratch and making delicious but healthy meals.

Most of all, the psychologist didn't know of James's heart, the driving force that compelled him to overcome every obstacle that life threw in his way. *She* knew of James's heart, she was his wife. She knew everything about James.

Except she didn't.

She knew he was from London. That when he'd been orphaned at the age of eighteen he'd moved to Carlisle and got his first kitchen job. Other than that, she knew virtually nothing of his origins.

Laura knew that James had issues with his early life. He suffered terrible nightmares in the last week of September, but never at any other time of year. She'd tried to get him to talk about it, but he just apologised for waking her and clammed up. A surprise trip she'd booked to London for the proverbial dirty weekend had had to be cancelled due to his refusal to return to the capital. He'd claimed it was too painful for him to be anywhere near his old stamping ground.

While she'd accepted his reasoning at the time, when she'd looked back at the conversation with hindsight, she'd classed it as the one time she was sure he was lying to her. Had everything else about him not been so perfect, she might have pushed the issue, but her pursuit of the happiness he brought into her life had been of more importance to her than one ruined weekend.

The psychologist was still droning on, offering forward coping mechanisms both for her and for James. She wasn't listening to him. Didn't care what he was saying. James's heart and her love for him would see them conquer whatever challenges lay ahead.

However, on a clipboard between her and the psychologist was the biggest challenge she'd ever faced. She knew what she had to do. Her brain was telling her that it was the right thing to do. It was her heart that was the problem. If she signed her name on the consent form for the operation to amputate James's legs, she'd be betraying him. Letting him down when he needed her most.

Yes, the doctors had told her that his lower legs were beyond repair and that James would never walk on them again, but they were his legs and she was his wife. How the hell could she give the surgeons permission to cut off parts of her husband?

She looked to her father for support. His face was grave, but the look in his eyes stoical.

'Darling, you need to think about reversing the roles here. What would you want James to do if you were in his position? I know it's awful having to sign that form, but the doctors have explained everything. If you don't sign it, they'll treat James as best they can, but when he comes round and learns for himself he'll never walk again without having his legs amputated and prosthetics fitted, what do you think he'll do? What would you do if you were in his position?'

Laura squeezed her eyes shut until they hurt. This was an impossible dilemma, but her father was making sense. James would prefer the challenge of learning to walk on prosthetics over being wheelchair bound. She opened her eyes and with a set to her jaw scrawled her signature in the box marked 'next of kin' on the consent form.

As she laid down the pen she offered a silent prayer that James wouldn't hate her for this decision.

CHAPTER TWENTY-THREE

Beth hung up the phone and began to process everything O'Dowd had just passed on to her. McKay had a quizzical look about him, but was too self-absorbed to enquire. She wouldn't keep the call secret from him, but she was damned if she was going to go running to the obnoxious sod with news of the two bodies that were currently being retrieved from the northern end of Lake Ullswater.

A farmer who'd had enough about him to recognise that the twin shapes floating in the lake weren't lumps of wood or some other kind of debris had called the police and in turn they'd contacted the coastguard. As soon as the PC who'd been sent out in the coastguard's dinghy had seen the head injuries on the bodies pulled from the lake, he'd radioed Control and suggested that FMIT be contacted. So far there was no identification for the men who'd been pulled out, but that would come soon enough.

As much as her blood chilled at the thought of at least one person being murdered, Beth also felt a rush of excitement at the possibility of a connection with the Sinclair case.

The best of it was that she'd been instructed to attend the post-mortem at 2 p.m. She'd learn then if her initial thoughts were right and if there was any foundation to the nasty suspicions growing in her mind.

'You gonna tell me what that call was about? Or was it a personal call you took when you should be focussing on the case?'

Beth gave him the facts she'd got from O'Dowd and kept her theories to herself. McKay wasn't the kind of sergeant who'd listen to opinions from a mere constable. He was too cocksure to believe that anyone of a lower rank could possibly contribute anything worth listening to. She'd met a few of his type during her career and they were all the same: arrogant, selfish and, for the most part, as far advanced in their careers as they were able to get.

'Right then, before you leave to go and flutter your eyelashes at all the doctors, we'll go and see this builder who's supposed to have fathered Drewitt's bairn. What's his name again?'

'Billy Craven.'

CHAPTER TWENTY-FOUR

A layer of snow topped the red transit van in the driveway of Billy Craven's home. Unlike the small cottages on the other side of the road, Craven's house boasted a second storey and a spacious garden. Beth was no judge of architecture, but she guessed the house was at least a hundred years old.

Stencilled onto the side of the van was 'Wm Craven. Paving and Groundworks Specialist' along with a mobile phone number. From the nature of his speciality, it was no surprise to Beth that he wasn't working today. With snow covering the ground, there was no way he'd be able to get on with any of his jobs. She thought it odd that he'd used a different contraction of his full name to advertise his business than he was known by. Wm was a shorter version of William that wasn't used as often as it used to be. Perhaps that was a clue to Craven's personality; maybe he was old-fashioned in his thinking.

A pleasant woman answered the door and led them into a kitchen where a tall man with a bald head was studying a pile of what looked like invoices and delivery notes. A sales brochure on the table caught Beth's attention. Craven's concentration on the task at hand meant he never heard their approach.

While McKay repeated the introductions, Beth assessed Craven. He was a big lump of a man. Strong and powerful, yet he seemed to be quite genial. The backs of his fingers bore patches of broken skin where he'd scuffed a knuckle on something, and below the sleeves of his faded Simply Red T-shirt, his arms were a riot of colourful tattoos.

For all his outward pleasantness, Beth sensed there was a dangerous edge to Craven; that if riled, his first reaction would be to clench one of those mighty fists.

As with Johnson, McKay took the lead and kept his only interaction with Beth to glances to make sure she was taking a note of Craven's answers.

Craven's responses were more articulate than Beth would have anticipated for such a lumbering hulk of a man. She knew it was wrong to judge a book by its cover, and that by having preconceptions she was neither being fair to Craven nor keeping an open mind about the investigation.

'Can I get you a cuppa?' Mrs Craven reached for the kettle.

'Please. Tea for me, one sugar and a dribble of milk. And don't worry about biscuits.'

Beth tried not to show her dislike at the way McKay used passive aggression to get some biscuits on the table as well. Craven had caught it too, his eyes narrowed for a moment, before his natural bonhomie returned.

When they were all cradling a cup, McKay barged into the interview with the same lack of tact he'd shown while quizzing Nicky Johnson.

'I beg your pardon? Are you asking me if I'm the father of Charles Drewitt's youngest?' Craven's shoulders trembled as he laughed in McKay's face. 'That rumour is a load of nonsense and is completely untrue. Jesus. I know you have to investigate what happened to James Sinclair and that by now you're probably aware of what happened in the pub on Saturday night, but Christ on a bike, you're a million miles off target with that.'

As McKay pushed at Craven for an explanation, Beth kept her eyes on the builder's wife. She was relaxed, comfortable. The look in her eyes spoke of amusement rather than anger at her husband's alleged infidelity.

'That rumour has been doing the rounds for years. It's a load of nonsense. I was working up there around the time she got pregnant and a couple of old busybodies put two and two together and made five.'

'So there's no truth in the rumour?'

'Not even the slightest hint of it.' Craven gave an easy shrug and nodded his head towards his wife. 'I have a beautiful wife at home, why would I risk losing her for a quickie with a woman so ugly it's a wonder Drewitt can distinguish between her and those pigs he keeps?'

Mrs Craven flapped the towel she was holding towards Craven's shoulder. 'Billy, don't be mean. She's nice enough when you get to know her.'

Again Craven nodded towards his wife. 'This one sees the good in everyone. Doesn't see what they're really like. Drewitt's wife is an ugly woman with a vicious tongue. He deserves a medal for marrying her and another one for each of the kids he's given her.'

The towel hit the back of Craven's bald head with enough force to create a slapping sound.

Beth flicked her eyes back to Mrs Craven expecting to see anger, but saw only exasperated fondness.

'Tell them, Billy. Tell them why you can't be the father of the Drewitt lass.'

Craven looked at his wife and then back at McKay. 'When Josie and I got together, we decided we didn't want kids. Josie couldn't take the pill, it made her ill, and condoms are horrible things, so I had the snip. The op was ten years ago and the lass is about five, so, regardless of the fact I've never slept with Drewitt's wife, even if I had, there's no way I could have got her pregnant.'

Despite McKay's body language telling her he was giving up on this line of enquiry, Beth had some questions she wanted answered herself.

'So you can't have kids, and you haven't slept with Mrs Drewitt. That doesn't mean you wouldn't be angry at James Sinclair spouting off. From what we've heard, Mr Drewitt was furious and tried to punch you. Why do you think Sinclair accused you of being the child's father?'

A shrug. 'That's typical of Drewitt. He judges her by his own standards. According to the rumour mill – which we've already established is a joke – he's had dozens of affairs. Whether it's true or not, I neither know nor care. Look, we were all pissed on Saturday night, and when Charles and James kicked off, everyone got drawn into it when James started mouthing off. James totally lost it. He was having a pop at everyone he could see. I think he brought up that rumour as a way to piss Drewitt off rather than have a go at me.'

'Fair enough.' Beth dragged her eyes away from the sales brochure she'd spotted on the table. 'Was it like James Sinclair to get mouthy with drink?'

'Not at all. Quite the opposite. He'd have a bit of banter and a laugh with everyone, but Saturday was the first time I've seen him like that. Or as drunk as that when I think about it. To be honest, it was a bit of a shock him chopsing off like that. It was almost like an explosion of pent-up anger.'

Beth took a look at the sales brochure again and made a decision. 'William Craven, I'm arresting you on suspicion of grievous bodily harm with intent…'

CHAPTER TWENTY-FIVE

Beth had to give McKay his due, he'd not questioned her once as they arrested a bemused Craven and arranged for a van to take him to Durranhill Station for a formal interview, but with the van now on its way towards Carlisle, he turned on her.

'Right then, young lady, you better have a good explanation for lifting him, because if you don't I'll make sure that any blame that comes our way for arresting the wrong man is directed straight at you.'

The term 'young lady' was enough to get Beth's back up without McKay washing his hands of any responsibility.

'I noticed a few things which, when you put them together, all suggested that he might be the person who assaulted James Sinclair.' Beth gave McKay what she hoped was a patronising look. 'I'm sure you noticed them yourself, but I'll list them for you in case either of us missed another clue. First there were the scuffs to his knuckles, which looked fresh to me. Naturally they could be a sign that he'd been fighting. Then you had the sales brochure on the table. It was open at a page which featured different masonry chisels.'

'What? You think that's what he used to attack Sinclair with, a hammer and chisels?'

'Think about it, sir. Masonry chisels won't be sharp like wood chisels, they're blunt because they're designed to break bricks and stone rather that cut wood. That explains the welts on Sinclair's body and the lack of blood from his wounds. I expect a forensic pathologist would use a term such as "concussion trauma" to describe each break as there's little actual damage to the skin and—'

'Hang on, what do you mean forensic pathologist? Has Sinclair died and nobody told me?'

Beth shook her head. 'He's not dead. We consulted the forensic pathologist as he has experience of identifying the cause of wounds. Third, Craven accused Sinclair of chopsing off. The only time I've heard the expression "chopsing off" was from someone who was in the army. This made me look at Craven's tattoos a little more closely. In among the death's heads and daggers there was one that looked like a cap badge. When we left I took another look at the picture on the wall of the hallway. It looked like a passing-out parade and it had a stamp on the white outer part that matched Craven's tattoo. There was also the inscription that stated they were "Royal Marine, 40 Commando". Craven isn't just a former solider, sir. He's a trained killing machine who as a builder knows how to use a hammer and masonry chisel.'

Beth could see McKay was floundering to keep up with her logic, and so far as she could tell from the way his face had registered each new piece of information, he hadn't made a single one of the connections for himself.

'But, why the brochure for new chisels?'

'Sinclair didn't bleed a lot, but he did lose some blood. I'd suggest that rather than risk having a trace of Sinclair's blood or DNA found on his chisels, Craven launched them into Talkin Tarn or dumped them somewhere else. There's also the chance that a nick or the shape of a chisel would identify them as the weapons used. All in all, another reason to get rid of them. As he uses them in his day job, he'd have to replace them.'

'You keep saying "them". Do you think he used more than one chisel?'

'Absolutely. According to what Dr Hewson told me, the wounds are symmetrical and when you think about the curve of someone's foot at the toe end, it'd make sense to use a smaller, narrower chisel to break each toe rather than a wide one to try and break them all at once.'

'I see your point, but I'm still o' the opinion that you've arrested the wrong man.' McKay looked at his watch. 'You run aff to your post-mortem, I'm gan to speak to Charles Drewitt and then the wife-swappers. I'll get you at Durranhill to interview Craven later.'

Beth left him to get on with what he was doing. In some respects she wanted to face off against Craven as soon as possible, but if her suspicions about the new victims were correct, it was better to wait until she'd attended the post-mortem, as the more information she had, the better she could grill Craven. The man was smart, behind the tattoos and the huge frame, he possessed a good vocabulary and an understanding of how things were.

The thing that bugged her most of all was that Craven had accepted his arrest without complaint. He'd even told his wife not to worry and that he'd be home before long. Either Craven was innocent and she'd leapt to a conclusion, or he was smart enough to know that beyond the coincidences she'd spotted, there was no real evidence tying him to either James Sinclair's assault, or that of the two men who'd been found in Lake Ullswater.

She'd find out at Durranhill Station, but first there was the matter of the post-mortems.

CHAPTER TWENTY-SIX

Dr Hewson was scrubbed and ready to begin the post-mortems when Beth arrived at the pathology suite in the bowels of Cumberland Infirmary. His face held that mixture of curiosity and remorse that was becoming all too familiar to Beth.

As much as Hewson dealt with death on a daily basis, Beth knew that he hated the murder cases as they always spoke of a life cut short. Usually in violent circumstances, and regardless of the killer's motive, the justifications never matched the fact that a man or woman had consciously chosen to end the life of another human being.

The counterpoint to this was the pathologist's need to find answers in those unfortunate enough to end up on his dissecting table. He'd made no secret of the fact that he enjoyed the challenge of working out what had happened to the victims and giving the police clues that could lead to an arrest.

Rather than speak, he gave her a terse nod and strode off towards his lab. As she fell in behind him, Beth told him about her theory about Craven being the one who'd assaulted James Sinclair, and when she got to the part where she told him about the masonry chisels, he stopped and turned to look at her.

'You know, DC Protégé, I think you just might be right. However, there are some differences between the two most recent victims and Mr Sinclair.'

'Before you tell me about the differences, are you aware that the two men fished from Lake Ullswater have been identified?'

Beth knew from experience Hewson liked to know who appeared in the pathology suite so he could refer to them by their given names. For him it was all about showing respect to the deceased.

'No, who are they?'

'Harry Anderson and Tommy Long.'

Beth thought about the telephone conversation she'd had with O'Dowd on the way to the hospital. While O'Dowd had been eager to get Beth's side of the story regarding Craven's arrest, Beth had also been excited to hear the DI's news about the two men.

They were a pair of low-level thugs best known by their nicknames of Harrytosis and Dippen due to Anderson's bad breath and Long's squint. Neither nickname was complimentary, but as both men operated on the fringes of society, they could expect nothing else. Political correctness might find its way into boardrooms, shop floors, and a thousand other places of work and social interaction, but it wasn't likely to take hold in the gangs which controlled crime.

As nicknames were rife in the underworld, the police often found themselves more attuned to criminals' nicknames than their real names. O'Dowd had used Harrytosis and Dippen when updating Beth and laying out the police records of the two men.

'Right then, DC Protégé, I have given these two gentlemen a preliminary examination and before we get started on my findings, I would like to identify who is who so that the recording of their post-mortems is accurate. Did Dowdy O'Dowd tell you about any identifying marks?'

'She didn't. But she did say that Tommy Long was nicknamed Dippen due to his squint and that Anderson was known as Harrytosis because of his bad breath.'

'No doubt short for dip and dazzle.' Hewson's eyes twinkled as he looked at her.

Beth had forgone her usual trick of smearing VapoRub on her top lip as she wasn't planning to stay around until Hewson began his dissection of the two men.

Hewson grunted and walked over to the nearest body. His gloved fingers caressed both eyelids and drew them upwards.

'I'd say this is Mr Long, wouldn't you?'

Beth leaned over and took a look at the corpse's eyes. The left eye's iris was centred but the right's was so high in the eye the edge of its pupil was tight up against the eyelid. As soon as she saw the differing heights in the irises she understood why he'd picked up his less than complimentary nickname.

'I would say so.'

'Good.' Hewson reached up and switched on the Dictaphone which hung from a cable above the steel table. 'I know you'll want to see what's been done to their heads, but first, I want to point a few things out to you.'

Beth followed Hewson's wave and joined him at Long's feet. She could see without being told that Long's right knee was bruised and misshapen. 'Would I be right in saying that happened pre-mortem?'

'You would. I took a quick X-ray of it and not only is the patella broken, but the anterior cruciate ligament has been snapped.' He bent over and used a pen as a pointer. 'If you look here, you'll see the point of impact shows a scuffing abrasion to the skin.'

Beth did as she was told and took a closer look. It was faint but she could see what Hewson was showing her. It was enough to allow her to start putting together the sequence of events.

'I see it. What else have you found?'

Hewson drew her across to the table bearing Anderson and positioned her by the head end. From here she could see the flattened top of Anderson's cranium but Hewson was pointing at the man's throat.

'This man's trachea has been collapsed by a blow to the Adam's apple. Other than what has been done to his skull, which we'll come to in due course, he bears no other injuries.' Hewson pointed at the throat. 'You'll see a slight patch of reddening, perhaps an inch wide.' Beth nodded to show she had seen it. 'That is synonymous with a hard blow being delivered. Mr Anderson would have died gasping for breaths that his ruined trachea wouldn't allow through.'

'So that's what killed him? Not what's happened to his head?'

'Precisely.' Hewson returned to Long's table. 'Now if you look at this gentleman's throat you'll see a similar set of markings that indicate he died the same way; however, if you look particularly closely, you'll see the reddening is incomplete.'

'What does that mean?'

'What do *you* think it means?'

Beth had grown used to Hewson challenging her this way, but try as she might she couldn't think of a solution, until she remembered the damage to Dippen's knee. She closed her eyes and worked through a scenario or two. The first was where the men were attacked one by one. A solid blow akin to a karate chop had been delivered to Harrytosis's neck which had crushed his windpipe. He'd have gone down and died at the feet of his attacker.

As for Dippen, maybe he'd blocked the karate chop and had then had his knee kicked outwards which would have caused the broken kneecap and the ligament damage. He'd have tumbled to the ground and then been killed with an unrestricted chop to the throat as he clutched his injured knee. This made sense on a certain level, as O'Dowd had told her that Dippen and Harrytosis were always together.

The second idea Beth had was that rather than being targets, the pair of thugs had started out as aggressors and had tangled with the wrong person. When she ran this through her mind she could picture the scene; Dippen's knee had been kicked out to disable him while their intended victim took Harrytosis down with a lethal chop to the throat.

Then it would be a case of delivering a similar chop to the throat of Dippen. Except there was a difference between the marks on the two men's throats. The marks on Harrytosis's throat spoke of a single blow, whereas the minute gaps between the markings on

Dippen's throat suggested either multiple blows or of him being struck in a different way with a different weapon than the edge of a hand.

Again she ran through the fight in her mind. This time she allowed for Dippen's reaction to what happened to his mate. If he'd seen Harrytosis gasping for air, he would have tried to protect his throat when their prey turned hunter. With his knee kicked out from under him, he'd either be on his back or his side.

Beth's hands rose to the side of her head as she acted out the movements she supposed Harrytosis had made. Her head ducked forward and her chin rested on the top of her sternum.

While she felt protected in this position she knew it was a falsehood. The muscles of the neck aren't generally that strong and a firm push on the forehead would tilt the head back enough to expose Dippen's Adam's apple. With Dippen's hands raised, a karate chop wouldn't be possible but there was still enough space for a fist to fly through the gap. If the person who'd delivered the blow that killed Harrytosis had meant to kill, there was a chance that they knew karate or another martial art, therefore they might have delivered the punch to Dippen's throat with extended knuckles. Beth nodded to herself; that was what had happened, it explained the different markings. The actual running order of things may be a little different, but in her mind that's how it went down.

Beth took a deep breath and then relayed her thoughts to Hewson. The way he smiled and nodded as she spoke gave her confidence she was on the right track.

'That's pretty much what I thought, DC Protégé.' Hewson's face turned grave again. 'There is one other question that you'll have to answer though. Once these two gentlemen were dead, why did their killer see fit to mutilate their skulls before dumping their bodies?'

As she waited for Hewson to move on to the wounds to their heads, Beth knew he was right to raise that question. She also felt he was right to show the people on his tables the respect he did. They'd never know he referred to them as gentlemen or ladies, but it showed his reverence and innate goodness.

Hewson pointed to the light box used to display X-rays. 'The switch is on the right-hand side. Before you look at the bodies, you might want to see the damage to their craniums that doesn't show externally.'

Beth flicked the switch and gasped in revulsion as she looked at the two X-rays.

CHAPTER TWENTY-SEVEN

While she wasn't familiar with looking at X-rays, Beth could see enough detail on both to understand the horrific nature of their injuries. The only sliver of mercy they'd been shown, was the fact they'd died before the killer had set about their grisly task.

Beth had no doubt in her mind that the pair of thugs had fallen victim to the person she was now starting to think of as the Chiseller.

The first X-ray showed Harrytosis's injuries. The bone was broken in a specific pattern that resembled a rugby ball, or would have done if the cuts hadn't carried on a further inch at one end. Although it was vertical, Beth recognised it as the fish symbol so often associated with early Christianity.

Beth shifted her focus to the second X-ray. It depicted a different tableau of destruction. Instead of a fish symbol, the top of Dippen's head had a triangle bisected by what looked to be an eye etched into it. Where the iris should be was a blank space of nothingness. To Beth it was like looking into the eye of a soulless killer.

The triangle overlaid with an eye was a symbol Beth had seen before, but she couldn't remember where.

She pulled out her phone to do a Google search only to find she had no signal in the bowels of the hospital. That detail could wait, although Hewson may be able to shed some light on it.

Beth cast her eyes towards the pathologist and found him looking her way.

'Your thoughts?'

'Sick. Twisted. Skilful. Iconic.' Beth didn't worry about the way she'd blurted out the random words. Hewson knew her well enough to know that there were times her brain took a moment to bring order to the multitude of thoughts that whirled around.

'I agree with the sick and twisted. That the person who did this was skilful at what they do, is beyond doubt regardless of how repulsive it is, but iconic. What makes you say that?' Hewson's tone held no censure, and his eyes twinkled as he waited for Beth's response.

'The triangle with the eye. It's familiar to me, but beyond knowing it's a popular image or graphic, I can't remember what it represents.'

'It's the Eye of Providence. It's an early Christian symbol, often surrounded by what are meant to depict rays of sunlight. The eye represents God watching over humanity. It features on the American one-dollar bill, several coats of arms and has been partially adopted by Freemasons as well as featuring in such places as a temple in Salt Lake City and the front page of the constitution of Serbia.'

'How do you know so much about it?'

Hewson wagged a finger in admonishment. 'Remember how I told you I did a preliminary examination? What do you think I did when I saw the Eye of Providence?'

'You did what I would do and googled it.'

'Correct, but I wasn't finished telling you about the eye and its most common association. Believe it or not, the Eye of Providence is widely understood to be a symbol of the Illuminati.'

'The Illuminati? What, are you telling me the Illuminati are alive and active in Cumbria? That a shadowy group of figures who may not even exist, and allegedly control the world through the media and via their vast resources, are bothering with a rent-a-thug like Dippen?'

'I'm telling you about the connotations associated with a design that's been carved into the top of someone's head. I'm not telling you anything beyond that. Personally I believe the Illuminati don't exist, and their myth is the creation of historic governments as a way to shift blame for their own failings. However, my opinion only counts for things that are medically based and what I've told you about the Eye of Providence is factual if Wikipedia is correct. The other one is obviously an early Christian symbol as well, although, considering where the men were found, it may well be a sick joke about sleeping with the fishes.'

Beth flapped an apologetic hand at the pathologist. 'Sorry, I didn't mean to snap at you. I've had a rough morning and I honestly thought you were saying the Illuminati had turned up in Cumbria.'

'All is forgiven.' A gesture towards Dippen. 'Shall we begin our examinations?'

Beth took up a position at Hewson's shoulder as he bent to examine Dippen's head.

From here she could see some areas where the thin skin of the head had split under the Chiseller's ministrations. There was no blood to be seen, but she hadn't expected there to be any. Dippen had been dead when his skull had fallen victim to the Chiseller's iconography and she knew corpses didn't bleed. Not only that, Dippen's corpse had been immersed in water for at least a few hours which meant that any trace of blood would have washed off as the gentle waves of Lake Ullswater pressed into him.

Now she could see the wounds in situ, Beth noted that the baseline of the triangle was not just level with Dippen's ears, but also with the table he was lying on. The top point of the triangle was above the nose and the one significant puncture wound was the iris in the middle of the eye in the triangle.

'Hmmm.'

Hewson picked up a probe and gently touched all the areas of Dippen's head that had been marked by the chisel.

Beth felt her stomach lurch as she watched the top of Dippen's head pulse under Hewson's touch. The pathologist's voice was soft as he described what he was doing for the Dictaphone suspended above his dissecting table. When he used careful movements to insert the end of the probe into the iris at the centre of the design, her stomach gave an almighty heave.

Fraction by fraction the probe went in until Hewson slid his fingers forward and pinched the probe at the point where it disappeared inside Dippen's skull.

When he withdrew it, there were a few globules of pinkish grey matter clinging to the stainless steel probe.

As Beth battled with the bile threatening to burst from her mouth, Hewson lifted a ruler and measured from the end of the probe to where his fingers were clasping it. 'Thirty-eight millimetres, or an inch and half in old money if you prefer.'

Beth nodded as she forced the bile down her throat.

Hewson laid down his probe and the ruler then turned to face Beth. 'I know you're struggling here, but are you able to hold on for a few more minutes while we take a look at Mr Anderson?'

'Of course.' Beth gave a sharp nod to accompany her words. The last thing she wanted was her body letting her down, but she knew she'd have to steel herself for the examination of Harrytosis.

She followed Hewson as he moved to the table which held Harrytosis. The only thing she could focus on was the top of his head. Where Dip's head had retained its shape, Harrytosis's skull had a sunken area where the body of the fish had dropped to rest against the victim's brain.

Unlike Dippen's head, Harrytosis's bore no cuts to the skin. It was a point she knew she'd have to take up with Hewson, but for the moment, she couldn't take her eyes off the flattened area in front of her.

Rather than imagining liquefied brain matter attempting to press the broken fragments of skull back to their rightful place, in her mind, Harrytosis's killer had done his work with the chisels and then used his hand to press the fish's body inwards.

'Have you finished your examination?'

'To be honest, I'm not sure what it is I'm looking for.' Beth tossed a pleading look at the pathologist. 'I'm trying to work out why they were killed, let alone consider the reasons why the fish and the Eye of Providence were carved into their heads. And that's before we consider whether these pair are connected to what happened to James Sinclair.'

'I can't answer all of your questions, but I can possibly answer one or two of them.'

'What, so you think—?'

'All in good time.' Hewson peeled his gloves off and tossed them in the bin Beth had planned to use if her stomach failed her. 'Let's go back to my office. I have a few theories and I'm sure you don't want to wait until the post-mortem is finished to hear them.'

CHAPTER TWENTY-EIGHT

Hewson plonked himself into the seat behind his cluttered desk and waved for Beth to occupy the visitor's chair on the other side.

Rather than sit, Beth remained on her feet and looked at the pathologist's grave expression. 'I'm guessing that as usual you're going to ask for my thoughts before you tell me what you think?'

'Of course I am.' An easy smile appeared on his face. 'You have a fine mind and a habit of seeing things others don't, and as such, you trigger ideas in my mind as well.'

Beth felt her cheeks colour at the compliment. 'Okay then, say I'm right about a masonry chisel or chisels being used to injure James Sinclair, beyond the symmetrical nature of the injuries, it wouldn't require an awful lot of skill to inflict those wounds. However, when you look at what's been done to the heads of Harrytosis and Dippen, to my mind that would imply a level of skill that's beyond most people.'

'I agree with what you're saying about the skill level and, for the record, like you I think it's fair to work on the assumption the same person who assaulted Mr Sinclair is also responsible for the two gentlemen we've just looked at. What else are you thinking?'

'The Eye of Providence, forgetting all the connotations for the moment, the skin was split in a lot of areas where it was etched into Dippen's head, but there was hardly a mark on Harrytosis's skull. Can you explain that?'

'Good question. Working on your theory about chisels, I would suggest that a fractionally sharper chisel was used to make the Eye of Providence than was used on Mr Anderson. Until I open them up, I can't say for sure, but the X-rays back up this line of thinking.'

'Do they? Other than the designs, I didn't see any difference between them.'

'And how many years were you at medical school?' Hewson's tone robbed his words of any offence. 'Mr Long's skull showed impact breaks which speak of a more direct contact, whereas Mr Anderson's displayed signs of concussive fractures synonymous with a blunter impact. There's also the cumulative effect of Mr Anderson's injuries. I wouldn't expect you to notice with the naked eye, but when I took a look at both gentlemen's X-rays with a magnifying glass, I noticed that the curved cuts were done via a series of cuts with a straight-edged blade. I'm no expert on the subject, but I shouldn't imagine there's such a thing as a curved stone chisel, and if there is, I should think it would be a small radius as its purpose would be to cut gouges into stone rather than circular shapes.'

Beth nodded along with Hewson's words as she absorbed them and their meaning. She hadn't got as far as thinking about the style of chisels used, but she knew that it would be something O'Dowd would want to know.

'What about the fish on Harrytosis's head?'

'I wondered how long it'd take you to get back to that. Sticking with the theory that a masonry chisel inflicted the wounds, I think it's worth considering the killer has a full set of chisels and knows how to use them.'

Beth nodded her thanks as she thought what O'Dowd would make of this. A Christian symbol on one head and an Illuminati symbol on the other. There was every likelihood the DI wouldn't know what to make of it, but other than the person who'd carved the symbols, who would? She could foresee long hours scouring the internet and various textbooks as she tried to understand the Chiseller's motive in leaving those symbols on his victims. It was the kind of research Beth enjoyed, but with the way things were going, she didn't know when she'd have time to start looking.

'Setting aside what the symbols represent for a moment, have you considered how the killer got them so perfect? I mean, the curves of the fish looked so smooth, and that can't have been easy to do on a head. Do you think he used a template or something?'

Hewson scratched at his arm as his gaze focussed on the ceiling. 'I can't say I have thought about that, but you raise a very interesting point. I'm not sure that you could get a template for that kind of thing, and unless the killer knew the size and shape of the victim's head in advance, there's no way he could have made one.'

'Okay then, did he draw them out on his victims before he picked up his chisel?'

'It's a good theory, but I didn't see any signs of pen marks on their heads.'

Beth thought about the two heads she'd just viewed. Neither had even the slightest trace of pen or marker where the killer had drawn out his designs. 'He must have done them freehand; that's even scarier, isn't it?'

'It is. Your killer has an understanding of geometry and shape as well as great skill with their tools. I wish you good luck with identifying and finding this person.'

'Is there anything else I should be asking you?'

Hewson's eyes twinkled brighter than she'd ever seen before. 'Their time of death? It's usually the first question I'm asked.'

Beth cursed herself for missing the obvious question. 'What is it?'

'Unknown because they were immersed in near freezing water for an unspecified period. An educated guess from their body temperatures would indicate some time around midnight give or take four hours.'

'When can I expect your report on the post-mortems?'

'As soon as I've completed them and typed it up, I'll email it to you and Dowdy.'

Despite the pathologist's vague answer, Beth knew better than to push for a specific time. Hewson would get it to her as soon as it was ready, but he wouldn't commit to an exact time as he couldn't know how long the post-mortems, and any lab tests he felt necessary to run, would take.

CHAPTER TWENTY-NINE

Sandi wrapped a scarf around her neck and flicked her hair out from underneath it. A quick fuss in front of the mirror and she was ready to go.

It was her birthday, and while Leo wasn't the greatest boyfriend she'd ever had, he wasn't so bad that he wouldn't take her out for a nice meal on her special day.

He'd climbed out of the taxi with a bag of presents which now sat on her sofa. She'd unwrap them later and if he played his cards right, she might invite him to stay over on a week night.

As was typical of Leo, he'd not booked a table anywhere, and she knew he'd be assuming that they'd get in somewhere without any trouble. She was a step ahead of him and had reserved a table at the Bridge Inn, one of her favourite local pubs.

She gave the taxi driver directions and waited for a reaction from Leo.

None came. Instead he asked about her day and played the part of an attentive boyfriend. When he turned on the charm like this, Sandi could feel herself falling for him, but she knew what he was like, had experienced his inconsistencies too often to have real faith in him treating her the way she felt she deserved.

With a delicious three-course meal washed down with two large glasses of wine, Sandi just wanted to get home, remove her Spanx and slob out on the couch, but she knew that was unfair on Leo.

He'd surprised her by having a bouquet of flowers waiting for her at the Bridge Inn and had admitted that he'd also booked a table, knowing that she wanted to dine there.

The way he was behaving made her feel as if she was the sun and he was orbiting her and radiating in her warmth. Tonight she felt more special than she had in years.

The only blight on her day had been the lack of contact from Kevin. He'd never failed to contact her on her birthday before. Regardless of the years they'd spent apart, he'd always wished her a happy birthday.

Sandi pushed Kevin from her mind. She was with Leo now. Kevin was the past and Leo, if not the future, was certainly the present.

She watched as Leo rose from his chair, one hand dipping into his jacket pocket.

Sandi presumed he was getting his wallet so he could pay the bill, when he knelt in front of her and lifted her left hand from the table.

'Sandi White, you have changed my life since the day we met. I know I haven't always been the boyfriend you wanted, but if you agree to be my wife, I promise I'll spend the rest of my life being the husband you deserve. Will you do me the great honour of marrying me?'

As she blinked in surprise at the proposal, Sandi noticed a waiter hovering in the background with a bottle of champagne in an ice bucket. To her left and right the people at the adjacent tables were watching her in expectation.

She looked at Leo again. He had an open ring box on the palm of his hand and hope in his eyes. The ring was a proper sparkler, although a piece of bling wasn't enough to sway her into such a momentous decision.

The hope in Leo's eyes turned to uncertainty as he waited for her answer. For Sandi, time was standing still. If a friend had asked her if she wanted to marry Leo, she'd have said no without even thinking about it. Yet now Leo was asking, it was a different question. When she ran her mind over his behaviour towards her over the last few months, she realised he'd let her down far less and treated her much better.

His proposal wasn't a pack of lies, it was the truth. Like a fine wine, he'd improved with age.

'Yes. Yes I will marry you.'

As Leo swept her up in a bear hug and kissed her, Sandi could hear the popping of a cork over the round of applause that swept the room.

When Sandi wiped the tears from her eyes, she was unsure if they were a symptom of happiness at having shaken off the past, or regret about the future she'd just chosen for herself. Whichever way she looked at it, at her age, Leo was her last chance of finding someone who'd be a father to the children she wanted.

CHAPTER THIRTY

Beth found O'Dowd stalking through the corridors of Durranhill Station. The DI's hair was unruly at the best of times, but today it looked as if it had been styled by a leaf blower.

O'Dowd listened as Beth related what she'd learned from Hewson. As she spoke, Beth could see the tightening of the DI's jaw and the narrowing of her eyes. She had to give the older woman credit for listening without interrupting, but she knew O'Dowd was itching to cross-examine her and vent some of the anger that was building.

When Beth finished speaking, O'Dowd fixed her with a stare. 'So, you think this Craven guy is the madman with the chisel? If you're right, I want the evil bastard nailed down for this. That symbolic shit carved into their heads is another level of sick. I'm going to let you and McKay take the lead with the first round of interviews. You can soften him up and then I want at the evil prick. Make sure you get everything from him. I want the connection between Sinclair, Harrytosis and Dippen exposed. I want the reasons for the symbols explained in a way that a six-year-old would understand. You got that?'

'Yes, ma'am.'

'Good.' O'Dowd thrust a folder at Beth. 'This is what we have on Harrytosis and Dippen. It's also got the report from Digital Forensics on Sinclair's iPad. Seems like he wasn't the goody two shoes everyone thinks. He's been doing a dead letter drop in an email account. Leaving messages in some weird code.'

'Have Digital Forensics cracked the code?' Beth felt her pulse quicken as she awaited the answer. Codebreaking wasn't normally the kind of puzzle she tackled, but if Digital Forensics hadn't used one of their programs to break it, she was more than happy to try and find the solution.

'No they bloody well haven't. They said that all codebreaking tasks now have to be sent to GCHQ to let the spooks at it. When I asked how long it'd take to get a response they laughed and said they were still waiting for an answer to one they sent back in September. Basically, if it's connected to terrorism in any way, it's top priority, other than that, they're not interested.' O'Dowd threw her hands up. 'What's the point of having a room full of geeks if they have their hands tied by bloody pen pushers and their bureaucracy?'

'I'll take a look at it, ma'am. I like that kind of thing anyway, so leave it with me.'

'Thought you'd say that. There's a couple of the messages in that folder, but I've asked for them to email all the others to you. Now, off you go and get yourself prepped for the interview. I'm away to find someone I can cadge a cigarette off.'

Beth found an empty desk in the CID office and sat down to read the file O'Dowd had given her. As much as she wanted to get on with cracking the code, Beth knew that the most pressing issue was preparing for the interview with Craven. All the same she still took a quick look at one of the two messages in the folder.

It was a single line of random punctuation marks, numbers and the odd letter, without any spaces.

?2E-G8+g"*-/"{+*&6-;"+)68?|?|+_G6"E-G~;+8+/

As she looked at the row of symbols, Beth could feel her curiosity piquing and replacing the anger and disgust she felt at the Chiseller. Sinclair had a secret and she would break the code to reveal it.

She turned her attention to the reports detailing the last movements of Harrytosis and Dippen. Both men had been drinking in The Boilermaker's at the bottom end of Botchergate where it became London Road.

Beth knew the pub from her days in uniform. It was a dive bar where drink was taken until the ability to walk deserted the patrons. It was one of Carlisle's havens for stolen goods and its clientele were either hardened alcoholics or low-level thugs. That Dippen and Harrytosis had frequented the place was no surprise.

They'd left together at 10.15 and hadn't returned. Triangulation of their mobile phones had shown they'd walked a short way before ducking into an alley. After that, their mobiles stopped sending out signals, which indicated they'd either been smashed or had their batteries removed.

The reports from the officers who'd visited their families were inconclusive at best. Fingers had been pointed at other lowlifes, but it'd take a lot more digging to uncover which of the accusations had factual merit and which ones were a settling of scores.

Beyond the basics there was little known about the movements of either man; both were unemployed, but they were also known to provide muscle for one of Carlisle's gangs. Their stock in trade was standing around intimidating people. One time, they'd been hauled in and questioned over their involvement in a protection racket, but the person who'd made the complaint had retracted their statement. It smacked of intimidation, but that was no surprise.

Beth knew that while the people the two men associated with would give nothing to the police as a matter of principle, they'd also be looking to find out who'd killed them for their own reasons. There would be fear of another gang moving into their territory, or that they'd be the next target.

Organised crime ran drugs and prostitution in Cumbria and while there wasn't too much trouble between the two rival groups, two members of a gang being taken out the way Harrytosis and Dippen had been was enough to spark a turf war.

Billy Craven was in the frame for the murders and the attack on Sinclair, but until she got answers from him, Beth couldn't think of a connection between the three victims. O'Dowd's instruction that McKay was to join her grated on Beth's nerves. The DS didn't believe her theory about Craven and she wouldn't put it past him to do little to support her during the interview.

Worst of all though, was the fact she'd already messaged Ethan to warn him that she'd have to cancel their date for tonight. She'd been looking forward to seeing him, but the way things were going it'd be late before she got home, let alone stopped working on the code. She knew that once she started work on it, she'd become absorbed and would block out all other noises and distractions. While Ethan wasn't a noise, he was a distraction she couldn't ignore.

With everything that was happening and could potentially happen with the case, it was imperative that she focus on her job, and cracking that code could just lay the whole case wide open.

When Beth had all the details from the files memorised, she rose to go and find McKay; the sooner the interview with Craven started, the sooner they might get some answers.

CHAPTER THIRTY-ONE

Everything about Billy Craven spoke of stress as McKay went through the formalities for the benefit of the recording equipment. His fingers were fidgeting as his eyes pinballed around the interview suite. The earlier calm he'd displayed nothing more than a faint memory.

Suspects being nervous meant nothing to Beth. Either they were guilty and were aware of how much trouble they were in, or they were law-abiding people who were innocent and were terrified of being convicted of a crime they didn't commit.

Beth had grabbed a quick word with the DS before the interview began. McKay had finished his visits with the alleged wife-swappers and Charles Drewitt, but he hadn't thought of any of them as being vicious enough to attack Sinclair and leave him in the state he'd been found, let alone take on a pair of thugs.

While this was reassuring and backed up her theory about Craven on one level, Beth wasn't sure she trusted McKay's judgement as he'd missed all the things she'd picked up about Craven who'd been trained by the army to kill.

Beside the restless Craven was a duty solicitor who'd earned Beth's respect if not friendship. Chloe Ezzard was a solid professional who did her job with aplomb, but what had earned Beth's respect was the way Ezzard had shown revulsion at some of the people she'd been obliged to represent. Ezzard had been too professional to let it show in the interview room, but had made her feelings quite clear when her clients had been returned to their cells.

'I'm not going to waste my breath telling you Mr Craven is innocent of the crimes of which you accuse him. He's more than happy to answer any questions you have that will prove his innocence.'

Ezzard's words were standard fare, although Beth suspected the solicitor believed her client's innocence and would fight to protect him.

McKay had decreed in their brief meeting that as it was Beth's idea to arrest Craven she should take the lead with the questioning. It had been an act of backside covering and Beth was aware McKay was distancing himself from her theory lest it prove to be wrong. Should it pan out that Craven was the Chiseller, she expected McKay would start taking part to insert himself into the case and draw the credit that the arrest would garner. It was all office politics, and while Beth didn't bother herself with such things, it infuriated her that people like McKay would always put their own interests ahead of the case's.

'We have a few questions we'd like answers to, Mr Craven.'

'Fine, ask away.' Anxious fingers drummed on the table.

'To start with I'd like to get some background. You were arrested fifteen years ago for affray outside the Purple Turtle in Reading. Would you care to tell me what that was about?'

Craven licked his lips and looked at Beth. 'It was a night out with a few mates. A couple of guys were hassling this lass. We told them to bugger off. They pulled out knives and went for us. One of my mates dropped one of them and I dropped the other. It was something and nothing, but because I broke the guy's jaw, he tried to press charges. The CCTV footage cleared me of assault as I was acting in self-defence.' His eyes flitted to the folder in front of Beth. 'That's what it'll say in there. I know you'll have run my name through your computers. You'll know that I was a Royal Marines Commando, and as such, I've been trained to kill people in a variety of ways.'

'It does say that.' Beth considered her next words with care. 'What it doesn't say is why you left the army and started your own business.'

'I'd had my fill of the army life. Met a woman I wanted to settle down with and, quite honestly, I didn't like some of the jobs we were getting. You're looking into me for the attack on James and apparently two murders. That tells me that you'll have had a good look into me and probably gone through my army records. I dare say that you'll have found some of them sealed. You're probably thinking I did something I shouldn't have and got cashiered out. I didn't do anything of the kind. The same way that I didn't attack James Sinclair and I certainly didn't kill those other two guys.'

Beth cast a glance at McKay who failed to meet her eye. She would have liked to have known about Craven's army file. To her the classified parts spoke of perilous missions where nerves would have been stretched. PTSD was a possible side effect and there was no telling whether he'd got a taste for killing that he'd brought to civilian life.

'You're obviously not a foolish man, Mr Craven. Why did you start a company working with your hands when you probably could have got an office job with ease?'

Craven looked at Beth with sincerity all over his face. 'In the army, there was always someone else telling me what to do. I'm my own boss now. I like to work outdoors; I'm not the type to sit in an office with a tie throttling me and all the bullshit that's office politics doing my head in. Most of all though, I like having a job that lets me stand back at the end of the day and see what I've achieved. You can't get that from a computer screen or a pile of papers.'

'Fair enough. Now, about the attack on James Sinclair. Someone systematically attacked him with what we believe are masonry chisels. He's had his bones pulverised in his lower legs and arms.'

Craven winced. 'Jesus! Poor bugger. I know what's it's like to hit a fingernail with a hammer; that sounds awful.'

'Tell me, when I was at your house earlier with DS McKay, why was there a catalogue on the table open at a page that showed a series of masonry chisels?'

'What? I was looking at a set of screwdrivers! I'm sick of my brother borrowing mine and not returning them, so I was going to get him a set of his own for Christmas.' Craven gave her a blank look as he tried to work out what she was getting at. 'Were there chisels on the same page? I don't know. I'm guessing you're asking because you think I got rid of my chisels after attacking James and those other guys. Have a look in my van, you'll find a yellow bucket at the back left-hand side. It has a couple of different-sized bolsters, two narrower chisels, a lump hammer, a string line and a trowel. You'll see for yourself that the bolsters and the chisels are worn with use.'

The explanation was simple enough that it made sense. As did his offer to check his van and his confidence that the chisels would show signs of wear.

'What is a bolster?' To Beth a bolster was a kind of long cushion or pillow.

'A wide stone chisel. It's what bricklayers use for cutting bricks and blocks.'

Like all of his other answers, this latest one came without any guile or hesitation. Craven may well be afraid, but he wasn't holding anything back when replying to her questions.

'Okay. Can you account for your whereabouts last night?'

'I was at a play. One of my friends is a playwright and their Christmas play debuted at the Theatre by the Lake in Keswick. I was there till gone twelve as we stopped behind for a drink with my friend and some of the cast afterwards.'

Beth's heart sank. If Craven was telling the truth there was no way he could have attacked Harrytosis and Dippen. Plus there would be countless people to give him an alibi. 'Can you prove that?'

'Yeah. There's at least half a dozen folk who'll vouch for me, although—'

'Yes?'

'If you get my phone and look at my Facebook feed, you'll also see I posted some photos from the after-party. I think the last one was around midnight.'

'I'll get it.' The legs of McKay's chair squeaked on the floor as he rose.

The triumph in his voice burned at Beth like a branding iron. McKay was the type to hold this miscalculation over Beth and remind her of it at every possible opportunity.

*

Beth escorted Craven out of the station and into the car park. He looked around at the industrial estate and saw his wife standing by a car.

She smiled at him and then shifted to toss a glare Beth's way.

'Before you go, Mr Craven. I'd like to apologise again.'

'Think nowt of it.' He hooked a thumb towards the station. 'I've always thought this place looked like the back of a grandstand and that made me wonder what it was like inside.'

Beth smiled at his gracious accepting of events although it wasn't the first time she'd heard the building described that way. As she turned to go back in, Beth steeled herself for the inevitable jibes McKay would fire her way. At least when he was finished his gloating, she'd be able to focus on cracking the code and learning Sinclair's secrets. With luck they would explain everything and point them towards the Chiseller.

CHAPTER THIRTY-TWO

*The lady who hands me the key to room five is a grandmo-
therly figure with rheumy eyes and a clear mind. She details
a list of things like breakfast time, parking and where I can
get a late meal.*

*'So, Alex, is it? Are you here on business or is this a plea-
sure trip?'*

*'Alex. Yes. Business, although I might take a look around
the town while I'm here.'*

*'There's plenty of things to visit and see while you're
here.' Arthritic fingers reach towards the stack of leaflets
behind the reception desk before selecting a couple to hand
my way.*

'Thanks.'

'Do you have any special requests for breakfast, Alex?'

*'Nothing unusual. A bowl of cereal and a fry-up is fine by
me, thanks.'*

*I'm used to situations like this. I never stay in the same
place more than once, and never for more than a night.
Everyone who does what I do does the same.*

*Tomorrow will see another B&B. The town of Keswick
is enough of a tourist trap to still have plenty of strangers
around, even during the depths of winter.*

*If luck is on my side, contact will be made tomorrow and
the next target can be dealt with. As scenic as Cumbria is,
I'm used to city life and miss the hustle and bustle that comes*

with throngs of people. It is always far easier to hide in a city than a rural town.

I could have stayed on in Carlisle, but after the fun I had with Squint and Bad Breath I felt it was prudent to abandon the border city in favour of somewhere else. Killing the pair of thugs and dumping their bodies wasn't an issue for me. So far as I'm concerned the world is a better place without lowlife scum like Bad Breath and Squint; bottom feeders who prey on the weak and vulnerable.

It had been disappointing to have to kill them without making them suffer first, but sometimes you have to play the hand you're dealt. At least I got to have some fun once they were dead. What I did to their heads took all of my skill, and while my profession isn't one I can brag about, I'm pleased with my work. What I wouldn't give to see an X-ray of their skulls so I could see just how good my handiwork really is.

The landlady at the B&B has prompted me to think of Grandmother for the first time in years.

As an only child, who'd been orphaned at the age of four, I'd never fitted in at school. Not with the kids. Not with the teachers. My coursework was completed sooner than any other pupil's, so I would sit and stare out of the window at whatever there was to look at until the end of the lesson. School holidays had been spent sitting quietly while Grandmother went from one house to another on her gardening round.

On my tenth birthday, Grandmother had deemed me old enough to be useful and from then on, school holidays were spent cutting grass, pulling weeds and raking leaves. Sometimes I would go with Grandad and help him to put up a garden shed or a fence, but for the most part, my days were spent with Grandmother.

Even all these years later, I can still hear Grandmother's admonishments – 'hurry up, Alex', 'lift it you weakling', *'why did I have to get saddled with a useless waste of space like you?' – and feel the sting of her belt. Crying hadn't been allowed and neither had slacking.*

Grandmother was the first person I killed.

It had started out as an argument over the volume of the music I was listening to and had ended with a violent shove when Grandmother was standing at the top of the staircase.

The cracks as Grandmother's neck and left wrist had broken as she tumbled down the stairs were the most exciting sounds I had ever heard.

I had checked Grandmother's pulse and found it missing.

Something else I've always found missing is emotion. I felt no grief at Grandmother's death. No anger or rage. Just indifference. Even the push which sent Grandmother tumbling was something I delivered without emotion. All I wanted was to listen to the music a little louder than Grandmother liked. Grandad had shown emotion and this had caused something inside me to click. Grandad's grief was normal, but even though I didn't share his grief, to not look upset would mark me as indifferent. Or worse, guilty.

The realisation had served me well and from that day on, I faked emotions to maintain an air of normalcy.

Grief, empathy, joy: I can fake any emotion I want to with ease.

CHAPTER THIRTY-THREE

Beth looked at the screen in front of her and sighed. The email from Digital Forensics held a great deal of technical jargon and few real details. Rather than send all the emails individually, they'd given Beth access to the account and told her where to look for the information she wanted.

The worst part of the email was the line which stated that while they'd been able to follow James Sinclair's trail to the email account, it had been impossible to trace the other users who'd logged in to it and saved their messages in the drafts folder as they'd used dynamic IP addresses.

Digital Forensics had made it clear that while static IP addresses could be traced to a fixed location with ease, tracing a dynamic IP address was a much trickier proposition that usually required warrants and could take several months if the provider of the email account dug their heels in. For a simple assault case, albeit one as violent as the attack on James Sinclair, there simply wasn't the budget available to pursue a lead that may pan out to be nothing more than a bunch of friends playing at spies.

Beth didn't agree with their assessment of James and the people he was leaving the emails for, but there was no point in picking a fight with Digital Forensics when FMIT were often reliant on their cooperation.

The first things she did were use the password Digital Forensics had given her to log into the email account. The guy at Digital

Forensics had already been into the back end of the account and had disabled the automatic notifications that were sent when a new device logged in. A look at the name on the email account told her nothing as it had been named "Contact Account". There were three folders in the drafts section, each with a different label: A, B and C. A quick look showed there were dozens of emails, going back nineteen years, saved in each folder. Beth noticed the email subject lines were letters. In the folder named A, the subject lines were either B or C. The emails saved in folder B had the subject lines A or C and the emails saved in folder C had used A or B in the subject line.

There was an inbox, sent items and a recycle bin, but a check of them found them all to be empty.

The best reason Beth could come up with for the three different folders was that there were three people using the email account and they'd post a draft email in their folder and use the subject line to indicate who it was intended for. On a number of emails, two letters were used, which suggested the author of the email wanted both of the other parties to read it.

Beth scanned down the first folder. She wasn't looking at the emails so much as the dates and times they were saved to drafts. The times didn't mean much but she noticed that there were certain dates when emails could always be found.

As a test she printed one of them out. When she looked at the sheet Beth was dismayed to find that it didn't print the date and time it was saved into the draft. This meant that she'd have to print out the sheets one by one and date them by hand. Altogether this was a much more laborious way to do things, but she knew she'd just have to buckle down and do things the long way round. As a rule she would have passed the task on to a member of the support staff, but there was only Jeanie working today and Beth didn't trust her to do the meticulous job she needed.

It took her half an hour to print off and date all the emails in folder A, but she felt a sense of satisfaction at completing the first of what she expected to be many steps.

Beth set to work repeating the steps with the other two folders and as she printed off the emails, she was already planning her next steps with regards to the code.

When she had three piles of emails, Beth got a ring binder and stored the emails from folders B and C inside it. She planned to work on A first and she wanted to make sure that the other emails were safely stored. Each folder's worth of emails was filed in date order, but when she began to start examining specific emails from folder A, Beth decided to organise them not just by date order, but also by intended recipient.

As she looked through the dates of the emails A had left in the draft folder for B, Beth noticed that there were common messages. On the twenty-fourth of December every year there was always a short message. A quick comparison between a few of the emails bearing that date showed her they all held the same combination of letters, numbers and symbols.

8+}}E*8;?|6/+|

Beth's pulse raced as she counted the symbols. Fourteen, just the same number of letters in 'Happy' or 'Merry Christmas' if there was no space between the words. That meant that the double } could either be 'p' or 'r' and the two | fit where the s's were in Christmas. When she added the letters she knew from working out 'Christmas' it confirmed that 8+}}E stood for 'happy'.

Beth sketched out a quick table and filled it with the twenty-six letters of the alphabet, leaving the spaces blank where she could add the corresponding symbol once she'd got it worked out.

A=+	N=
B=	O=
C=*	P=}
D=	Q=
E=	R=;
F=	S=|
G=	T=6
H=8	U=
I=?	V=
J=	W=
K=	X=
L=	Y=E
M=/	Z=

The next thing Beth did was scour the remaining emails for more matching dates. She found two sets of matching dates over the years each with a similar message.

8+}}E{?;68)+E)G)"
8+}}E{?;68)+E{+{"|

As the first thirteen letters of each message were the same, and they'd all been sent on the two dates over a number of years, they could correspond to birthday wishes. She'd already worked out that 8+}}E was code for 'happy'. The next parts to work out were)G)" and {+{"|. From the 'd' in birthday, the words became clearer: dGd" and bab"s giving her enough clues to realise the words were 'dude' and 'babes'.

If James Sinclair was the email author of folder 'A', then 'B' was the person he called 'Dude', which left 'C' as 'Babes'. She could be wrong and Sinclair could be the person using the 'B' folder, but until she'd gone through more emails, she wouldn't know for certain.

The fact Sinclair was secretly messaging a woman he called Babes made Beth give an inward wince for his wife. Whether or not there was any sexual or intimate contact between Sinclair and the mystery woman, he was still contacting her behind his wife's back.

The name Babes suggested intimacy. It wasn't the kind of name a man would use for a sister, aunt or cousin. It was a lovers' term and even if Sinclair wasn't the author of the emails in 'A' folder, he was still messaging a woman without his wife's knowledge.

Beth hated infidelity and had seen its effects throughout her career. Husbands and wives at war while their children cried endless tears at their arguments, spouses and lovers beaten to a pulp by the person who'd been wronged. Once or twice things had got so far out of hand that a murder investigation had to be launched and it was all because of a drunken fling, or someone not having the strength or guts to get out of a relationship that had gone bad.

So far she'd never been cheated on, to her knowledge, but she knew that if it ever happened, she'd finish the relationship at once. As she dropped a teabag into a cup Beth realised her own hypocrisy. She was due to meet with Neck Kisses tomorrow night and while she had no intention of being intimate with him in any way, she knew that she'd behaved in a way that had led him on a little.

There was also the question of how Ethan would feel about her meeting another man behind his back. She knew she'd be devastated if he was to meet someone, even if it was for the same reasons she was using to justify her actions. For all they'd been dating for a few months, neither she nor Ethan had spoken of love. Beth loved Ethan but she was afraid to tell him in case he didn't say it back. For once in her life, she was happiest not knowing the answer to something.

Beth leafed through a couple more messages until she found one that was longer than the ones she'd already dealt with and fitted in the letters she'd decoded.

It took a few minutes but she was soon able to guess what enough of the words were to work out which symbols, letters and numbers represented all of the alphabet apart from Z and Q.

A=+	N=:
B={	O=-
C=*	P=}
D=)	Q=
E="	R=;
F=2	S=|
G=~	T=6
H=8	U=G
I=?	V=g
J=£	W=<
K=&	X=,
L=_	Y=E
M=/	Z=

With her table almost complete she began to decipher each of the emails. Her stomach rumbled as she worked, but with dozens of emails to go at, she paid it no heed. She could grab a pizza or something on the way home; for the time being, she had work to do.

She bent to her task and tried not to think of food. Or of Ethan and how much she wanted to be able to tell him about Neck Kisses. Her fear was that he wouldn't understand. It had been five years since Neck Kisses had deflected that broken bottle into her cheek. While he'd escaped justice at the time, he wasn't the one who was wholly responsible for the scar on her face. He held a certain amount of blame for starting the fight, but the man who'd smashed the bottle and thrust it towards Neck Kisses was the real culprit of the piece.

Beth found herself deciphering the emails on autopilot as she thought about Ethan and Neck Kisses. By the time she'd decoded five emails, she'd decided that once she'd met Neck Kisses tomorrow, she'd tell Ethan everything. Not just about her clandestine meeting, but about how she felt about him, as she believed he had a right to know. She hoped that he'd understand and that his feelings were as strong as hers.

CHAPTER THIRTY-FOUR

Beth slouched into the office and tried for the umpteenth time to rotate her head in a way that would ease the crick in her neck. McKay was in Thompson's seat, but the only sign of O'Dowd and Unthank were jackets hanging on the back of empty chairs.

When McKay cast his eyes her way he glanced at her face, but as she eased her winter jacket off her shoulders, she caught him staring at her chest.

The pain in her neck was exacerbated by a lack of sleep. She'd pushed on with the emails as long as she could, but had had to call it a night at 2 a.m. She'd arrived home tired and hungry. A bowl of cereal had been guzzled down and its sugar content had given her enough of a boost to keep her awake until well after four. Tired as she was, her mind had continued chewing at the emails she'd decoded.

When she'd read one detailing how the author was getting married, she'd worked on the assumption that James Sinclair was the author as the date it had been sent was six months before the wedding date Laura Sinclair had mentioned. This confirmed that the author of the emails in folder 'B' was the person James referred to as 'Dude', while the email sender of folder 'C' was 'Babes'.

To give her a bad start to the day she'd slept through her alarm and had woken up too late to even spend ten minutes doing stretches and aerobic exercises.

'Well, well, well, look what the cat's just thrown up.' McKay eyed her with suspicion. 'Either you were on the piss last night, or you spent the evening arresting more innocent people. So come on then, Missy, which was it?'

The term 'Missy' was one which Beth disliked with a passion. In her mind it suggested that she was a little girl but in a way that held a lot of derogatory connotations.

'I was—'

'You were what? You know, they told me about you. Told me that you were sharp as a tack as well as being beautiful. They were wrong. From what I've seen, you're nothing more than a pretty face, and considering the bags hanging from your eyes, you don't even have that to fall back on.'

'Actually, sir.' Beth made sure her anger could be heard in her voice. It may have been more political to go with meek and polite, but she didn't think McKay would understand nuanced tones. 'I was here until after two. I cracked the code in the emails and deciphered almost a third of them. Would you like me to explain how I cracked the code or would you prefer to insult me again? Perhaps you'd even like to tell me how you spent your evening. Did you cuddle on the couch with your wife? Or maybe you fell asleep in your chair and had to be woken when it was bedtime. But my guess is that you went back to an empty house, ate a takeaway and spent yet another lonely night refilling the well of bitterness that overflowed yesterday. I may only be a DC, I may have made a genuine error of judgement in arresting Craven, but that's no call for you to get personal. So if it's all the same with you, *sir*, I think all comments you make to me should be strictly professional, otherwise I'll be forced to share my opinions on the way you've never missed a chance to try and ogle me. I saw you trying to eye up Craven's wife when you thought she wasn't looking. Now, can you imagine how it'd go down if I was to share those opinions? Perhaps I'd choose to only share them with you, believe me, you wouldn't want to hear what I think of you, but that wouldn't be as bad as me sharing my opinions with my boss, would it? Just think about that for a moment. DI O'Dowd would be obliged to pass them on to Professional Standards. They'd look into you, speak to other female officers you've worked with. How do you think that would go down? Do you think they'd describe you as a good guy, or one whose eyes wandered over them in a way that made their skin crawl? It's up to you, you can either be professional, or risk me speaking my mind.'

'That's blackmail.'

Somehow McKay's voice held a mixture of anger and fear. The fear told Beth that she'd rattled him.

'Call it blackmail if you like. But think on it, if a female colleague has to blackmail you to stop you being lecherous and unnecessarily rude, it says a damn sight more about you than them, doesn't it, *sir*?'

McKay gave Beth a hard stare as he rose to his feet and pulled his cigarettes from his shirt pocket. He was slow and deliberate with his movements, but there was no doubt in Beth's mind that he was furious with her.

Beth let him go without saying anything, glad he was out of the office, and although she was aware she'd just made an enemy, she didn't want to let McKay dominate her thoughts. Until she saw O'Dowd, she planned to carry on with the emails.

Of all the emails she'd gone through last night, none had piqued her interest with regards to the case. They'd all been banal messages, congratulations about a new job, updates about his own work, but never any details about where; there had even been a recipe or two.

As was to be expected with any form of letter writing, the frequency had decreased over the years, and Beth was pleased for Laura's sake that Sinclair's email messages to 'Babes' had dropped to just birthday and Christmas wishes since he'd told her of his impending marriage.

'Dude', on the other hand, got a message on the first of every second month. Not a long one due to the code, but it was a regular thing. Whoever 'Dude' was, he was close to James.

CHAPTER THIRTY-FIVE

The thud of brogues on industrial-grade linoleum announced O'Dowd's arrival. She was ushering Unthank and McKay before her and her face was as unruly as her hair.

'Right my little band of reprobates, today is the day that we achieve two things. Number one, we find out who likes to take a hammer and chisel to people, and number two, we get the press off our backs. How the bloody hell they've got so much information about the case is beyond me. If I didn't know better, I'd wonder if they had an in with one of you.'

Beth's first thought was that McKay was the person feeding the press. His presence on the team was a temporary attachment and there was a quality about him that made Beth distrust him. All the same, she knew that her suspicions weren't founded on fact. A look at his face showed he still wore the same expression of consternation he had when she'd given him a piece of her mind.

'What's the Hampden roar, boss?'

'I take it you mean score?'

McKay nodded his answer.

'First off, update time. The brass, and by brass I specifically mean Chief Superintendent Hilton, is worried that with Harrytosis and Dippen getting killed the way they did, that this is only the beginning. The pair of them were known to do stuff for the RF and the chief super is getting antsy they were killed because of this, and that rightly or wrongly the RF will blame the Currockers and take revenge on them. We need a collar and we need one soon, before there is civil war in Carlisle.'

Beth agreed with the chief super's assessment. While the two dead thugs were on the bottom rung of the criminal ladder, they represented the RF, as the Raffles Firm was now known. Named after the Raffles estate in Carlisle where it had grown during the eighties and nineties, the RF shared Carlisle's illegal activity with the Currockers, a gang that hailed from the Currock area of Carlisle. For the most part there was an observed truce and the two firms kept to their agreed boundaries, but that didn't mean to say that a turf war couldn't break out at any time for a perceived attack.

There was always the possibility that this was the first battle in what would become a war, although if it was, Beth couldn't see where James Sinclair fit in.

Unthank looked O'Dowd's way as he eased himself into his chair. 'What do you want us to do, boss?'

'The chief super wants a presence where it counts.' O'Dowd pointed at McKay. 'You and me are going to go see the leaders of the RF and the Currockers, tell them we're watching them and that we'll not tolerate any more violence. I doubt it'll work, but we have to try and warn them off.'

'Paul, Beth, I want you to go see the families of Dippen and Harrytosis again. Go over everything that's already been gone over and put your brains towards finding me a killer. Any questions?'

Beth didn't mimic Unthank and reach for her coat. 'Not a question as such, ma'am. But as you were speaking, I ran a search on HOLMES.'

'And?'

'I was looking for victims whose injuries were similar to our three victims.'

McKay's top lip curled into a snarl. 'Fuck's sake, DC Young, will you get to the point?'

'Hoy!' O'Dowd whirled to face McKay, her extended finger a fraction of an inch from his nose. 'I don't know who the hell you think you are, but if you ever speak to one of my officers like that again I'll nail your bollocks to the nearest desk and then set the damn thing on fire. Do I make myself understood?'

'Aye.'

'I beg your pardon, sergeant.'

Beth watched in silence as O'Dowd's glare morphed into a glower and McKay capitulated with the expected bad grace. 'Yes, ma'am.'

'Don't forget DC Young.'

'Sorry. But you were drawing it out a bit.'

The sneered justification for his conduct washed off Beth. She'd heard worse, been called all kinds of names and had her face spat on while arresting people. What galled her was that he thought it was acceptable behaviour. Fair enough, bollock someone if they're out of line, but to be abusive through impatience was unnecessary and spoke of an inner anger. Still, she planned to get a dig of her own in as retaliation.

'I wasn't drawing it out, I was explaining what I'd done. And, if you hadn't interrupted me, I'd have told you what I found by now.' Beth caught the wink from O'Dowd, but rather than press her point home, she reverted back to the information she'd found. 'As I was saying, I looked for victims with similar injuries. Over the last six years, fourteen bodies have been found with similar injuries.'

Unthank was the first to respond to the news. 'What? Where were these victims? How come we've never heard anything about them?'

'All fourteen were in London. Nine were known gang members and four of the others were suspected to have gangland connections. The fourteenth and final victim was the owner of a small hotel. After his body had been found, his wife sold up to a development company which was owned by a shell corporation. Apparently he'd spent years refusing to sell to them.'

'Jesus. Did the London victims have any shapes or symbols on their bodies or were they like Sinclair?'

Beth bent to her computer to look for the answer to O'Dowd's question. She could feel the eyes of the others on the top of her head, but she didn't worry about rushing. Better to take her time and get the right answer, than rush and give a half-baked one. McKay's impatience filled the room like a malevolent spirit, but she resisted the temptation to draw her search out just to wind him up.

'The hotelier was the only one to have a symbol. All the others were similar to Sinclair. All had a variety of broken bones. Apparently the cause of death was a single blow to the temple in all fourteen cases.'

'What was the symbol?'

'According to the notes it was a pair of overlapping triangles on his forehead.' A check of the notes on the screen. 'The triangles formed the Star of David and it's no surprise the hotelier was Jewish.'

Beth left them to think about the murdered hotelier and the fact he'd had the symbol of his religion etched into his forehead. She still had information to impart, but knew they'd need a moment to process what they'd heard.

Unthank tossed a look her way. 'Does the report say anything about whether they've got any suspects for these murders?'

'They have nobody in the frame, but they've heard rumours about a mysterious hitman known as the Sculptor and well...'

Beth didn't need to finish her sentence. The Sculptor was a fitting name for a hitman who used a hammer and chisel to kill his victims, and the connection was too obvious to pass up.

O'Dowd rattled a pen in the handle of the mug she used as a desk tidy. 'Right, it would appear that we possibly have a hitman from London operating on our patch. I'll let DCI Phinn know, but otherwise, that little snippet isn't to leave this room. On the other hand, it should be fuelling your questions. Thoughts, please.'

'Thoughts, please' was O'Dowd's way of turning a briefing into a general discussion. McKay half sat on the corner of a desk with his arms folded and an inscrutable expression on his face, so Beth ignored him and addressed O'Dowd and Unthank.

'Are we sure it's a hitman and not a hitwoman, ma'am?'

'Good point.' O'Dowd nodded at Beth's question. 'All the intelligence that the SOCA team have amassed on the Sculptor suggests he's a man.'

'Takeover. Freelance. Too far.' Beth flapped a hand at her outburst. 'What I mean is, it's possible there's going to be a takeover of the RF. The Currockers are the prime suspects as they're the RF's biggest rivals and Carlisle is way too far from London for a London firm to bother muscling in. There's also the fact that by London standards, the organised crime in Carlisle and Cumbria will be chicken feed. A London firm wouldn't expand to Carlisle, they'd target places which are much nearer and far more lucrative. Therefore if the Sculptor *is* behind the two murders and the assault on James Sinclair, he's either freelancing, or has been sent by the firm he works for. Whether a deal has been struck with the Currockers or not doesn't really matter. He's here and he's killing.'

'Agreed.' O'Dowd used her pen to point at everyone else in the room. 'Get on to any CHISs you have and see if you can find out if anything is going down.'

Beth only had one Confidential Human Intelligence Source. She'd tried to cultivate others, but hadn't been able to recruit any more. It was a skill that was beyond her as she didn't like the blackmail elements that had often crept into the negotiations. A former colleague in CID had been legendary for the way he used to collect CHISs by getting dirt on people and using it to extract information from them in exchange for not arresting them. To her this process was wrong on every level. To inform was a risky business and most criminals knew when they were in for a slap on the wrist from the CPS and when they'd be facing jail time. A slap on the wrist didn't worry them, and Beth's own moral code made it impossible for her not to follow the letter of the law when it came to dealing with criminals.

Beth pulled her scarf round her neck and shucked on her jacket with a feeling of dread balling in her stomach. It'd be bad enough dealing with the families of Dippen and Harrytosis without having to go and speak to Greasy Bob as well.

CHAPTER THIRTY-SIX

The drive to Carlisle was a gauntlet of swirling snow and idiots driving too fast. Twice Beth passed abandoned cars that had slid from the road and ended up on the embankments at the side of the motorway.

Unthank had spent the journey on the phone. He was alternating between sending messages and calling his own CHISs.

Beth had to sneak glances at his face when the driving conditions allowed, but to her it seemed that he was smiling at the messages he was getting despite the fact the sides of the conversations she heard yielded no positive results.

This made her think about Unthank's behaviour over the last few weeks. Like James Sinclair, Unthank was a private person, but she knew he was a romantic at heart and was happiest when he was in love. Over the last couple of weeks he'd had a spring in his step, and he'd been far cheerier than he had during the months he'd spent chasing anything in a skirt after being dumped by his fiancée. Therefore, Beth surmised, he must be in a relationship once again. The texts he was smiling at would be from his new girlfriend and while it was wrong for him to not focus on his job, other than making a few calls, there wasn't a lot that he could be getting on with.

Beth pulled off the M6 at junction 44 and navigated her way along Carlisle's bypass. It was a constant series of roundabouts as various roads spidered in towards the great border city.

As she drove, Beth was hoping against hope that Greasy Bob would be at his usual pitch on the A595 which led to west

Cumbria. The snow wasn't lying as much at Carlisle due to the proximity of the Solway Firth and the salt air it carried with each tide, but the same snowstorm that had impeded her drive from Penrith was still sending flurries swirling with a galactic fury. She'd always likened driving in snow to those moments in sci-fi films when a spaceship travelled at warp speed and the stars streamed past the windscreen.

As soon as she'd seen the familiar boxy shape of Greasy Bob's roadside stand in the lay-by two miles from Carlisle she'd felt a sense of relief. With the weather as foul as it was, she'd wondered if he'd bother setting up, as people weren't likely to stop for a bacon or sausage roll in the middle of a snowstorm.

The proof of her theory was in the emptiness of the lay-by. Other than the burger van and the battered 4x4 Greasy Bob used to tow it, there were no vehicles, and the dusting of snow covering the tarmac was devoid of any wheel marks to indicate recent customers.

Beth had to force her door open against the wind driving the snowstorm. Unthank was about to do the same, but she waved him back. 'Stay warm. No point us both getting frozen and he'll probably clam up if you're there.'

'Cheers.' A look like a puppy enveloped his face as Unthank fished in his pocket and produced a fiver. 'Grab us a bacon roll, will you?'

As much as she could, Beth wrapped up against the driving snow, but the wind propelling it still whipped her hair and spiked her skin with icy droplets of sleety snow.

'Sorry, darlin', we're shut. Alls I have left is a bit of sausage.'

Greasy Bob's voice was as oily as his moniker. He firmly believed addressing females as love, darlin', sweetheart and a dozen other casually sexist terms was complimentary. Beth had learned there was little lecherous intent about him, he was just stuck in old ways that didn't resonate with modern sensibilities. She'd met plenty like him and knew Greasy Bob wasn't the worst example of his generation.

'I'll take it, Bob. Have to say, I was surprised to find you here.'

Greasy Bob leaned forward and squinted at her. 'Oh it's you. So what brings a pretty little thing like you out on a day like this? Is it really the last bit of sausage you're after, or are you here to pick my brains again?'

'A little of both if I'm honest.' Beth always let his flattery roll off her without comment. There was never any serious intent behind it. 'I take it you've heard about Dippen and Harrytosis?'

'I heard. Bad business that. They were no loss to society, but the pair of them were a handful and if what I've heard was right, whoever took them out without hardly leaving a mark on them must have been a more than capable fighter.'

Greasy Bob flipped a square piece of sausage onto a roll and used a dirty fingernail to scratch at some of the lank white hair poking from beneath the woolly Carlisle United hat that topped his head.

'As they say in all the cheesy films: What's the word on the street?' Even Beth winced at her poor attempt at humour.

Before he answered, Greasy Bob cast his eyes sideways as if looking for someone who might overhear him speak, then opened the door at the tail end of the burger van.

'Get yourself in here, lass. There's lots to say and you'll be frozen out there.'

'Cheers.' Beth grabbed the sausage-filled roll, squirted a blob of brown sauce at it and strode back towards her car.

With the roll passed through the window to Unthank, she climbed into the back of the burger van and tried not to touch any of the grease-laden surfaces. Being inside the burger van might be a few degrees warmer than being outside, but when Beth took a moment to look around her, she saw enough dirty areas to make her fear for Unthank's health after eating something cooked by

Greasy Bob. The smells assaulting her nose were mostly chip fat and BO when they should be of sizzling bacon.

'You got rid of that a bit sharpish.'

There was accusation in his tone, so Beth flashed him the brightest smile she could. 'It wasn't for me, my colleague is eating it in my car as we speak; I've already eaten otherwise I'd have had it and stuff him.' Eating Greasy Bob's food as she prised information from him was the price she usually had to pay, and there only being one piece of sausage left meant she didn't have to worry about food poisoning. That was Unthank's gauntlet to run.

'Fair enough.' The look he gave her was still filled with suspicion even though he'd appeared to accept her explanation. 'They killings. Them was bad lads, but I'm not sure they was bad enough to warrant being killed. 'Specially not if what I've heard about their nappers is right.'

'Why, what have you heard?'

'That both o' them had symbols cut into their nappers and the top of one o' them's napper was damn near battered flat.'

Beth gave a tiny nod. There was little point denying what had already got out into the public domain. A porter or cleaner at the pathology lab will have heard about the kills and passed the news on for a few quid. It wasn't just the police who had informants, the press and criminals all had their own networks.

'What's the RF saying about it all? Are they planning a retaliation against the Currockers or do they have another target in their sights?'

There was an audible rasp as a liver-spotted hand rubbed across a stubble-laden grimace.

'Alls I heard is they're charging round like napperless chickens. 'Parently, soon as word of Dippen an' Harrytosis got out, the Currockers got in touch with the RF. They's not working together as such, but they's not fighting each other 'bout it neither.'

This made sense to Beth. If the Currockers had nothing to do with the murders, they'd want to make sure they didn't cop for the blame and end up in a turf war that neither party would profit from. An even greater reason for the unprecedented cooperation was the fact that if the Currockers were innocent, another firm may be trying to muscle in on RF's turf and if they were successful, it'd only be a matter of time before this new firm turned their attention to the Currockers' territory. Either way, if an outside firm was involved, the Currockers and RF would be stronger if they stuck together.

'Thanks for that. What's the consensus? Are the Currockers setting up to eliminate the RF as a rival, or is it something else?'

A shrug that dislodged a suspicious crumb from the front of Greasy Bob's apron. 'Beggared if I know, sweetheart. Some say it's the Currockers and others say both gangs is running scared. Alls I know is, this isn't over. Not by a long chalk. They're both looking for someone called the Sculptor and from what I've heard, he's a London hitman.'

Beth gave a nod as confirmation she'd understood what he was saying. The fact the underworld knew about the Sculptor being in Cumbria didn't bode well for anyone. As much as they might try to find him, the London police had never managed with all their resources, so there was little chance of the two Carlisle firms having success.

There was also the worry about who the Sculptor would target next. Would it be a mysterious civilian like James Sinclair, or more of the low-level thugs attached to the RF or Currockers?

With luck the Sculptor would return to London before taking any more lives in Cumbria, but Beth found herself agreeing with Greasy Bob's assessment that the situation would worsen before it got better.

'Thanks for everything, Bob.' Beth handed him a twenty and didn't bother waiting for change. It was how she always paid him.

She'd buy something from the burger van and then overpay. The bacon or sausage roll would always be eaten as slowly as possible so the majority of it could be dumped in a bin, but having seen the inside of his burger van, she wasn't sure she'd ever be able to eat or drink anything he sold her, even if it was pre-packaged in a factory.

CHAPTER THIRTY-SEVEN

The house on Henry Street was part of the old Raffles estate, and while it was a lot better than it used to be in the eighties and nineties, Raffles had retained enough bampots and ne'er-do-wells to maintain its reputation as an unsavoury place to live.

Built in the 1920s as social housing, it had been a desirable area in the beginning until more and more of society's flotsam were allocated council houses on the estate. At one point it was a no-go area where residents who had a problem with their neighbours would go out and buy a weapon. Significant amounts of drugs had been discovered in the estate over the years and despite the millions of pounds spent redeveloping the estate in the noughties, it still wasn't classed as a safe area for strangers.

The house listed as Harrytosis's address was mid-terrace and fronted a narrow road. The weed-strewn patch of grass at the front of the house was no larger than a king-size mattress and there was a sense of despair about the area that had nothing to do with the untimely death of its occupant. Like so many of the original houses, it was brick built and its upper floor had been coated with a coarse roughcast that had once been painted white.

Beth knocked on the door, while Unthank stamped his feet and turned his back on the weather.

The woman who answered the door was a hard woman. Beth could tell as much from her first glance. Her face was set in a sneer and there was no mistaking the fact her body language was instructing Beth to eff off.

Before Beth could introduce herself the woman went on the attack.

'What do you want? You caught the bastard who killed my Harry, have you?'

'I'm afraid not. We're still working the case, which is why we're here.'

'Ain't got nowt to tell you. Told everything to the other pigs what was here yesterday. You should be out there looking, not doing what's already been done.'

'To a point I agree with you.' Beth noticed the stunned look on the face of Harrytosis's widow. Agreeing with someone was a tactic she often used to take the fight out of them. Once they'd calmed down they were more receptive to opposing ideas and fresh questions. 'But, Yvonne, if you don't mind me calling you that, I have some different questions for you. Ones which have arisen during the course of our investigation.'

'Better come in then. Bloody house is cold enough without having the door open all day.'

Beth followed Yvonne into a living room that made her long for the comparative sterility of Greasy Bob's burger van.

Yvonne had plonked herself into a chair, but neither Beth nor Unthank did. The mess and smell of the house explained how Yvonne tolerated her husband's legendary bad breath. If she could withstand this level of stench without doing anything about it, bad breath would be the least of her concerns.

'C'mon then, what's these other questions you have for me?' A cigarette was pushed into the sneer and lit.

'First of all, we're not going to feed you any bull. We know what your husband was, who he worked for and what he did. We're not interested in any of that beyond what we need to know to catch his killer. The next part is up to you.'

'What do you mean, up to me?'

'You can either tell us what we need to know, or you can play dumb and clam up. That won't see your Harry's killer caught. It'll see him go free. Your choice.'

'Hang on, DC Young. You're right, it is Mrs Anderson's choice as to whether she helps or not, but you're not taking into account the fact she might be mixed up in his killing herself. I mean, you've seen his record. Right handy with his fists he was. I reckon that he wasn't averse to giving his wife the odd slap, to keep her in line, like. If that was the case, then perhaps she had a hand in his murder. Mrs Anderson here has been round the block herself, she knows how the game is played and I reckon she'll have many of the same connections her husband had. Just look at her record. Three convictions for soliciting, four for dealing dope and as many arrests for dealing stolen goods as you can shake a stick at. And all that's before you look at the arrests for assault and affray.'

Yvonne's sneer twisted into an expression ugly enough to turn the stomach of a gargoyle enthusiast. When she spoke her voice was a half decibel away from a full-on shout. 'You bastard. You fucking pig bastard. My husband's been murdered and you've got the cheek to stand beside his chair and accuse me of having him murdered. You're scum, complete and utter scum. Get out. Get out of my house.'

Before the woman could rise to her feet and get physical, Beth put herself between Unthank and Yvonne. It had been a gamble for Unthank to go quite so far with the bad cop routine, but as the one playing good cop, it was up to her to rein in Yvonne's anger and redirect it towards the investigation into who this mysterious Sculptor was and who'd ordered the hit on Harrytosis and Dippen. As she looked at the grieving woman she could see bright unshed tears in her eyes. Beth knew pride would stop them rolling down her cheeks in front of the police.

'I'm sorry, Yvonne, but as much as it hurts and angers you, he's not the only one who'll be thinking that way. Other cops will be and what I want to do is to get to the truth. I don't think you're involved, but to prove you're not, we need to learn who killed Harry and why. It's rough on you to be accused, I know that, but if you work with me, we can catch his killer.'

Beth tossed a look at Unthank and saw her own uncertainty reflected in his eyes. This was the crucial moment, the one where Yvonne would either clam or open up.

Yvonne's jaw clenched and her eyes flitted around the room as she worked out for herself that she was better off giving the police the information they needed, rather than reverting to type and maintaining her silence. 'So, what I tell you won't get me into trouble?'

'Not exactly. We can't give you a free pass if you've been involved in anything illegal, but depending on what you have to say, we can either turn a blind eye, or make a point of playing down your role in proceedings.'

Even as she spoke, Beth loathed herself for the fact she was offering to turn a blind eye to something illegal. Yvonne may well have been recently bereaved, but she was no angel and the state of her house was making Beth afraid she'd start gagging, and it was all she could do not to scratch at the thousands of imaginary itches assaulting her body.

'Well, like, Harry and Dippen had this la'al job they was planning.' A plea hit Yvonne's eyes as she looked at Beth. 'I knew about it, like, but I told Harry it wasn't a good idea. Told him to keep me well out of it.'

Beth had heard a thousand statements like the one Yvonne had just made. It was always the same when someone was about to grass on someone else. There was the disassociation, the desire to be believed when they were lying, to distance themselves and, most of all, there was the fear their admission would come back to bite them in the form of violent retribution. More often than not, short-term cowardice won over long-term fear, but Beth

was aware that one wrong word from her or Unthank would see
Yvonne clam up.

'What was the little job?'

'You know that they did stuff for the RF, right?'

'We do.'

'Well they done a bit of delivering for them. Usual kind
of things, a box of this here and the odd person got a lift to
somewhere. They also spent a bit of time providing muscle to the
escorts the RF had running.' Beth nodded for Yvonne to continue.
It was standard behaviour for escorts to have a bit of muscle in
a back room in case one of their punters kicked off. 'Apparently
the girls weren't as busy as they used to be. Well, the pair of eejits
only decided to try recruiting some of the girls with the aim of
setting up a brothel.' A hand lifted. 'Mind, they wasn't totally
stupid about it. They cleared it with the RF before they spoke to
any of the girls.'

'Why did they want to set up a brothel? Surely they would
know the risks.'

'They thought it'd be easy money. Thought that by offering a
choice of girls they'd get lots of trade.' The look Yvonne gave Beth
said everything.

Soliciting for sex was illegal and brothels were doubly so. The
get-out clause for sex workers was escorting. Escorts would meet
the punter, and they'd be paid a set fee for their 'companionship'.
The sentences for those running a brothel were far steeper than
the sex workers would get, but even so, most stuck to escorting
so they didn't fall foul of the law.

'How close were they to setting up their brothel?'

Beth flashed a look at Unthank as she didn't want him asking
questions. Yvonne had opened up to her and she needed to preserve
the fragile trust the woman had given her.

'Nowhere bloody near. None of the girls they spoke to were
up for it. All they had was a bill for renting a house on Airbnb.'

Beth got the whole picture at once. She'd heard of this happening at other locations around the country. A sex worker would take a rental property for a week and then use it as their base while providing services to a specific area. Firms like the RF and Currockers would have a number of properties around the city where they'd house sex workers for a few days at a time before they moved on to another city. There would be a smattering of local independent escorts working in the area as well, but for the most part, prostitution or escorting was controlled by organised crime.

In all reality, it was lucky for the two men that their scheme hadn't got off the ground, as they'd have either been caught or ended up paying a cut to either RF or the Currockers. On the other hand, as they'd been speaking to the girls and had run the idea past the RF, it wasn't impossible that a pre-emptive retribution had been dished out by either firm.

The counterpoint to that theory was Greasy Bob's statement that both the RF and the Currockers were running scared. The more she looked at it, the more confused Beth got.

She tried a few more questions, but Yvonne had nothing else to tell them.

*

Unthank fiddled with his phone until Beth got her car going and set off for the short journey to Cumberland Infirmary.

'What do you make of it then?'

Beth pulled a face as she didn't have an answer. Before visiting Yvonne Anderson they'd spoken to Dippen's partner. She'd not been as abrasive as Yvonne, but she'd told them a lot less. Whichever way they'd tried to prise information from her, she'd shaken her head and denied any knowledge of Dippen's illegal activities.

'I don't know. It's possible the RF got rid of them for wanting to branch out in a way that may impact their takings. They may even be planning to try and use their deaths as a way to go to war with the Currockers. The same could be said for the Currockers, as one of the sex workers they approached could easily have passed on or sold the information. On the other hand, the Sculptor being in town adds another dimension and that's before you even try and work out where James Sinclair fits in.'

Unthank shook his head. 'It doesn't seem likely to me that the RF would kill two of their own men before going to war. It'd make sense to maybe use them as bait or sacrificial lambs, but it's not like they'll have hundreds of people at their disposal.'

'I was thinking the same thing. Also, if he really is a hitman, who's paying the Sculptor? If it's not one of the local firms, then it must be someone looking to oust them. Again though, it doesn't explain what happened to James Sinclair. There's also the nature of his injuries. Dippen and Harrytosis were killed then had those designs etched into their heads, whereas the attack on Sinclair was brutal, but his life was spared. Why? It'd have been easy to kill him, and in all reality, much safer for the Sculptor to not leave a witness, yet he wasn't killed. What's that about?'

Unthank didn't give an answer and they travelled the half mile to the Cumberland Infirmary in silence. Beth's thoughts meanwhile were on the questions she'd have to ask Laura Sinclair and how best to minimise the impact they might have on a woman who was already distraught.

CHAPTER THIRTY-EIGHT

They found Laura sitting outside the coffee shop in the atrium of Cumberland Infirmary. Her father was with her but it was clear to Beth that Laura was alone in her thoughts. Her eyes were unseeing and the cup of tea in front of her had formed a skin on its surface.

She'd lost weight. Her face was gaunt and her eyes were sunken pits of despair. Wherever she was in her mind, it looked like a private hell.

Beth didn't know whether she ought to feel guilt for disturbing her thoughts, or empathy for the nightmare Laura was enduring. The questions she had to ask weren't likely to offer any support or peace of mind unless Sinclair had shared his secret with her.

'Hello, Laura. Do you have a few minutes so we can talk again?' Beth aimed for breezy and upbeat without going so far as cheerful. She wasn't sure she'd achieved it until she got a wan smile from John.

Laura didn't look up. Didn't speak. John nudged his daughter's arm but she remained in her own orb of consciousness.

'Hello, Laura. Do you have a few minutes?—'

'He's in theatre. They're cutting his legs off as we speak. My husband is having his fucking legs cut off and you're here with more of your stupid fucking questions. He may die at any moment. He may even be dead now, and yet here you are, Little Miss Copper with her big book of stupid questions.'

John's tone was soft but his words showed his opinion. 'That's enough, Laura. The detective is just doing her job. There's—'

'Maybe she is. But my heart is breaking in two and she's not even asked how James is.'

'You didn't give her chance.'

As Laura shook her head, Beth mentally berated herself. Laura may have snapped at her, but Beth knew in her heart that she was in the wrong. Her focus had been so intent on the case, that asking after the woman's husband hadn't even entered her mind. To Beth the lapse in her humanity was unforgiveable and she hated the idea that she'd been so cold. Yes, it may have been unwitting and unintentional, but it was still wrong of her to not put the victim first, second and third.

She took the chair beside Laura and prayed she could find the words to rescue the situation. Not for herself or the case, but for Laura's sake. As much as grief was making Laura lash out, Beth knew she'd made herself an easy target.

'You're absolutely right, Laura. Asking how James is should have been my first question. For not asking right away, I apologise.'

'So you bloody well should.'

'Agreed. However, it's my job to be objective, and being objective, I have to say that if the surgeons are removing James's legs, then, as horrible as it is for you and him to deal with, it tells me that they don't just believe he'll survive his injuries, but the surgery as well. And while it sure as heck doesn't seem like it, it still has to be taken as a good sign regarding his long-term prognosis.'

'I know all that. They're still cutting his fucking legs off though. Every footstep I hear makes me wonder if it's a surgeon coming to tell me the operation has been a success, or to take me off somewhere quiet so they can tell me he's dead. Can you imagine what that's like? Can you? My head's full of mince and I'm terrified of every foot-fucking-step I hear.'

Tears streamed down Laura's face as she spoke, but she made no attempt to wipe them away.

Beth's heart was breaking for Laura, and she recognised the woman wasn't fit to answer her questions. 'I'm so sorry, Laura. I'll leave you in peace.'

'Oh no you don't. You're not just up and fucking off. You came to ask me questions, so bloody well ask them. Maybe, just maybe, they'll help you catch the man who attacked my James, and if they don't, they might stop me thinking about bone saws, prosthetics and coffins for a minute or two.'

Beth gave a nod and hoped for Laura's sake that she knew about the secret emails her husband was sending to the people he called 'Dude' and 'Babes'.

CHAPTER THIRTY-NINE

Laura gripped the cup in front of her as tightly as she would the last parachute on a doomed plane. She wanted to launch it across the hospital's atrium and see it smash against the far wall in a shower of pottery and cold tea.

As much as she loved James and was petrified of him not surviving the surgery he was undergoing, all she felt was betrayed and abandoned. He was her husband and she was his wife. He knew everything about her. Her moods, her hopes, dreams and aspirations. She'd even told him about the time in her schooldays when she'd got caught shoplifting. He knew about her exes and about the couple of one-night stands she'd had. Every part of her life had been shared with him and for what? For him to betray her with secret messages to someone he called 'Babes'.

Whoever Dude was didn't matter. It'd be a guy. But that James had been messaging a woman and calling her 'Babes' was eating at Laura's heart like a ravenous shark. 'Babes' was the term he used for her. She was 'Babes' and he was 'Honey'. The pet names weren't hugely gushy or soppy, but they were how they referred to each other.

The scar-faced copper had said that James had been emailing Babes and Dude for years, but that just made it worse for Laura. She wasn't even a replacement for Babes because apparently James was still in contact with her. So who was this Babes? James had no family, so it couldn't be someone innocuous like a sister or cousin. It *must* be an old girlfriend he still kept in touch with.

It was as she tightened her knuckles to grip the cup even tighter that she felt her father's hand on her forearm. He wasn't pressing down as such, but there was enough pressure to prevent her from lifting the cup and hurling it at the far wall.

Laura relaxed her grip and pushed the cup to the far side of the table. She couldn't look at her father. Couldn't face seeing the questions in his eyes.

One way or another James had betrayed her. Taken her trust and honesty and smashed them into smithereens. If Babes was an old girlfriend, he'd lied to her. And actually, even if Babes was a previously unmentioned relative, he'd still lied to her, still kept things from her.

More than anything though, it was James's secrecy which made her feel betrayed. The way he'd kept that part of his life not just secret, but so secret he'd used a code to contact these others, meant that if she had found out about the messages, she'd still never have been able to read them.

As the first wave of angry tears pricked her eyes, Laura was aware that a lot of her anger was at herself. James had been lying to her for years and she hadn't spotted a single one of his lies. She blinked away the tears and tried not to wonder just how much of her marriage was a sham. Laura's heart was breaking over what had happened to him, but she was damned if she was going to shed a single tear over his lies.

If James survived the operation, he'd have to be honest about everything if he wanted their marriage to survive. That included her meeting Babes and Dude and hearing their side of whatever story James told her.

As much as she loved James, if she couldn't trust him, she couldn't be with him.

The limbic part of Laura's brain kicked in and she went from being in an unknowing funk of anger, to a state of heightened awareness. Footsteps were approaching. Not the slippered shuffle of a patient heading for the door so they could have a cigarette, or the pocking of a secretary's heels as they strode across the atrium. No, the footsteps she could hear were the purposeful steps of a doctor.

Desperate to know and afraid of the answer, she turned to look. The consultant who'd been managing James's treatment was walking her way with an expression she couldn't read.

CHAPTER FORTY

O'Dowd's face twisted as she listened to what Beth and Unthank had to say. It was obvious to Beth that the trip to speak with the two gang bosses had left the DI in a less than sunny mood.

When she heard about the scheme Harrytosis and Dippen had planned, O'Dowd shook her head while muttering about the stupidity of some people.

Beth finished up her report with an update on her conversation with Laura Sinclair.

'So, she knew nowt about her hubby's secret life, eh?' McKay crinkled his nose like a rabbit. 'Lucky bugger. If I so much as stop off for a pint on the way home, my wife knows before I've had a sip of the bloody thing.'

'No wonder. Heaven help me for saying this, but if I was married to you, I wouldn't trust you either.'

McKay shot a glare at O'Dowd but kept his mouth shut when she returned his look with interest.

Unthank cleared his throat. 'I've been thinking, what if there isn't a connection between James Sinclair and the other two? I agree that it looks like this Sculptor guy is responsible for all three, but when you take a step back and look at the bigger picture, Sinclair was super squeaky clean whereas Dippen and Harrytosis were low-level thugs. There's also the fact that he let Sinclair live but killed the other two. He's obviously very skilled at what he does, the Eye of Providence and the fish tell us that. However, what happened to Sinclair was different. It was unnecessarily brutal whereas the other two were killed before there was any chiselling. What's that about?'

'Come on then, Paul, tell us your theory.'

'I think that James Sinclair was done by a local who knew about the planned hit on Dippen and Harrytosis. I also think it was done for the sole purpose of messing with our heads. So that when the turf war kicks off, we waste time trying to work out Sinclair's connection instead of nicking the RF and the Currockers.'

'Interesting. It's a hell of a conspiracy theory, though. You're also crediting the local hoods with more intelligence that I would.' O'Dowd cast her eyes towards Beth. 'What does your sideways-thinking brain make of it?'

'Wrong. Complex. Secrets.' Beth sent an apologetic look Unthank's way. 'Sorry, Paul, but I think you're wrong. I think the connection is much more complicated than you're suggesting and it has to do with James Sinclair's secrets. I don't know how or why, but when you look at the emails he sent, in the very first email he tells Dude and Babes that a certain subject must never be mentioned. We need to find out what that subject is and hope that it explains everything for us.'

O'Dowd gave a terse nod. 'That makes more sense to me. What do the other emails say?'

Beth gave a helpless gesture. 'I don't know. I haven't translated them yet.'

'Then get on it as your number-one priority. Unthank, you get on to any copper you can who's worked on a case involving the Sculptor. I want to know everything about him including the hunches they don't put in their reports. McKay, you're to speak to all the detectives based within twenty miles of Carlisle, I want to know what whispers they've heard and who was doing the whispering. Understood?'

As Beth and Unthank reached for their keyboards, McKay lifted his jacket from the back of his chair. 'If there's no overtime on this case, I'll see you in the morning.'

The fury on O'Dowd's face at the way McKay had put his own agenda before the case was something Beth shared, but the fact was, unless there was a budget, overtime was voluntary and unpaid. In some respects, she could almost understand McKay's point of view. There was a lot of indifference in the police and justice system to what they often referred to as 'scum-on-scum' crimes. And the murders of Dippen and Harrytosis would only bring tears and outrage to their very nearest and dearest. However, the rest of the team were staying back, therefore it was only fair to assume that McKay might do the same. Even if it was for only an hour or two.

'Ma'am.'

'Yes, Paul?'

'I also have plans for this evening. Ones I can't really change.'

A grimace from O'Dowd. 'Fair enough. Can you both give me until seven?'

On hearing that Unthank had plans, Beth gave a little smile to herself. This backed up her theory that he was in a relationship again. It also reminded her that she too had plans.

It was tonight she was meeting Neck Kisses, although she knew she had to stop thinking of him that way and start thinking of him as Richie.

Even as she bent to the task she'd been given, she was thinking about how she'd conduct herself with Richie and how she could get the information she needed from him without getting herself into a dangerous situation.

Beth logged on to James's secret email account and was about to click on the folder marked B when she noticed something which sent a shot of adrenaline through her entire body.

The number of messages James had sent was now one higher and it had both B and C in the subject line meaning it was intended for both 'Dude' and 'Babes'.

<" :"") 6- /""6 6"__ /"<8";" +:) <8": +:) ? <?__{" 68";"

Beth grabbed the piece of paper with her translation of the code and set to work cracking the message. There's no way it could have been James who sent it. He was back in intensive care after his twin amputations. Therefore it must be someone else who'd written it.

The message said:

WE NEED TO MEET TELL ME WHERE AND
WHEN AND I WILL BE THERE

'Ma'am, you need to see this.'

As Beth looked at the message a second time, everything became that little bit clearer. If Sinclair had been a deliberate target, his attacker had tortured him to reveal information about the two people who he was in contact with.

Beth couldn't see Dippen and Harrytosis dealing with secret codes, so it stood to reason the people referred to as 'Dude' and 'Babes' were as yet unknown. If she worked on the assumption that it was the Sculptor who'd attacked Sinclair, then he'd learned how James had contacted 'Dude' and 'Babes' and this was his way of flushing them out.

O'Dowd bumped Beth's shoulder as she leaned over her back. 'Shit, shite and buggeration. That's not good. We need to find out who these other two people are and damned quick. Go and do whatever you have to do tonight, but I'm warning you now, there'll be overtime available tomorrow and I expect you both to be here until I say otherwise. Beth, can you keep an eye on that email address? I want to know within minutes if one of them replies.'

As she got to work, Beth's mind wandered towards her meeting with Richie. She didn't have his number, so she couldn't call to postpone. It felt wrong putting her vendetta against him ahead of the case, but other than asking her to monitor the email address, O'Dowd had as good as given her the evening off. In the end she decided that the couple of hours spent away from her desk could be made up after she'd met Richie.

CHAPTER FORTY-ONE

Beth dumped the pile of emails on her coffee table and ran upstairs where she stripped off as the shower was warming up. She had half an hour to get changed and travel to Langwathby. The journey itself would take a good twenty minutes as the snow had again thickened and there was now a slushy layer on every road.

She'd stuck it out in the office until the last possible minute. Every one of Dude's emails she'd tried to decipher had resulted in a stream of gibberish until she'd realised that he must have a separate code. As a test she'd picked one of Babes's emails at random and had tried to decode that using the code Sinclair used. Again, she'd been left with unintelligible words.

Unlike James, Dude hadn't bothered with birthday or Christmas greetings, so she'd had to cross reference the emails he'd exchanged with Sinclair and try to guess what his response might be to Sinclair's messages.

As much as she'd enjoyed the challenge of the puzzle, she'd grown frustrated by her failure to crack Dude's code as quickly as she had Sinclair's. By the time she'd left the office, she'd pinned down eight letters and was desperate to keep going, but ever since her brutal injury, she'd dreamed of finding Neck Kisses and getting the answers she craved, and nothing was going to stop her meeting him tonight.

Her thoughts drifted to Ethan as she showered. He'd be furious if he ever found out about her meeting Richie. She hadn't told him about her search for the man with the twin kisses on his neck, but she had told Ethan how her cheek had been scarred. She'd never forget the look in his eyes. There had been sorrow at first but it had soon been replaced with a simmering rage.

When she'd towelled herself off, Beth dressed in skinny jeans and a thick fisherman's style sweater. The one bonus about the weather was that she could dress in clothes that were deliberately unsexy while going on what Richie presumed was a date. Had this been the middle of summer it would have been much harder for her to mask her femininity while playing on Richie's assumptions to further her own ends.

As she zipped up her boots, she started to mentally rehearse how she planned to play the evening.

The last thing she did before picking up her keys was check the secret email account. She'd accessed it on her phone so she could keep tabs on it, but so far there had been no responses to the new message. She crossed her fingers it would remain that way for the next couple of hours and locked the front door behind her.

CHAPTER FORTY-TWO

The bar of The Drover's Rest was quiet when Beth entered. Apart from Richie there was one other customer and from the battered Land Rover she'd seen in the car park and his clothing, she guessed the other guy was a farmer.

Richie was dressed in a smart shirt and a pair of jeans that cinched on a trim waist. His chin was freshly shaven and his hair looked shorter and much cleaner than the last time Beth had seen him.

When he saw her, he climbed off his bar stool and walked towards her with a nervous smile. There was also a look of apprehension about him, but Beth put it down to first-date nerves. She was nervous herself although it was for a different reason altogether.

'Glad you made it. I wasn't sure you'd get here with the weather being the way that it is.'

Beth gave a shrug as she steeled herself to play the role she knew she must assume. 'Me neither, but I don't have your number and having been stood up myself, I know how humiliating it can be, so I made sure I got here.'

'I'm not sure if you're paying me a compliment, or making an excuse to turn round and leave.' His smile dimmed a few degrees and Beth detected uncertainty in his voice. 'Can I get you a drink?'

'A tonic water, please.'

Regardless of the weather, or the work she knew she'd have to do later, Beth had planned to not drink alcohol when meeting Richie. She wanted all of her wits about her and there was no way she wanted to loosen her inhibitions with alcohol. Tonight of all nights, she had to be in total control, not just of her emotions, but of how every situation played out.

Once the drinks were bought, Beth let Richie lead her to a table in the opposite corner from the farmer, where they'd be able to talk without being overheard.

Richie put down his pint and looked at Beth in a way that made her feel uneasy. 'So, do you want to tell me a little bit about yourself?'

'I'm Lisa Reid. I'm a secretary from Penrith and, um… I like puzzles and eighties hair metal.' Beth kept as much truth in her response as she could while still playing a part.

'Really? Because I thought your name was DC Beth Young and that you were a detective with the Force Major Investigation Team. You might have thought I didn't recognise your scar and acknowledge my part in you getting it, but I did.'

Beth didn't know what to say. What to do. She wanted to get up and run out but her entire body had seized to the point where it felt as if she were encased in concrete. She couldn't speak, couldn't think. She could see though. Richie had leaned back in his chair and was watching her with quiet patience.

CHAPTER FORTY-THREE

Sandi had spent the day at work oscillating between the joy of showing off her engagement ring and telling her colleagues every detail of Leo's proposal, and the dread she felt at the thought she should tell Kevin about her engagement.

Once she heard the creak as Leo climbed into the tub, she removed the bottom drawer from her sideboard and reached into the envelope taped to its back. With her codes resting on the cushion beside her, she fired up her iPad, opened a private browser tab and accessed the email account.

As she created the jumble of punctuation marks, numbers and letters, Sandi was telling herself that this was a significant day in her life. She wasn't so much erasing the past as burying it and rebirthing herself for the future.

Tears pricked at her eyes as she typed the final sentence and saved the message into her iPad rather than leaving it in her folder in the drafts section. It could be left at a later date when she felt less emotional.

There was a new message in her folder, but she closed down the browser window without reading it. Maybe she'd read it tomorrow, or at another time in the future if her resolve failed, and maybe she'd never read it.

Sandi closed the private browser window, opened a new tab and typed 'wedding venues'. The tick of her biological clock was getting louder, and knowing Leo was keen on having children too, she wanted to get married as soon as possible so they could start trying for a family.

The more she thought about the message from Kevin, the more she had to fight the instinct to read it. So much time had passed now. What if, after all these years, he was finally coming to his senses and realising he couldn't live without her?

CHAPTER FORTY-FOUR

It took Beth a full ten minutes to gather her thoughts and ask the obvious question. 'How did you know who I was?' Richie had spent the time watching her, but his scrutiny had been non-threating, it was almost as if he was observing an animal in a zoo. Or at least it would have been, had there not been a look of latent guilt in his eyes.

'First off, I've got to say I'm sorry for what happened to you. It was a terrible thing and I can see the damage it's left. I'm genuinely sorry. To answer your question, I read the reports in the paper after that night, which was when I learned your name. I know I should have come forward back then, but the truth is, I didn't have the guts. And then so much time had passed, and I hadn't, and even though I spent weeks, then months waiting for the knock on my door, it never came.

'But then finally, years later, when I had started to believe that knock would never come, I saw you in here. I knew who you were right away. You'd just done that case about the killer – and you did a press conference that got shown everywhere – so I knew you'd become a copper. You were with a boyfriend that first day I saw you, and another time after that. But then when we met the other day and you sort of flirted with me, I knew you were up to something. Your eyes never left the tattoos on my neck. Most people glance at them, make a decision about whether they like them or not and then move on. So, what's it going to be? Are you going to slap a pair of cuffs on me or do you have a posse waiting outside to give me a good kicking?'

Beth's thoughts tumbled like boulders at the head of an avalanche, each one propelled by an unseen, yet irresistible force. 'Neither. I'm here because I want answers. I blame you and I don't blame you. I've had a lot of thoughts about this, but at the end of the day, I was an innocent bystander who was unlucky enough to be near you when you deflected the bottle that was coming at you. What you did in protecting yourself was a human reaction. Ninety-nine per cent of the population would have done the same thing. I guess I can't blame you for that human reaction, however much pain and misery it caused me.'

'Thank you.' Richie may have spoken the two words softly, but the expression in his eyes was saying a whole lot more than two words. There was, of course, gratitude, but there was also the receipt of absolution. He'd known all along that Beth was playing him when setting up this meeting, yet he'd come anyway, despite wondering if he was going to be arrested or beaten up. He'd turned up to face the music and had been prepared to listen to Beth's tune.

She wasn't letting him off that easily though, she still had a goal to achieve from this meeting and now that his cards were on the table it was time to play hers. 'Hold up a minute, it's not that simple. While I don't blame you for defending yourself, you were clearly the one who started the fight which ended up with me being bottled. The person you were fighting escalated things when he broke the bottle. I want to know who he was and why you were fighting with him.'

A nod. 'Don't blame you. In your shoes I'd want—'

'Stop right there.' Beth lifted a hand from the table in a 'halt' gesture the way O'Dowd so often did. 'You don't get to be in my shoes. You don't patronise me, and you don't ever, ever get to tell me you understand. You lost those rights when you picked that fight.'

'Sorry.' Richie lifted his own hands in apology.

'From the start, tell me about that night beginning with the point where you walked into that bar.'

Before he opened his mouth to speak, Richie pulled out a photograph and passed it across to Beth.

The picture was your typical family picture. Mum, Dad and the two kids. Richie looked to be in his early twenties and his sister was around fifteen or so.

Beth didn't speak, she just waited for Richie to say his piece.

'That was my family. They died in a car crash on the way home from my sister Isla's parents' evening. They were killed outright, which I suppose was a blessing, but the car that hit them was driven by a young lad. You know the kind of thing, lowered suspension, full bodykit and a stereo pumping out a bassline. The lad who owned the car was pissed, but when the police got there they were told it was his girlfriend who was driving. She was sober and got done for dangerous driving. The lad is the one I was fighting with 'cause I'd heard on the grapevine that he was the one who was actually driving.' Richie paused and looked at the ceiling, but Beth could tell he was reliving a memory. 'I heard about the crash and went there to see for myself. Dad's car had been shunted off the road and had rolled down a bank. It was dumb luck the crash happened where it did, but if that little fucker had been sober and not showing off to his girlfriend, the crash might never have happened.

'A few months after the crash I was on the piss in Carlisle when I saw the lad. He was laughing and joking with his friends like he didn't have a care in the world. It was him I was fighting with. Him who pulled the bottle. He killed my parents and my little sister. Isla could be an annoying brat at times, but I loved her. I'm nine years older than she is and when I was in my teens, she used to sit outside my bedroom door so she could listen to the music I was playing. I wanted him to pay for killing them. When I saw him in that pub I wanted to smash him to a pulp. He picked up a weapon. What happened, happened. As soon as I saw the blood pouring from your face, I lost my nerve and legged it. That little coward was already gone. I wanted to come back and apologise. Explain to you, but I was afraid of what would happen to me. Being honest, as much as I was dreading you ever finding me, I'm glad you have. You've given me the chance to apologise to you myself and that's not something I'm sure I deserve.'

Beth didn't speak until she'd processed some of what he was telling her. It could be a cock-and-bull story, and it could be the truth. Richie's voice was laden with emotion and his eyes were filled with moisture as he told his story. However, he'd fooled her once by pretending not to know who she was and that made Beth doubt her ability to read him. She'd learned a certain amount about body language throughout her career, both during training and from on-the-job experience, but having been fooled like this grated at her and she vowed to learn more about body language and facial expression so she wouldn't make the same mistake again.

'I'm sure you're wondering if I'm telling the truth about the car crash. You might think it's a sob story I'm using to soften you up. It's true.'

Richie pulled out his wallet and with great care unfolded a newspaper clipping and passed it across to her along with a small photograph that depicted Richie, Isla and his mother all pointing and laughing at the lipstick kisses they'd left on his cheeks.

Beth gave the clipping a quick scan and when she saw Richie was telling the truth, her heart went out to him.

The photo said a thousand words and each one of them told a tale of loss. As much as she knew it was rude of her, Beth found herself staring at the kisses tattooed on Richie's neck. The scarlet one spoke of full lips while the smaller, pink one told a tale of a child becoming an adult. As she pulled her eyes from Richie's neck, Beth got the whole picture. The tattoos were a tribute to his mother and sister. A reminder of happier times spent enjoying the company of his family.

He'd been twenty-five when he'd lost his parents and sister. His entire world would have changed in that moment and it was understandable that he'd wanted to seek retribution against the driver who'd evaded justice for the deaths of Richie's family.

It still didn't answer the most important question though.

'I'm very sorry for your loss, but what was the name of the lad who was driving the car?'

'Dane Kenyon. You've probably heard of his father, Walter.' A shrug. 'The next morning, after your… you know… three of Walter's associates paid me a visit and advised me that I should forget any issues I had with Dane or things would get ugly.'

Walter Kenyon was a name that was well known to her. He was the head of the Currockers and while she'd never encountered him, she was well aware of the man on a professional basis.

The Currockers were something of a new firm in Carlisle, but what they lacked in longevity, they more than made up for in brutality. Their rise to power was well documented by the police, but while the police were aware that Walter Kenyon was the main man for them, they'd never been able to pin anything on him. Kenyon senior was slipperier than a greased eel, and if what Richie had said about Dane getting a girlfriend to take the blame for the crash was true, it would appear that his son was just as bad.

Beth closed her eyes and thought about what Richie had gone through. Her own experience had taught her what it was like to not receive justice, but she'd not lost anything like as much as Richie had. To have then seen a chance for retribution end up with an innocent injured and a threatening warning, it was little wonder that he'd agreed to meet her and accept his fate.

Even as she was thinking of Richie's frustrations and grief, her own situation was present in her mind. With the man who'd held the bottle turning out to be a gangster's son, her own quest to earn justice for herself was now looking harder than ever to achieve.

'So, where do we go from here?'

'Forward. Together. Justice.'

'You what?'

'Sorry. We go forward, we work together and we get justice for your parents, for Isla and finally, for me.'

'How?'

'I'm not sure yet.' Beth took a drink of her tonic water and pulled a face at how bitter it now tasted. 'There will be a way though. It took me five years to find you, and if it takes me another five to catch Dane Kenyon, I'm prepared to wait.'

Richie looked up from his pint. 'Thank you.'

Beth gave a nod and kept her mouth closed as she worked through her kaleidoscoping thoughts.

First off, she had a name for the man who'd held the bottle, although it was a blow he was the son of a brutal gangster, and as such, would be protected by his father's power and the threat he carried. Second, Richie had recognised her straight away and there was every possibility Dane would do the same. Even if he didn't, the fact he was from a criminal family and she was a police officer would mean his instincts would probably tell him what her job was, if not who she was specifically, before she'd even spoken to him. Third, as a police officer she couldn't go around waging a personal vendetta against someone. Without evidence she had no reason to even pick him up and interrogate him. Fourth, the only help she had was from Richie, who determined and well intentioned as he might be, was someone who repaired stone walls rather than compiled evidence, sifted through data and built a case.

It was as she reasoned this last point out that she had an epiphany.

'Can I ask you some questions about a case I'm on?'

'Huh?' As much as his single word, Richie's face expressed his surprise at the question.

'Sorry. My mind is leaping all over the place and that came out without me properly thinking about it.'

'Don't sweat it. But before you ask me anything else, can I ask you a couple of questions first?'

'What is it you want to know?'

'How do you feel about your scar now? Does it still hurt? And… how does it affect your life?'

Rather than give a glib or flippant answer, Beth took a moment to compose her thoughts. It was a personal question, but she felt strangely compelled to answer it.

'I've had it for five years now. Whether I like it or not, it's a part of me, part of who I am. Dealing with the pain – which has mostly passed now – was one thing, but I've also had to deal with people's reactions to it. There's pity, I get a lot of that, shock, and on some occasions, revulsion. I've learned how to cope with the way people react to my scar though, and I've found it helps me judge their character. Don't get me wrong, I wish I didn't have it. But I don't let it define me.'

Richie nodded and gave her a long assessing look. To Beth, the way he was looking at her was unnerving, not in a physical sense, but an emotional one. One of the perpetrators of her scar was examining it, questioning her about it and looking as if he carried the world's guilt on his shoulders. As much as she'd wanted to bring about his downfall when she arrived at The Drover's Rest, she now found herself empathising with and pitying him. She'd been dealt a bad hand by the events that had bound them together, but his was far worse.

'You're a far better person than I am. I expected you to scream in my face and call me all kinds of shit, yet you've been very gracious. What was it you wanted to know from me? It's way too little and way too late, but if I can help you in any way I will.'

Beth noticed that Richie didn't so much lean back into his chair but sink into it as all the tension leeched from his body.

'You work with stone, right? You cut it and work it with chisels and so on?'

'I do, although I don't do owt fancy, I just split big stones into smaller ones to fit the place I want to put them.'

Beth explained about the injuries to Sinclair and the two Carlisle hoodlums without giving names. The word was out about what had happened to them, and was sure to be in the press tomorrow, which made Beth confident she wasn't disclosing anything she shouldn't.

As she spoke, Richie's eyes widened in horror and his head shook side to side. When she finished speaking he sat back in his chair for a few seconds before leaning forward again.

'That's some sick shit you're talking about. I'm fairly handy with a hammer and chisel, but to carve symbols into someone's head is way beyond what I could do. Bones are brittle and you would need an exact strike to break them in any sort of specific way, wouldn't you? You also said there weren't a lot of cuts where the blows had been struck?'

'That's right.'

'Well, to get defined breaks like the ones you've described, you'd have to have a fairly narrow edge, but if it was too narrow it'd break the skin. I've broken a finger between two stones on a couple of occasions and my skin was broken.'

'Don't forget the symbols were done post mortem.'

'Unless skin thickens after death, it wouldn't matter. Maybe they wouldn't bleed, but skin is still skin.'

'Damn. How do you think it was done then? Or rather, if you wanted to do it, how would you go about it?'

Richie scratched his chin as he thought. His eyes were unfocussed, but the flicks they gave told Beth that his mind was working.

'I'd use a damper to lessen the impact and I'd grind the point of the blade until it was a shallow rounded shape. For the damper I'd use a piece of thick leather which would probably prevent the chisel from cutting the skin but would still allow the bone to break. A rubber matting might work, but I reckon it would be too stiff and would most likely spread the area of impact too much.' A hand scratched at his leg. 'This is sick, but if I was doing it, I wouldn't start at one point and keep going, I'd miss a couple of chisel widths so that I wasn't putting too much stress on any one area. Then come back and join the dots so to speak.'

What Richie was saying made a lot of sense to Beth and it also explained how the cuts could be so accurate. If a piece of heavy leather was taped to the two men's heads, it could have the symbols already drawn onto it which'd make things much easier for the Sculptor. As for his statement on how he'd do it, that too was logical although she knew nothing about carving or cutting. She did know that although bone was strong it was also brittle, which is why she agreed with his proposed methodology.

Beth talked a little longer with Richie, but she was conscious of the weather conditions, so she cut the conversation short a little sooner than she wanted to. She swapped numbers with Richie and before leaving went into the lounge so she could use the ladies.

A young couple were cuddled up in a corner and she paid them no attention until the man turned to see who'd entered the room.

It was Unthank and from the expression on his face he was surprised, and not too happy, to see her.

'Paul.'

'Beth.'

He didn't make an effort to introduce his girlfriend, so Beth kept walking and didn't push the issue. Beth didn't need an introduction though, because she'd recognised the other woman. Teri Veitch was a reporter for the *Evening News & Star* which covered the north of Cumbria and parts of Southern Scotland. She was a dogged reporter who asked pertinent questions rather than accepted the statements issued by the press officer. It was no secret that she wasn't above using her feminine wiles to get a story, and seeing her draped over Unthank made Beth think the worst.

It wasn't that Unthank was stupid and would go out of his way to give her what she wanted from him, but he was susceptible to flattery and while he was a private person, she knew he was always happiest when he was in a relationship. The question was, should she let O'Dowd know?

CHAPTER FORTY-FIVE

Beth pulled herself awake and answered her mobile. For some reason the ringtone she'd assigned to O'Dowd seemed angrier than usual.

'Ma'am, what's up?'

'*Open your bloody door and I'll tell you what's up.*' The DI's words were backed up with a series of bangs on Beth's front door.

Beth didn't have a clue what O'Dowd was so riled up about, but there was only one way to find out. She opened the door and stood aside as the DI barged her way in before an invitation could be given.

'Listen to me, young lady, I want a full explanation and I want it right now. Do you understand?'

Beth shook her head to try and clear the sleep-spun cobwebs. It was a mistake. O'Dowd interpreted the shake as a refusal to talk.

'We can discuss this in an interview room if you prefer.'

'Whoa, now hold on a minute. I haven't got the foggiest what you're on about, so you're going to have to fill me in from the start.'

'What? You're saying you know nothing about it?'

'About what, ma'am?' Beth gestured at the pile of notes strewn across the coffee table in her lounge. 'I was working on the code and took a minute to rest my eyes and the next thing I know you're banging on my door and demanding I tell you about something. What the hell that something is, is fucking well beyond me.'

Beth wasn't in the habit of swearing at O'Dowd, but she hadn't liked the way the DI had barged into her house in the middle of the night and threatened her with the interview room. It showed a complete lack of trust and as much as Beth respected O'Dowd, she now felt disappointed in her boss.

'So you've been here all night, have you?'

'No.' Beth wasn't sure why O'Dowd was asking, but she'd already worked out that whatever the DI was asking about must have happened since she'd left the office. 'I went out to meet someone.'

'Aye well, that someone has been found with the shit kicked clean out of him. The investigating officers spoke to the landlord of The Drover's Rest and guess who he described as spending an hour and a half having a very serious conversation with one Richie Booth?'

O'Dowd pulled a face that would terrify an entire shoal of piranhas.

'Me.'

'Yes, you. You met the man with two kisses tattooed onto his neck. The man you've identified as being there the night you got bottled, and lo and behold, look what happens, he gets seven different shades of shit kicked out of him.'

'I didn't do it. I know nothing about it. I met with him, we talked and then we went our separate ways. If you must know, ma'am, you've got it all wrong. Back when I got bottled he was fighting someone who'd stolen his girlfriend. What happened to me wasn't his fault. He didn't even know the guy's real name, he just knew him as Beaky.' Beth hated lying to O'Dowd, but she had to keep the real perpetrator's name a secret until she'd worked out what she was going to do regarding Dane Kenyon. 'How is Richie?'

'He's black and blue. He says he has no memory of the attack, but because you were with him, you and those connected to you are in the frame for it.' O'Dowd met Beth's eyes with a withering look that pierced her. 'Who did you tell you were going there?'

'Nobody. If I'd told Ethan or my dad about it, they'd have done exactly what someone else has and kicked the shit out of him. That's why I didn't tell them. Richie getting a good kicking won't remove the scar from my cheek and them getting into trouble for giving him a hiding won't help anyone.'

O'Dowd flopped into a chair. 'Okay. I believe you. But what possessed you to meet him without someone to look out for you? God's sake, Beth, if you'd asked me I'd have gone over and sat in a corner in case you needed me.'

Beth almost mentioned Unthank being at The Drover's Rest, but she hadn't yet decided whether she ought to share that news as it'd certainly be traced back to her when O'Dowd challenged him about his new girlfriend.

'It was my past, ma'am. I had to silence its echoes myself.'

'Whatever. You're just lucky they called me before arresting you. Even so, the duty sergeant wants to see you down the station for a formal statement.' O'Dowd stood. 'He means now, and you want to think yourself lucky he had the decency to call me first, otherwise there's every chance you'd be going there in handcuffs.'

As she went upstairs to get dressed, Beth's mind was considering who might have attacked Richie. Her father and Ethan hadn't known about the meeting, so there was no way it could have been them. All the same, they were the most likely candidates. If she found out it was either of them, they'd be getting a piece of her mind.

CHAPTER FORTY-SIX

Beth didn't care that it was three in the morning as she banged on the door. The duty sergeant had gone over her story the same way O'Dowd had, but the DI had vouched for her so she was allowed to leave once the sergeant was satisfied she had nothing to do with Richie being attacked.

Ethan's face was bleary when he answered the door. At first Beth thought it was sleep that had caused it, but she caught the strong smell of stale alcohol on his breath and revised her opinion.

'What is it? What's up?'

Rather than rage at him the way O'Dowd had gone at her earlier, Beth took Ethan's hands in hers and looked at his knuckles. They were swollen and bruised.

'You beat him up, didn't you?'

'What are you talking about, Beth?'

There was no conviction to his words. No denial of beating anyone up, just a deflecting question.

'Ethan, this is huge. You beat him up, didn't you?'

A curl appeared on Ethan's top lip. 'You mean that lowlife who bottled you? Yeah, you're bloody right I beat him up. What in hell possessed you to meet with him? Why the hell didn't you tell me you'd found him? You're forgetting I was there the night you found him. You maybe thought I didn't see him, but I did. I saw how you stiffened. Saw the way you reacted to him. I've been waiting for you to tell me that you'd found him, but oh no, you never thought of sharing that little detail.'

'Wait a minute. You knew about me searching for him? Who told you, because it wasn't me.'

'One night when I saw her in town, I asked Steph why you're always scanning the crowds. I guessed you were looking for someone, but until I asked Steph, I didn't know about the tattoos.'

Beth sent a mental bollocking Steph's way. She'd purposefully not told Ethan about the tattoos as she didn't want him going all macho and getting himself into trouble, yet her friend had given away the identifier.

'So, how did you know where he was, were you following me?'

A grimace. 'Not following exactly. One of the paramedics lives at Langwathby. He told me he'd seen you at The Drover's Rest by yourself from time to time. I asked him to tell me whenever he saw you there. I knew *he* lived out that way. We talked about going back, but after you saw him you pooh-poohed us ever going back. You did though. You lied to me about going there. I can't believe that you didn't trust me.'

'I was right not to trust you. You went and did exactly what I didn't want you to do. I'm a police officer and I can't have you running around kicking the shit out of people who've wronged me. Fuck's sake, Ethan, I've just spent two hours telling a sergeant and my DI that there was no way it could have been you who beat Richie up and yet it bloody well was. My job could be compromised if they trace it back to you. How's it going to look when a cop's boyfriend goes round attacking people?' Another thought struck Beth. 'And you were having your friends spy on me. That's nice, real fucking nice.'

'Don't start with that holier than thou shite. You're the cop. You're the one who went to meet him. You're the one who spent an hour and forty minutes talking to him.'

Realisation hit Beth hard. 'You followed me, didn't you? You sat outside the pub and watched us talking, didn't you? What did you think I was going to do, sleep with him?'

'No, of course I didn't think that, but yes I followed you. Yes I sat in my car and watched you talking with him. When you left, I waited until he was going home and I jumped him. I'm sorry if it affects your career, but I'd do it again tomorrow.'

'Why? Why did you feel the need to batter him when you saw that all we did was talk?'

'Isn't it obvious?'

'Not to me it bloody well isn't.'

'I did it because I love you. Because he's one of the men who scarred you. You are the most wonderful and remarkable person I've ever met, and he hurt you. I wanted to punish him.' Beth pulled away when Ethan reached for her hand. 'I'm not sorry for beating him up, but I am sorry that I told you I love you this way.' A shrug. 'I wanted to tell you months ago, but I was waiting for the right moment. It never came and when you didn't say it to me, I wondered if you loved me.'

Beth wiped away the tears that were filling her eyes. Ethan had made such a mess of things. But while she didn't agree with what he'd done, she could see it from his point of view. At this moment in time, none of his actions mattered. Only his words did. He loved her and she loved him. Yes, she was still mad at him, but now she knew how he felt, she'd be able to forgive him. He was also right, she should have trusted him and not gone behind his back.

'Do you really love me?'

Ethan held her gaze. 'With all my heart.'

'Good, because I love you too, but, after what you've done tonight, we have to talk.'

CHAPTER FORTY-SEVEN

Beth tried to hide her yawn, but O'Dowd spotted it and fired yet another scowl her way. By the time Beth had finished talking with Ethan, she'd only had two hours to grab some sleep. A phone call to Richie had given her a slice of good news, as he wasn't too badly beaten up and he genuinely hadn't seen his attacker.

A couple of PCs were doing door-to-doors looking for witnesses, but just as Beth was starting to feel there was a strong chance Ethan would get away with his attack on Richie, she remembered Unthank's presence at The Drover's Rest. If he'd seen anything he'd surely recognise Ethan, as Unthank had bumped into them a couple of times around town. The counterpoint to this was Unthank's own relationship with the reporter. A private person, he wouldn't want his personal life discussed and certainly not put under the scrutiny it'd get when O'Dowd learned he was dating a tenacious journalist.

O'Dowd banged a stapler onto her desk to get their attention. 'Right then. Paul, what have you got from the London officers?'

'Not much yet. I spoke to a few last night and have a list to go through today.'

'Good. Get on with it then. Beth, how's your code cracking coming along?'

'Not bad, ma'am. I should have the second code done in an hour. Two tops.'

'Make sure it's an hour. Were there any new messages?'

'I haven't checked yet.'

'Do it now then.'

Beth was aware she deserved the glower O'Dowd sent her way. With everything that had gone on with Ethan and Richie, she'd not kept up with checking the email account.

'McKay, you crack on with speaking to the local teams. If something is brewing, I want to know about it before it happens, not after. Right, all of you get to work. If you need me, I'll be upstairs making excuses to the DCI and chief super.'

O'Dowd's last comment was her barbed way of telling them she was covering for them, but they needed to get some results soon because the pressure on the team was building.

McKay left the office which gave Beth the chance to speak to Unthank, or as much a chance as she could get. He had a phone to his ear and she knew that he wouldn't want to talk about his relationship with Teri Veitch.

Rather than worry about it, Beth decided to let the matter drop. She had more than enough to deal with as it was, without bothering herself with Unthank's love life.

She accessed the email account and her pulse quickened when she saw there had been two new messages sent by whoever was posing as Sinclair and three from Dude.

Beth grabbed her notes and deciphered the two messages from Sinclair as quick as she could.

In chronological order they were:

MUST BE FACE-TO-FACE SOMEWHERE
SECLUDED SO WE ARE NOT SEEN TOGETHER

YES THAT SOUNDS PERFECT TEN SUITS ME

Beth looked at her watch. It was five past eight, which meant that she had an hour and fifty-five minutes to crack the code and then scramble a team to wherever the meeting was due to take place. Her pen bounced off Unthank's shoulder. When he looked at her Beth mimed that he should cut the call he was making.

'Forget what you're doing and go get O'Dowd. Bring the DCI and chief super if you need to. They've set up a meet.'

Unthank didn't bother with a reply, instead he just scurried out of the office to run the errand.

She bent her focus to the first of Dude's three messages

£;'>>~~;;1<£|>+;%&

Using the letters she'd already worked out for Dude's code, Beth got the message to be

£O'EETTOODA£|E+O%&

Beth tapped her fingers on the desk as she tried various letters against the symbols until she had a sentence that made sense.

NO MEET TOO DANGEROUS

She filled in the table she'd created for Dude's code and then moved on to the next coded message.

)$~:)+@1|><~);%&~><1:@^^

As before she put in the letters she knew and tried to make sense of what was in front of her.

)$T:E)R@DGEAT)OUSTEAD:@^^

O'Dowd stormed into the office with the bullish DCI at her heel. 'What's this about new messages, Beth? What do they say? Paul said there is a meeting arranged.'

'There is.' Beth showed her the notes she'd made on a notepad. 'Where's it at?'

'I'm working on it.'

'Let's have a deeks.' O'Dowd took the notepad from Beth and looked at it. Her face scrunching as she tried to understand it. 'Bloody hell. How the hell do you make sense of that?'

'With peace and quiet.' Beth took the notepad back and placed it onto the scanner at the top of the printer then set the machine to print six copies. 'Please, ma'am, the meet is set for ten o'clock, so give me peace to work out where it is before we're too late.'

Beth took her notepad from the printer and marched back to her desk.

'You heard the, lass.' O'Dowd grabbed the copies of Beth's notes then crooked a finger at Unthank and the DCI. 'Let's leave her in peace. Beth, call me as soon as you have it cracked. Sir, I think we need to have response teams ready at Carlisle, Penrith, Kendal, Workington and Barrow. Both plain clothes and uniform.'

Beth tuned them out and then bent her head to the jumble of letters and symbols.

)$T:E)R@DGEAT)OUSTEAD:@^^

If her thinking was right, the last four symbols would spell out a word like 'hall', 'hill' or 'gill'.

She checked the list of letters she'd already worked out and saw that 'A' and 'G' were present so she struck 'hall' and 'gill' from her possible last words and added 'hill' in at the end. Next she used the 'H' and 'I' from hill to replace the corresponding symbols earlier in the code.

This left Beth with a partial message:

)$THE)RIDGEAT)OUSTEADHILL

Had she been working this for fun, she'd have kept going at the puzzle by herself, but with the ten o'clock deadline spurring her on, she took a shortcut and ran a Google search for 'OUSTEADHILL'.

Before she'd even set the search active, Google was suggesting 'Boustead Hill'. With the 'B' from Boustead replacing ')', she was left with:

B$ THE BRIDGE AT BOUSTEAD HILL

Beth couldn't help but read the words aloud. 'By the bridge at Boustead Hill.'

She pulled her phone from her pocket and called O'Dowd. As she relayed the information, she checked her watch. 9.18 a.m. Forty-two minutes to get a team from Carlisle to Boustead Hill. A Google search told her the journey could be done in twenty-six minutes, which left sixteen minutes spare.

They'd need every one of those minutes due to the weather conditions, but at least they had a cushion.

Boustead Hill was located on the Solway Estuary at the point where a narrow country road met the coast road. Beth went into Google Street View and saw there was a bridge leading to the coast road. That would be the meeting point.

With only three drivable routes from the bridge, it should be straightforward to capture Dude and whoever he was meeting. Beth wanted to believe it'd be the Sculptor, but she'd learned the hard way not to make assumptions.

As she waited for O'Dowd to reappear and tell her whether she wanted her to travel up to Carlisle for any interviews which may arise, she turned her attention to the final message.

With so much of the code already cracked, it only took her a minute to solve it. When she had it decoded she cursed.

MAKE IT HALF NINE

It was now 9.20 and there was no way the police in Carlisle could get to Boustead Hill in time. Maybe they'd get lucky and the meeting would still be taking place or there would be an officer or two already within the vicinity, but she wasn't hopeful.

She picked up her phone to let O'Dowd know of the change of meeting time and braced herself for the DI's onslaught. Had she not been distracted with everything that had happened with Richie and Ethan, she would have picked up on these messages last night, or would have been up early to check them this morning, and there would have been ample time to install a surveillance team. As she dialled the number, she gave her fingers a mental crossing they'd be able to get there in time to save Dude, whoever he was.

CHAPTER FORTY-EIGHT

Capturing Owen Grantham had been simple. He'd been expecting to see his brother Kevin, but the isolated meeting point coupled with the weather meant I could be swaddled with hoods and scarfs. Getting close enough to take him down had been straightforward. One throat punch with extended knuckles had dropped him into a spluttering gasping heap. Two cable ties, a strip of duct tape and a mighty heave later and Owen Grantham was bound and gagged in the back of my van.

The sounds of Owen's thrashed attempts to escape are filtering through to the front of the van, so I turn the radio up.

The coast road is deserted as I drive west. With the marshes of the Solway Firth hidden beneath a layer of snow and more falling, I feel a wonderful sense of isolation in the desolate landscape. It's like I'm the only person in the universe.

A road appears on the left, and while I have no idea where it will lead, the junction still gets taken. Perhaps there'll be an abandoned house, or an unused shed somewhere along the road. I don't know Cumbria, and had had to google Boustead Hill when Owen suggested it, but that wasn't a problem. What matters is finding somewhere where I can start sculpting Owen Grantham.

I've never liked the idea of leaving alive witnesses to my work, but the fee for this contract is a cool half million. Like his brother Kevin, there is a special remit from the client for Owen, and Michaela when I find her. They have to be crippled with life-changing injuries. So rather than a quick clean death, they have to suffer unimaginable agony and then a lifetime spent coping with the disabilities me and my chisels have wrought upon them. As I'd done when dealing with Kevin, I'll wear the balaclava to hide my face and put on that Irish accent again. Yes, it may have wobbled towards Geordie or Scottish from time to time, but their pain would be of far greater worry to them than my attempts at an accent.

There is still the matter of finding Michaela Ingles, or 'Babes' as she is called on the email account. I know that if Owen knows where to find her, he'll tell me.

Failing that, I can keep sending the woman emails.

I could have well done without having to play detective, but for half a million, I'm prepared to do whatever needs doing. Besides, it's wonderful fun to inflict the crippling injuries. The fear and pain in Kevin's eyes was beautiful to behold and I have to admit, I'm looking forward to seeing it replicated when I go to work on Owen.

A few turns later I see the ruins of a small farm through the snowdrifts.

Perfect.

I draw into the weed-strewn farmyard and back the van up to one of the outbuildings, where an open door reveals a stone floor. A hard surface beneath Owen is imperative if the bones of his limbs are to be suitably broken. This particular job may be all about doling out a punishment, but that doesn't mean I can't enjoy myself and take pride in my work.

CHAPTER FORTY-NINE

Beth kept her back straight and her eyes to the front as the chief super made his points. Chief Superintendent Hilton wasn't a shouter who ranted and raved at his officers. His style was to ask questions that couldn't be answered without dropping yourself further into the mess.

Hilton's bollockings were never abusive, but what they lacked in angry verbiage, they more than replaced with quiet condemnation. In a lot of ways, Beth equated them to her father's shaking head and muttered, 'I'm very disappointed in you'. Whenever she'd been in trouble as a child, she'd always preferred her mother's strong admonishments to her father's quiet guilt trips.

The chief super paused in front of O'Dowd. 'So, let me get this right, you had a hot lead with the email account, and you didn't get the night shift to monitor it. Can you tell me why you chose that course of action? Perhaps while you're at it, you can explain why the emails pertaining to the meeting this morning were not picked up, let alone deciphered, until it was too late.' He leaned forward until his quiff was an inch away from O'Dowd's unruly mop. 'Come on then, let's hear it.'

Beth knew she might regret speaking up, but it was unfair for O'Dowd to carry the can for her failings, so she opened her mouth before the DI could respond. 'Sir. I was supposed to be monitoring the email account.'

Hilton's head snapped her way and while she'd earned a certain amount of credit with the chief super on previous cases, Beth could see that she'd just shot back into negative equity. Rather than speak he raised an eyebrow and waited for her to continue.

The only thing she could do was tell him the truth. Or at least the pertinent details. 'I checked it here until I left for home around seven. I met a… a friend for a couple of hours and planned to check it when I got home. Unfortunately though, the conversation I had with my friend led to some personal problems and I totally forgot to check it again when I got home.'

Hilton's other eyebrow joined the first in the middle of his forehead. 'Totally forgetting is not a good excuse. If you weren't able to check it, then at the very least you should have passed it on.' He gave a heavy sigh. 'I fully appreciate that there wasn't an overtime budget for this case and that you were monitoring it in your own time. But someone may have been brutally attacked if that meeting went ahead as planned. You do understand that, do you?'

'I do, sir.'

'Well, as disappointing as all of your collective efforts have been so far, we still have a killer out there and the ever-increasing possibility of a turf war. There is now an overtime budget. Personal problems, family meals and everything else that may be thrown in my face as an excuse for inexcusable lapses, all of them are to be ignored until this Sculptor has been caught and the population is safe. I trust that none of you has an issue with that.'

Beth joined the chorus of 'No, sir' with the others, but at the back of her mind was a planned meal on Saturday night. Ethan's parents were on a round-the-world trip to celebrate their pearl wedding anniversary, but they were back in time for Christmas and she was supposed to meet them for the first time on Saturday. While she knew Ethan would understand the vagaries of the job, it wouldn't look good to his parents if she had to call it off.

CHAPTER FIFTY

'It was very noble of you going all Spartacus on us in front of the chief super, but don't for one minute think it's got you off my shit list. You're acting like a stupid cow who keeps making mistake after mistake. How you got on to FMIT in the first place is beyond me. What was it you were doing last night? Shagging your boyfriend or bawling your eyes out over some chick flick?'

'That's enough, *Sergeant*.' O'Dowd put enough steel into her voice to emphasise her point, while glaring at McKay. 'Beth made a mistake, but she's a full-time member of FMIT whereas you're a temporary replacement. Besides, even with the mistakes she's made, she's still contributed more to this case than you have. Do me a favour and bugger off and do the job you were asked to do last night.'

Even as he nodded acquiescence to O'Dowd, McKay was sending a scowl Beth's way.

When he'd left the office, Beth gave O'Dowd a nod of her own. 'Thanks, ma'am.'

'He's not wrong about you making mistakes, but it's my place to bollock you, not his.' A hand flapped in exasperation. 'We've too much to do to waste time arguing. Consider yourself bollocked, but not forgiven. Not yet. Right, let's move forward. From the car abandoned at the bridge at Boustead Hill, we have a possible name and address for whomever Sinclair referred to as Dude. Beth, Paul, get yourselves over to Cockermouth where this Pete Benson lives. I want you speaking to his wife and kids if he has them, work colleagues and neighbours, if he hasn't. I want to know everything about him. Especially if he's as bloody secretive as James Sinclair was. Paul, you're to drive; while you're travelling, I want Beth to be working on that last code. If Babes responds to the email she got, I want to know what she says within seconds of her saying it.'

Beth grabbed her notes and took a moment to wind a scarf around her neck as she thought about the Sculptor's potential next victim. An initial search told her Pete Benson was in his late thirties, and had no police record of any kind, neither as a suspect nor a witness. Just like James Sinclair, he was a ghost as far as databases were concerned. His entire file, which was the bare minimum, was nondescript and bland.

With luck they'd get a decent lead and a picture of Benson's life that might help them find him. But if the Sculptor *had* taken him, it didn't bode well for his health, or even survival.

CHAPTER FIFTY-ONE

As much as she wanted to focus on the notes on her lap, Beth couldn't help but keep glancing up as Unthank drove along the A66 to Cockermouth. Because the snowfall was worsening into a full-on storm, the gritters and snowploughs working to keep the road clear were fighting a losing battle.

At best Unthank was doing forty miles an hour and there were times he had to slow to a crawl where snow had drifted on to the road or a vehicle had become stuck.

She counted five cars which had left the road due to the icy conditions, and as much as she trusted Unthank's driving, there were enough variables for her to feel uneasy.

The one bonus she had was that the emails from Babes weren't too hard to crack. Like James Sinclair she'd sent birthday and Christmas greetings with regularity; however, the date she wished James Sinclair a happy birthday was completely different from the date that was listed as his date of birth.

Another look out of the window revealed nothing but white and the fog lights of the car in front of them. It was a form of sensory deprivation, and Beth didn't envy Unthank the task of driving in such conditions.

They were alongside Bassenthwaite Lake when Unthank's mobile rang. He pressed a button on the steering wheel and tossed out an introductory greeting.

A disembodied voice came back through the car's speakers.

'DI Monkton of the Met here.'

'I'm driving in a snowstorm just now, sir, but my colleague DC Young is here.'

'Okay. You put a query in about the Sculptor. My team and I have been tracking him for years.'

Beth's pulsed quickened. It sounded like Monkton was the very person they needed to speak to. On the other hand, if he'd spent years pursuing the Sculptor without success, he might not be able to help them.

'DC Young, sir. What can you tell us about him? We have three attacks that match his style here. Two fatal and one which has led to life-changing injuries. We think he may be operating in the area for one of the two local firms, or possibly he's been sent to stir things up between the two firms so someone else can step in and take over.'

A hesitation then Monkton began speaking again. 'I'll be honest, I don't have much on him at all. He's like a wraith. Flits in and out, does what's needed and then leaves. There's never been any forensics on his kills and anyone we've interrogated who knows of him, has either not known the full story, or been too afraid of the Sculptor to share it with us. I have extensive files on him that are full of nothing but speculation and rumour.'

'Anything you can tell us will be a help, sir.'

'He's been operating for around five years that we're sure of, but for all the victims we know have been attributed to him, we're convinced there are at least as many again that we don't know of.'

'Do you know if he has an affiliation to any particular gang? HOLMES suggested he does, but as someone who's been on his trail, I thought you might have a better handle on it.'

'None so far as I'm aware. I can't say for certain without proof, but I'm convinced two or three of the bigger gangs have used him on several occasions.'

'Against each other or other targets?'

'Other targets. My thinking is that he doesn't piss off customers by acting against them. Although, I dare say that if the right offer was made, he'd take on anyone. To me he seems amoral and apolitical.'

'Thanks. Do you have a psych profile for him?'

'I do indeed. If you give me your email address I'll ping it and everything else I have on him through to you.'

'Thanks. One last thing, sir, I know that there's only one recorded instance of him leaving a design on one of his victims, but have you heard any whispers of him doing something similar or having any kind of agenda? I only ask because his two fatalities up here had the Eye of Providence and a fish symbol cut into their skulls. The symbols might suggest the Illuminati and Christianity respectively.'

'Hmmm. Not noticed anything like that with him before other than the Star of David. He might be getting cocky or may just be yanking your chain. I'll have a think about it and get back to you if I come up with anything. What's your email address?'

Beth gave him her email and thanked him.

Unthank cut the call and said nothing, so Beth went back to her task. By the time they pulled in to Cockermouth Beth had cracked Babes's code barring X and Z.

Before she left the car, she checked the email account again and saw that Babes hadn't yet replied to the email asking for a meet.

CHAPTER FIFTY-TWO

Owen lies broken at my feet. He'd been stubborn at first. Resolute in his determination not to talk. A sharp blow on his kneecap had changed his mind and he'd started talking.

Nothing he'd had to say had been meaningful though. Like his brother Kevin, or 'James Sinclair' as he was calling himself, he'd denied any contact with the other two people who made up their triumvirate – other than via the email account.

Even with the bones of his left leg below and including the kneecap smashed into fragments, he'd not given me any clue as to where Michaela Ingles now lives. I'd even tried rotating his mangled foot through a hundred and eighty degrees, but he'd done nothing beyond scream so loud I had to get my ear defenders from the van.

My information is sketchy at best. So far as I'm aware, Kevin Grantham had only been discovered due to a social-media post that had been spotted by one of the lackeys employed by the people who'd contracted me for this job.

The Facebook live video had been taken by a junior chef and had shown his big-eared boss telling him to put down his phone. A hand had been raised to shield the chef's face and that had been the clincher.

The lackey had watched the video a few times and then shown it to his boss. Enquiries had been made and I was contracted to extract the whereabouts of Michaela Ingles and

Owen Grantham and then leave all three of them with life-changing injuries.

I don't know why the contract has been issued on the three and I don't care. All that matters to me is the £500,000 contract. As payouts go, it's large even by my standards, but I guess that if the punishment should fit the crime, the people who hired me were also certain whatever crime the triumvirate had committed against them fit the punishment.

With Owen yielding no information on where Michaela might be, I had given up questioning him and had concentrated on meting out the rest of his punishment. Like his brother, I pulverised both of Owen's legs and arms below the elbow and kneecaps and shattered his ribcage with a wide bolster.

When I'd finishing sculpting Owen, I smashed the ice on a water trough and washed the blood from my chisels.

With my tools loaded back into the van, my last act was to carry four hay bales from a nearby shed and arrange them in the shape of an arrow on the road.

Owen has to be found before he dies so he doesn't miss a lifetime of suffering.

I climbed into my van and drove off without a backward glance. With luck, Michaela will read the email addressed to her and respond soon. When that happens, I can complete the contract and vanish back to London.

CHAPTER FIFTY-THREE

Like so many of Cumbria's towns, Cockermouth was an ancient market town, and it took its name from the fact it was located where the River Cocker joined the River Derwent. For Beth, the one overriding thing she remembered it for was the ever-present smell of hops from the Jennings Brewery.

Beth shivered and yawned with an equal fervency. The lack of sleep was taking a toll on her, and while the buzz of activity earlier had given her some spikes of adrenaline to keep going, now she was in a warm car after trudging through snow-filled streets, her body was reacting to the cold and her tiredness.

She and Unthank had grabbed a hot pie from a bakers on the main street by way of lunch, but hers hadn't begun to give her the warmth her body craved. Being tall and slim, her circulation wasn't brilliant and her toes each felt as though they'd been blast chilled.

The time spent in Cockermouth looking for, and trying to locate, Pete Benson had brought the worst kind of news. He'd not been at the small cottage he called home, nor had he been at the café where he worked. Like James Sinclair he worked in a kitchen, but rather than being a head chef with a mouth-watering menu, Pete Benson served fry-ups, chips and a handful of other unhealthy dishes in a place that was little more than a greasy spoon.

An elderly neighbour had used a spare key to let them into Benson's cottage and had been eager to tell them what she knew about his life.

Pete Benson lived alone and hadn't been in a relationship for the last few years, to the neighbour's knowledge. When the subject of Benson's relationships had been broached, the neighbour had looked around in a furtive manner before dropping her voice to a whisper and confiding that Benson was 'one of them gays'. As much as the neighbour's attitude was out of date, the woman was a product of her times, so Beth didn't pass any mental condemnation for the outdated attitude.

Benson's home was a masterclass in austerity. No two pieces of furniture matched, and each one looked as if it had been bought second-hand. Even the TV fixed to the wall didn't look fancy, and would at most have a thirty-inch screen.

What did draw attention were the sketches Blu-Tacked onto the walls. Beth didn't know much about art, but from what she could tell the proportions and shading of the sketches told of the artist's skill. Some were countryside scenes and others were of people or pets. The one that really stood out to Beth had been placed centre stage above the fireplace: unless she was very much mistaken, it was of a young James Sinclair. As much as the email communication, it proved the two men were connected. She used her mobile to take a picture of it for future reference.

The discovery of Sinclair's picture had sparked an idea in Beth, so she'd asked the neighbour a specific question and got the answer she expected. Like Sinclair, Benson had a London accent. This tied them closer together again, and if it was Sinclair in the only sketch to be framed, he was either a former lover of Benson's or a close relative. Beth's guess was that he was a brother or perhaps a cousin as they were of a similar age, but she didn't discount the idea that he was a former lover.

It was when Beth clocked that all the electrical items were on shelves at least five-foot high that she'd understood why the furniture was all second-hand. Benson's cottage was near enough to the river to be in the flood zone and he probably could no longer get insurance for his household contents. Therefore, the expensive electrical items were kept up at a height and he bought cheap second-hand furniture which could be easily replaced after a flood. She'd already noted that rather than a carpet or laminate flooring, Benson had tiled floors. Another measure to combat the damage and expense caused by floodwater.

Floods were a permanent risk and Beth knew that both the neighbour and Benson would have been watching the snowfall with a fearful eye. If the snow fell deep and melted quickly, it would swell the waters of the Derwent and Cocker, and once again, their homes would be deluged with the irresistible force of rampaging floodwater.

For it to happen at any time of year would be bad, but it seemed especially worse in the short, dark days of December. This was a time of year for looking forward to family occasions, to spending quality time with loved ones free from the stresses and strains that affected the rest of the year.

Benson's boss at the café had been furious at him not showing up for work, although when Unthank had asked if it was a regular occurrence, she'd calmed down after admitting he'd never before left her in the lurch in the six years he'd worked there. Like the neighbour, the café boss was adamant Benson wasn't currently in a relationship, and her initial anger had turned to worry by the time Beth and Unthank had left.

As a matter of course, they'd bagged Benson's iPad for Digital Forensics to go through. When Beth had found a statement from his mobile provider, she'd tried calling his number only for it to go straight to voicemail. She relayed the number back to O'Dowd so its whereabouts could be triangulated on the unlikely chance he'd met someone else at Boustead Hill and wasn't in any danger.

Like everything else about the case it had come back negative. A text from O'Dowd had informed her that Benson's phone had been found buried in a snowdrift at the side of the road near the bridge at Boustead Hill.

The drive back to Penrith was even more treacherous than the journey to Cockermouth had been, and there were many occasions that Beth feared they'd either become stuck or find the road impassable due to other vehicles having been unable to manage the wintry conditions.

In addition to the blizzard, it was now late enough in the day that what little sunlight had permeated the snowstorm had been replaced by utter blackness.

Beth was deciphering Babes's emails as they travelled, but the constant slipping and sliding, coupled with the frown of concentration furrowing Unthank's forehead, made it hard for her to keep her focus when she expected to either crash or become stranded at any moment.

One thing she was sure of, when she braced her feet against the footwell as Unthank went into yet another slow slide, was that the case was being blown apart in a lot of different ways, and that their best chance of solving it was to go right back to the beginning and start over again. Once Babes's emails were done that's what she planned to do, even if she had to do it in her own time.

CHAPTER FIFTY-FOUR

Sandi kicked back in her chair and smiled at the sleeping form of Leo. After wolfing down a large portion of cottage pie, he'd got himself comfortable in front of the TV and had started with his soft snores within ten minutes of the football match he'd planned to watch kicking off.

As soon as she was certain he was asleep, Sandi had grabbed the remote control and switched over to a soap in an effort to distract her from her thoughts.

All day she'd puzzled over what she should do regarding the email from Kevin. Should she read it, or should she be true to the words she'd written but hadn't left in the drafts folder for Kevin to read and move on? Many years and a lot of water had travelled under that bridge, and now she was getting married, she wanted to put that part of her life behind her for once and for all.

Leo was her future. Kevin and his brother Owen were her past. She still paid for that past on a daily basis, but she now had a chance of a bright and happy future with Leo. Sure, he wasn't perfect, but he was essentially a good man who'd look after her and hopefully give her the children she so craved.

All the same, her natural inquisitiveness was compelling her to know what he was messaging her about. It was too early for his usual Christmas message and since he'd married, he barely contacted her other than to offer birthday or Christmas greetings.

Against her better judgement, she retrieved her codes, logged into the email account and pulled up Kevin's message.

It took her less than a minute to transcribe the email from Kevin and when she did, she felt her blood chill despite the fact the heating was on full.

WE NEED TO MEET ASAP

What does he mean by that? Has his marriage failed and he wants me back? Does he want me back in his life? Do I want him back in mine?

Of all the questions pummelling Sandi's brain, the last one was the only one she had an answer for. Having Kevin back in her life after nineteen years of absence wouldn't work. She'd spent years grieving the break-up of their relationship, but had finally moved on and found someone who wanted to spend their life with her.

Sandi bit down on the sob of frustration for all the things which might have been, closed down the email account and clicked on to the Victoria's Secret website. Just because she and Leo weren't married yet didn't mean they couldn't start trying for a baby. With luck, whatever she bought would be here in time for Christmas and she could spend the holiday period both securing her future, and burying her past.

CHAPTER FIFTY-FIVE

The first thing Beth did after dumping her notes on her desk was to flick on the office kettle. Unthank's car had been toasty warm by the time they made it to Carleton Hall, but her fingers and toes still felt numb. A cup of tea would go a long way to restoring some internal body heat and would give her something warm to hold onto while there was the inevitable debrief.

She made a cup for Unthank and a coffee for O'Dowd, but nothing for McKay. After his earlier outburst, he could bloody well make his own.

He scowled when he noticed that she'd omitted him, so Beth gave him a sweet smile knowing it would annoy him further. *Let him realise for himself that I'm here to contribute a lot more than being his maid.*

O'Dowd accepted her coffee with a thumbs up as she rose from her seat and went to the office whiteboard. 'Right, to bring you two up to speed, DS McKay has spoken to a lot of the officers in and around Carlisle. They're all hearing whispers about the RF and the Currockers running around looking for someone, anyone, to blame. So far their uneasy truce is holding, but it's a tinderbox that'll go off at the slightest spark. Needless to say, the brass have everything crossed that it doesn't end in a full-blown turf war.'

McKay leaned back in his chair and adopted the smug expression of someone who was satisfied with his day's work. His smug nonchalance irked Beth as it was unfounded. All he'd effectively done was canvas the opinions of others and round them up into a simple statement of fact.

Beth was aware that the animosity between McKay and her would tarnish her opinion of anything he'd done, but she and Unthank had been out in a snowstorm and had got a picture of Pete Benson's life. On top of that, she'd cracked Babes's code and had made a start on deciphering the woman's messages.

O'Dowd carried on with her briefing. 'So far, Pete Benson hasn't been found, but while others are conducting that search we need to stop being reactive and start being proactive.' A hand was waved at Unthank and Beth. 'We know he's not at home or work, therefore we have to assume the Sculptor has him and that Benson is either already dead or will be soon. What we have to do is work out who this Sculptor is and where they'll have taken Benson.' O'Dowd picked up a marker and turned to the whiteboard. 'Ideas, please. I don't care how stupid you think they are, spit them out.'

O'Dowd's line at Benson either being dead or close to death skewered Beth. Since her lapse in checking the email account had come to light, she'd battled with her sense of guilt and it was a fight she wasn't winning. Benson was in his current predicament because she'd taken her eye off the ball due to being so wrapped up in speaking to Richie and then the fallout of Ethan's attack on him.

Rather than speak up and give McKay another chance to mock her, Beth let the two men throw their ideas at O'Dowd first.

'Some weird religious thing. A broken body and then the Eye of Providence and then a symbol used by early Christians? No idea what's next, but maybe Benson's corpse will hold the clue we need.' McKay leaned back in his chair.

'Gambling debts. I'm talking about private card schools, not online sites or anything like that.' McKay again.

Unthank looked pensive as he added his thoughts. 'Retribution. All the victims are male. Maybe they've all slept with the same woman and her husband has found out. Dippen and Harrytosis were gang members, so it's possible the woman in question is the wife or daughter of one of the gangs. Hence the hiring of the Sculptor.'

'Not bad so far. Keep them coming.' O'Dowd spoke without turning round.

Unthank: 'Someone instigating a gang war.'

McKay: 'Protection racketeering. A pair of hoods and a guy who worked in a place worth targeting. We already know Dippen and Harrytosis were looking to branch out on their own. Maybe they were further along than anyone knew and got caught out.'

'Good points.' O'Dowd turned and glanced at Beth. 'You're too quiet. I don't believe you've not got any ideas. Come on, let's have your thoughts.'

'Wrong. Emails. Links.'

'Here we go again.'

Beth ignored McKay's sneered comment and focussed her attention on O'Dowd as she pulled her thoughts into coherent sentences. 'I think all of those ideas are wrong. The first one about religion is the only one which has some merit, but I'm still not sure about it. The symbols on Dippen and Harrytosis have religious meaning, but only to a point. From what I understand from the brief online research I've done, the Eye of Providence may have started out as a Christian symbol but it's now more Illuminati than anything else and the fish was an early symbol of Christianity that was used in secret to begin with, or they could just be the Sculptor showing off.' Not for the first time, Beth wished she'd had the time to properly research both symbols. 'Geometrically speaking, it'd be tricky to create either design on a head. If we go back to my friend's theory that a damping agent such as a piece of thick leather was used to cushion the blows and reduce actual damage to the victims' skin, then add my own suspicion the designs were already drawn on to the damping cloth, it makes logical sense. Where the broken man comes in, I don't know. Sorry, but I don't know a lot about religion. I don't even know if there is a broken man in the Bible or if that's the correct term to use. To me it sounds more like the name of a tarot card. As DS McKay used the phrase, perhaps he knows more about it.'

Beth looked at McKay, but all she got was a glower then the shake of a head.

'Okay, I see your point.' O'Dowd tapped the marker pen in her other hand. 'What about the other points?'

'If, as DS McKay suggested, it's to do with card schools, then it doesn't make sense that James Sinclair and Pete Benson are exchanging secret messages for years, but are in the same card school when the messages clearly state that they daren't ever meet.'

McKay rose to his feet, a finger was extended at Beth and triumph filled his voice. 'They could be in separate card schools and the Sculptor was giving warnings so they'd pay their debts.'

'Possible but it seems unlikely. There wasn't enough time for the warnings to travel to the correct ears if what you say is right. Plus, it looks like the Sculptor has been specifically hunting down Pete Benson and the woman we know as Babes. If they were involved in a card school, someone would know who they were. Ergo, it can't be that idea.' Beth took a slug of her tea and pulled a face at the fact it was now lukewarm. 'The idea that they'd all been sleeping with a gangster's wife or daughter is preposterous. One, Dippen and Harrytosis wouldn't dare. Two, they were both overweight, unattractive and had bad breath and a squint between them. Three, while James Sinclair's picture shows him a decent enough looking man, he's been described as intensely private and there's no way I can picture him doing anything which may draw attention to him from anyone, let alone a gangster. Four, Pete Benson is apparently gay and Babes is probably a woman, so you're looking for a gangster's wife or daughter who likes secretive men, unattractive and smelly men, gay men and also women. I'm not sure such a woman exists, but perhaps DS McKay knows of one.'

McKay's top lip curled into a malicious sneer. 'Careful, Detective Constable. I am still your sergeant.'

'Actually, you're only here on a temporary basis and considering the way you ripped into her earlier, I'd say she's being remarkably polite. All she's doing is giving her opinion on your theories.' O'Dowd ran a hand through her hair that neither tidied nor messed it further. 'The fact you're picking at her last sentence rather than the preceding ones tells me that you can't argue with her logic.' A wave of the hand holding the marker. 'Go on, Beth.'

'The gang-war aspect troubled me at first, but while the first and last victims…' Even as she classed Pete Benson as the last victim, a spear of guilt pierced Beth's heart. '… have a connection, and the middle are connected to each other, there's no connection beyond the Sculptor linking the four of them. It's possible that it's to do with a gang war, but that still doesn't explain why the Sculptor is hunting Pete Benson and Babes. As for the idea that it's all to do with Dippen and Harrytosis setting up on their own, I'm sorry, but I think that's a total non-starter. They had an idea and ran it past their boss at the RF. They got a green light, because it was a stupid idea that wouldn't work. They were hired muscle and while I don't want to speak ill of the dead, not a lot of that muscle was between their ears. And again, it doesn't explain the Sculptor hunting Benson and Babes.'

Beth sat back in her chair and drained the last of her tea as the rest of the team digested her reasoning. Unthank looked chastened, but McKay was clearly furious at all their ideas being shot down.

He rose to his feet and crossed the office so he could tower over Beth as she sat at her desk. 'Come on then, you're so bloody smart, what do you think the connection is?'

'I don't know. I'm not even sure there is one. I think we have to go right back to the start of the investigation and begin again. One thing that's been troubling me though, is where Dippen and Harrytosis were put into Lake Ullswater. We've never looked at that and we should have.' There was a thud as O'Dowd's hand connected with her desk. Even McKay looked a little guilty, but that didn't matter to Beth as she pressed on. 'We know the Ullswater flows north and forms the River Eamont at Pooley Bridge, therefore they must have been put into the water somewhere south of the place where they were picked up. The A592 might run along parts of the west bank, but I can't think of anywhere that you could tip someone straight into the lake from the road, and besides, yes it might be the middle of winter, but that road will still see a bit of traffic; it'd be way too risky to dump bodies along that road. Glenridding is at the southern end of the lake, which only leaves us one place: the road that goes south from Pooley Bridge.' Beth cast a glance at O'Dowd. 'Correct me if I'm wrong, ma'am, but isn't there a small yachting marina along there?'

'Dammit, Beth, you're right. It'll be deserted at this time of year, but there's houses along the road to it. For once on this bloody case we might just get lucky and get a witness who saw something suspicious on the night Harrytosis and Dippen were dumped.'

Before anyone could respond, the phone on O'Dowd's desk rang.

Beth used the distraction to check the email server again and found that while Babes had read the email from the Sculptor, she hadn't replied.

O'Dowd's voice was soft as she spoke into the phone. When Beth looked at her the DI had her eyes closed and a sorrowful expression on her face. She didn't need the DI to speak to know that Pete Benson had been found. The only question whose answer mattered was if he was alive or dead.

CHAPTER FIFTY-SIX

Beth checked the email account for what seemed like the millionth time that day. After cocking up last night, there was no way she wasn't going to spot the next message coming through. O'Dowd had already arranged for an officer on the back shift to check the account every half hour from ten o'clock, but even though that handover was only fifty minutes away, Beth had no plans to abandon it until her head hit a pillow.

As it was she was yawning hard enough to crack her jaw. McKay had been dispatched to speak to the nearest minister he could find, and Unthank had just been sent home while the road to High Hesket was still open.

O'Dowd was outside for a smoke, which meant that Beth was alone for the first time in hours. With nobody to put on a brave face for, Beth thought about the implications of her mistake. Pete Benson had been found in a semi-derelict farm with identical injuries to James Sinclair.

The farmer who'd found him had called for an ambulance, but due to there being so many snowdrifts on the isolated country roads near the Solway Coast, the ambulance had been forced to abandon its mercy dash a mile away and the paramedics had got the farmer to transport them in on his tractor. With the snowstorm making it impossible to summon the air ambulance, they'd made an executive decision and had administered enough painkillers to keep Benson unconscious, loaded his broken body on to a stretcher and the stretcher on to the tractor's trailer.

Benson was still alive when he reached Carlisle hospital, but his grip on life was tenuous at best and the doctors and surgeons who'd attended to him didn't expect him to survive the night.

Beth wanted to cry for Benson, to give way to the temptation to break her heart for the selfishness which had distracted her from monitoring the email account, but the tears wouldn't come. A logical part of her knew that she wasn't as guilty as she believed she was, but there was no escaping the fact that if she hadn't allowed herself to be sidetracked by events in her own life, Benson would be alive and well and the Sculptor would be behind bars. Beth vowed that regardless of what it cost her personally, she wouldn't allow the same fate to befall Babes.

O'Dowd reappeared in a swaddle of scarves and swearwords about the weather. Before the DI could get started with one of her customary rants about the lack of a smoking shelter, Beth got her idea across first.

'Ma'am. You know how we're always behind the Sculptor instead of ahead? I have an idea. Two ideas actually.'

'Go on.' O'Dowd looked at her with suspicion. 'What is that sideways-thinking brain of yours suggesting we do?'

'My first idea is that we message Babes ourselves. Explain who we are, why we're contacting her and tell her she must go to her local police station and call us immediately. We might lose the Sculptor over it, but we'd at least be able to guarantee Babes's safety.'

'And your second idea?'

'We message the Sculptor with Babes's code and arrange a meet of our own. We'd be able to set up a proper sting operation and then we'd be able to take him down. Then once he was in custody, we'd be able to get Babes to come forward and help us work out what the hell has been going on.'

'Those are good ideas. I like the second one the most as I want this Sculptor off the streets. I think we should plan that for tomorrow, providing nothing breaks during the night. The way this bloody weather is going, we may have to wait a day or two anyway as we could end up with half the county snowed in.' O'Dowd pointed at the various pieces of paper strewn across Beth's desk. 'What have you got there?'

'The messages between James Sinclair, Pete Benson and Babes.' Beth made a dismissive gesture. 'They are all blah blah this blah blah that messages that don't say anything other than menial stuff about new jobs, James getting married and Babes getting her heart broken a couple of times, there's nothing of substance, let alone use, to the investigation.'

'And what about Monkton's files on the Sculptor, what do they say?'

'A whole hell of a lot and nothing at all. There's lots of conjecture, some speculation and a shitload of rumour, but nothing substantial. The psych report Monkton had commissioned is pretty much standard fare. According to the criminal psychologist who studied these files and the details of the Sculptor's kills, the Sculptor is most likely to be a single male, mid-twenties to late fifties. He'll have trouble forming meaningful relationships due to his utter amorality and he'll be a textbook psychopath who has no emotional interaction with anyone. He also stated that it's likely he came from a broken home or was possibly raised in the care system which meant he was never shown love as a child.'

O'Dowd lifted an eyebrow. 'Sounds familiar.'

Beth got what she meant. It was frustrating that without specific details about an individual killer, many criminal psychologists hedged their bets and made their pronouncements based on statistics rather than a definitive understanding of the killer's mind. It was their way of safeguarding their reputations, and being fair to them, Beth knew that without details to fuel insights, it was damn near impossible for them to be specific when they didn't have enough information to base a proper assessment on. The problem was, that unless the police could provide the necessary details, every psych evaluation came back with the same profile. Young to middle-aged man. Broken home or part of the care system. Psychotic tendencies. After a while the profiles all blended into one interchangeable document.

She was pleased that O'Dowd had liked her idea of sending messages to either Babes or the Sculptor. Should it come to it that a sting was set up, Beth was more than prepared to put herself forward should anyone be needed to play the role of Babes. After all, it looked as if her mistake would cost Pete Benson his life, so it was only fair that she took on any risk associated with catching the Sculptor.

CHAPTER FIFTY-SEVEN

Beth made sure the first thing she did when she got home was give Ethan a quick kiss. She'd messaged him as she'd left the office and as per her request, he'd come round to see her. The next thing she did was check her phone. There were no emails waiting in James Sinclair's folder, but there was a text from Unthank.

He was apologising for the way he'd not mentioned seeing her the previous night and thanking her for not telling O'Dowd he was dating the tenacious reporter.

Beth smiled to herself when she read his text. To her mind it was clear what had happened. After getting home he'd spoken to Teri and related his day to her. Whether or not she was using Unthank as a source, she'd have been worried about the implications of Beth informing O'Dowd of their relationship. When she'd heard Unthank hadn't addressed the subject with Beth, she'd have prodded him to do so.

Ethan went into the kitchen and put the kettle on while Beth tucked into the chicken kebab she'd picked up on the way home. Eating after eleven at night was never a good idea, but she was ravenous and at least a chicken kebab was a little bit healthier than the other late-night offerings available.

When the kebab was finished she related her day to Ethan. He winced and looked shamefaced when she told him about Pete Benson, but she held up a hand when he tried to apologise. His fight with Neck Kisses might have distracted Beth, but it was

Beth who'd been tasked to monitor the email account, and had failed to do so.

'There is something I need you to do for me, Ethan.'

'What is it? Say the word and I'll do it.'

'It's easy to say, maybe not so easy to do. We talked long and late last night. I meant everything I said. No more secrets, no more lies and definitely no more kicking lumps out of people.'

'Agreed. No more of any of that. Just us having fun and being honest with each other.'

'About that.' Beth swallowed, unsure how Ethan would take this piece of news. 'Unless we've caught the killer by Saturday night, I may have to cancel on your parents. If that happens, I'll pay for us to take them out somewhere for a meal. Somewhere nice.'

'You do know that I won't allow you to do that, don't you?' Ethan pulled her close until her head was resting on his chest. 'Besides, I've already warned them we may have to postpone. I did it as soon as you got this latest case.'

Beth levered herself off the couch, dropped a kiss onto Ethan's forehead, took his hand and stumbled upstairs; she was already three parts asleep. Her brain dead from all the thinking, and in the case of Pete Benson, overthinking. The last thing she did before closing her eyes and snuggling against Ethan was check the email account. Just in case there was a new message.

CHAPTER FIFTY-EIGHT

The bedroom door creaked as Sandi opened it and got ready to sneak downstairs. Leo was doing his usual sleep thing of alternatively mimicking a corpse and then thrashing like a drummer in the middle of a huge drum solo.

It wasn't his fault Sandi was awake. The full blame for that lay halfway between her and Kevin. She'd found it impossible to send the goodbye email, and she knew that until things were finalised between them, she wouldn't be able to quell the suspicions in her mind as to why he wanted to meet, let alone move forward with her life.

She pulled her dressing gown tight around her and tucked her legs beneath her bum as she sat on the couch. Her house had cooled in the time since she and Leo had gone to bed and the heating wasn't due to kick back in until morning.

Sandi read the message from Kevin again, although she'd imprinted every one of the words onto her brain. Of the three of them, Kevin had always been the most insistent that they must never meet. Whatever had caused him to request a meeting was a mystery that Sandi couldn't solve no matter which way she looked at it.

Despite the potential risks involved, Sandi couldn't turn down the chance to see Kevin one last time. She'd tell him about Leo face-to-face. Hear about his wife, maybe even his kids.

Sandi tapped out a reply to Kevin's message, closed the program down and sat alone and silent. Her thoughts a jumble of speculation and anticipation.

She wanted to know everything about Kevin, how he was, if he was happy. She wanted to hear his laugh again, and feel his arms around her one last time before she married another man.

As she'd done so many times since last seeing him, she wondered what he looked like now. Would he have greying hair or a receding hairline? Maybe he'd gone properly bald and maybe he'd given up the fight and shaved his head. Had he put on weight as he'd aged, or was he still stick thin? However he was, Sandi couldn't wait to see him. Kevin had been full of enthusiasm for life twenty years ago and she didn't see how that could have changed as it was his very essence.

With the message sent and her thoughts of Kevin becoming increasingly sluggish, Sandi padded back upstairs and slipped under the small part of the duvet Leo hadn't claimed.

She was getting married and she'd see Kevin again soon. It might be snowing outside, but she could only see blue skies in her future.

CHAPTER FIFTY-NINE

Beth lifted her elbow and pushed backwards, but the shaking of her shoulder didn't stop. If anything it got worse. There was a noise as well. Familiar, but out of place. She was in a summer meadow having a picnic with Ethan. Noises like an angry hornet and shakes on the shoulder had no place here. It was quiet and tranquil; a place of laughter and fun.

'For God's sake, Beth, will you wake up. Your phone's ringing and it's your boss's name on the screen.'

Beth snapped into something that resembled the first stages of waking and put the phone to her ear. 'Mmngth?'

'Beth. It's Zoe. She's only gone and bloody replied to him in the middle of the night.'

'Who?' Clarity hit Beth hard enough to make her sit upright in bed. 'Babes?'

'Aye, Babes. Get your arse out of bed and get me that message deciphered.'

O'Dowd ended the call and that was fine by Beth. She was already climbing out of the bed so she could wash the sleep from her face with cold water.

When she came back for her dressing gown, Ethan was pulling his jeans on.

'What, are you going home?'

'No, I'm going to put the kettle on. You've obviously got to go into work or at the very least do some work here. You were frozen when you came in and if you have to go out at this time of the morning, it's a fair bet there's some kind of flap on. Having a hot drink inside you won't do any harm, so I'm making you one.'

Beth leaned in and gave Ethan a quick kiss. 'I love you.'

A minute later Beth had the email account open on her phone and had a pen and a piece of paper on her coffee table. She could have fired up her laptop, but she was too impatient to wait the five minutes it took for it to boot up. The table she'd created with all three codes on it lay on the arm of her chair.

Because Beth had gone through this process many times, she had the message decoded in record time. Her haste and sleepiness caused her to make an error with the odd letter, but it was easy enough to substitute the correct letters without resorting to her table.

O'Dowd answered after the first ring. 'Well?'

'The basic gist is that she's agreeing to meet.'

'Shite. Meet me at Carleton as soon as you can get there and keep an eye on that bloody email account.'

'Yes, ma'am. What about the others, do you want me to call them for you?'

'Don't bother. McKay's bloody useless and if we're starting this early, I want Paul rested so he can cover the backshift. From now on I want a member of FMIT all over that email account.'

As she went upstairs to get dressed, Beth couldn't help but flash back to the meeting the previous day where O'Dowd had got everyone's theories and had then asked her opinion on them all. She'd felt bad shooting down all the ideas, but to her logical mind none of them were anything like correct as they all missed part of the picture.

Beth was sure there had been an element of Machiavelli in O'Dowd asking her opinion of the others' ideas. In particular McKay had looked furious to have his ideas rubbished by a DC. As Beth pulled on her boots, she wondered if it was the DI's way of proving her worth to McKay so he'd stop giving her a hard time.

Whatever it was, it had backfired, as McKay seemed to hate her more than ever now.

CHAPTER SIXTY

Beth beat O'Dowd into the office by less than five minutes. As a matter of course, she filled the kettle and set it to boil. O'Dowd was grumpy enough at eight without coffee, at four thirty she'd be insufferable.

She checked the account again. No response from the Sculptor, but that didn't mean anything. It was the middle of the night and for once they had the opportunity to get ahead of events.

O'Dowd breezed into the office with her mobile pressed against one ear and hair like an electrocuted Einstein. When she peeled off her jacket, Beth was amazed to see her DI was wearing a smart dress with knee-high boots. Given O'Dowd's usual rumpled suit and frumpy tops, it was overdressing. But at this time of the morning, it made Beth wonder if the DI had been at a party and hadn't returned home by the time the call about the email came in.

Beth could only hear O'Dowd's side of the conversation, but there was little doubt that the DI was speaking to whichever senior officer whose turn it was to be on call this week.

Exceptional circumstances and major incidents would see gold, silver and bronze commanders appointed and these could go as high as the chief constable depending upon the severity of the incident. For something like this, the senior officer on call would be the one to make the decision, but Beth didn't expect a bronze commander to be appointed until they had a firm fix.

There was also the second part of Babes's message to consider. She'd agreed to the meet but had stated that she was at work all the next day, so it'd have to be after 6 p.m.

O'Dowd ended the call and flumped down in a heap of frustrated sighs and sequins. 'Not a word about the dress, right. Bloody washing machine's on the blink and this was the first clean thing I could find.'

Rather than get drawn into commenting on the DI's clothing or laundry woes, Beth asked what their course of action was to be.

O'Dowd pointed at the phone. 'That was the chief super I was speaking to. As Babes is saying after work, he reckons we've got time to formulate a plan, so for the time being, we're to sit on our hands regarding action. Needless to say, we've to keep a watch on the account in case anything changes.'

'Fair enough.'

'Oh no you don't. Don't hit me with one of your "fair enoughs". You only ever say that when you disagree with something. Whatever you're thinking, spill it and spill it now.'

'I'm just thinking out loud here, okay?'

'Beth, it's half four in the bloody morning, I'm dressed like I'm going to a bloody cocktail party and we've a hitman targeting the people we're paid to protect. Let me know what your weird but wonderful brain is thinking and be done with it.'

'I can't explain it all, ma'am, but I'll try. Some ideas are still forming in my mind so please, don't interrupt me.' O'Dowd's frown bounced off Beth. She'd worked with the DI long enough to know when she was angry and when she just wanted to get some answers. 'I think we should try and imagine every possible message that might go between Babes and the Sculptor and pre-empt some responses so we can swoop in with our own email and take control in an instant. I may have cracked those codes, but it still takes a few minutes to decipher each message and will take as long to compose one. I say we should have some ready so we've got the jump on either Babes or the Sculptor should we need it.'

'Good point. What else?'

O'Dowd listened without interrupting as Beth outlined her ideas. As tired as she was from three nights back-to-back where she'd had less than three hours' sleep, Beth's brain had dusted itself off and hit top speed. It was always like this for Beth when an investigation was building. Her brain went into overdrive as it assimilated all the separate pieces of information which it had amassed during the case.

When Beth finished speaking, O'Dowd had made her usual jumble of notes on the desk pad she used and had made them both a cuppa.

'Right, you start going over the things you wanted to take a second look at, and I'll start working on the responses.'

Beth took a sip of her tea and hid the wince at how weak it was. Being a staunch coffee drinker, O'Dowd never left the teabag in long enough for Beth's liking.

The first thing Beth did was go back to the spreadsheet she'd created for the attack on James Sinclair. She had some suspicions about various aspects of the case, but they weren't yet formed well enough in her brain to take a shape. To bring them into a sharp focus, she needed to refresh the details and look for the connections.

As she looked over the various boxes in the spreadsheet, Beth's initial focus was on the statements of all the people they'd interviewed about the fracas in the Coachman. Nothing jumped out at her, but she cross-referenced as many details as she could until there were no further avenues to explore.

The investigations into the deaths of Dippen and Harrytosis had been hampered by the nature of the victims and the people in their circle. Thugs like Dippen and Harrytosis hung out with their own, which meant all of their acquaintances shared their suspicious view of the police. Beth suspected that most of the details in the statements from those who'd been drinking with them in The Boilermaker's were half-truths at best.

She tried to read between the lines and get a picture of what had gone on that night. On the surface of it, the pair of thugs had been in there having a drink and had left only to turn up in Lake Ullswater with symbols cut into their heads.

Beth had learned from their files that both men were players. Each had had domestic call-outs due to arguments with their spouses over alleged infidelities. They planned to set up a brothel and Beth was under no illusion as to how the interview process would go for the girls they would need to hire.

A common denominator from the statements gathered from those in The Boilermaker's was that there were some women in the bar and that both Dippen and Harrytosis had been chancing their arms with them.

One statement stood out from the others. It was one taken from an old man who'd been described by the interviewing officer as a barfly who'd been swatted by life. His statement intimated that the pair of thugs had left soon after a big lad and a woman. The interviewing officer had put notes into his report doubting the veracity of the old man's memory as he'd been drunk when interviewed at lunchtime, but to Beth it was a clue which pieced together a chain of events.

Dippen and Harrytosis had left the pub shortly after a woman had and then their fate had befallen them. None of the people in the pub had mentioned either of the thugs being out of order, and the women they'd interviewed said the two victims had tried chatting them up, but had got the message when they were told to get lost.

There were four people alleged to have been in The Boilermaker's who the barman didn't know, but that wasn't unusual for any pub. There would always be strangers as well as locals, although Beth would have liked to have had statements from the strangers who had no loyalty to, or grudge against, Dippen and Harrytosis.

A sequence of events in Beth's head was starting to take shape. Dippen and Harrytosis had been frustrated by their lack of success with the other women in the bar and had followed the unknown woman on purpose. Whether they intended to persuade her to join them for a drink elsewhere, or they had a more sinister plan in mind, would never be known, but at this stage Beth was working on the assumption they weren't planning to rape the woman. Neither had form for it, and even a pair of meatheads like them knew the chances of being identified by the police investigating the sexual assault charge were way too high.

All the same, they could have been pestering the woman, intimidating her as a way of petty revenge for rebuffing them.

Somewhere around this point the Sculptor must have entered proceedings. In Beth's mind, it was possible that he'd been in the Boilermaker's as well and had seen what Dippen and Harrytosis were up to and had followed them in case they were getting overly fresh with the mystery woman. He'd saved the woman from a mugging, or worse, and then exacted a violent revenge upon Dippen and Harrytosis.

This train of thought put a different perspective on Beth's thoughts about the Sculptor. If she was right in the way she'd reconstructed the chain of events, the Sculptor came across as a vigilante saviour rather than a stone cold killer. Killing gangsters for gangsters might be a scum-on-scum crime, but it still ridded the streets of scum. Was he some kind of white knight when he wasn't a killer for hire? Maybe he'd just happened to leave at the same time as the woman, and it was him that the pair of thugs had followed. They'd not taken to his accent, or they'd seen a challenge in his eyes and had tried to exert some dominance only to find themselves outmatched by a far superior opponent.

Quite where the squeaky clean James Sinclair fit into the picture was unknown, as was the quest to trace both Pete Benson and Babes, but the way that Sinclair had been secretive had been echoed when they'd looked into Benson's life. Beyond basic details, neither Benson's neighbour nor boss had known about his past.

When asked if they'd tried to discuss it with him, both had claimed that he'd politely changed the subject.

The secretive behaviour of Benson, Sinclair and the woman Babes was intriguing Beth, but she couldn't get her head around it in a way that made any kind of sense. Was Babes the woman who'd been followed out of The Boilermaker's?

The more she thought about it, the more she doubted that Babes was that woman. The Sculptor was looking for her and if Babes had been the woman in The Boilermaker's she'd surely have fallen victim to his chisels by now.

But if they could find the woman who'd been followed from The Boilermaker's, she may be able to give them a description of the Sculptor, which was something none of the London officers had managed to get. Even Monkton who'd been pursuing the Sculptor had failed to get even the most basic details such as an age group, height or general build, let alone facial features.

'Here, what do you think of these?'

Beth took a look at the various responses O'Dowd had composed and made a couple of suggestions based on her experience of the different voices used by the three different people. Babes was wordy, Sinclair brief but polite and Benson brief with occasional spelling mistakes. To convince Babes or the Sculptor they were really conversing with the person they thought they were speaking to, they had to mimic their speech patterns.

Once they'd agreed on the content of the emails, Beth shared her thoughts with O'Dowd.

A hand rubbed at O'Dowd's lined forehead then disappeared into a clump of hair. 'God's sake, Beth, it's bad enough that we've a twisted killer on the loose, but if the public find out he's some kind of avenging angel, we'll end up getting criticised for stopping him or not catching his victims for whatever their crimes were before he got to them. Once, just the once, can you please come up with a theory that doesn't land on my head like a bird of prey and shit down the back of my neck?'

Beth ignored O'Dowd's grumbling and started translating the messages, while trying not to picture the aforementioned bird of prey trying to find a landing spot among the disaster zone that was O'Dowd's hair.

To distract herself from the imagery, Beth called Cumberland Infirmary to see if Pete Benson had survived the night.

CHAPTER SIXTY-ONE

Unthank and McKay trooped in as a pair, and while there was an obvious disparity in their personalities and age, they were both wearing dark puffa jackets and woolly hats which made them look like twins at first glance.

Unthank tossed greetings around while McKay issued scowls.

'Right then, you two. Beth and me have been here half the night...'

Beth tuned out the chatter as O'Dowd brought the two men up to speed. She had O'Dowd's messages transcribed and loaded onto her computer so they could be sent within seconds, and she'd checked the account for a response from the Sculptor. So far there hadn't been one, but both she and O'Dowd had a theory that the Sculptor would push for an earlier meeting as the ASAP in the message to Babes suggested urgency.

The counterpoint to that thinking was that there was a chance the Sculptor would accept the delay as the snowfall around the county had increased, and many roads were now either impassable to anything less than a 4x4, or were blocked by snowdrifts or vehicles which had become stuck. This meant that rural meeting points such as Boustead Hill were no longer accessible. It was possible that the Sculptor would suggest a more urban meeting point, but if their plan was to snatch and then attack Babes, it stood to reason that another rural setting would be chosen.

Beth put a call in to Traffic, to see what the state of play was with the roads, but when she was brushed off with a terse 'we're not the bloody Met Office' she hung up without further comment. As a backup, she fiddled with her phone until Radio Cumbria came on. It wasn't as up to date as the information Traffic would have, but at least their travel updates would give them some idea of which roads were and weren't passable.

The other problem the weather created was that the adverse conditions ate up a lot of manpower dealing with blocked roads, arguments about crashes and, most important of all, rescuing people who'd got themselves stuck.

Beth kept half an ear on the radio as she tried to delve deeper into the lives of the Sculptor's four Lake District victims.

Dippen and Harrytosis had attended school together, but neither of the other two victims had. All four were in the same age bracket, but only James Sinclair had gone to Carlisle College. This fit with his job, and while it made no sense for the two thugs to have sought higher education after being expelled from secondary school, Beth checked anyway.

To Beth it seemed there were two separate groups of victims. The secretive Sinclair and Benson, and the thuggish Dippen and Harrytosis. By definition, the two groups were totally different characters. The first group seemed to be doing all they could to fly under the radar, while the second were known to use their reputation to intimidate.

Beth checked the email account again, while she listened to the latest travel update.

'… *A66 closed at Brough but currently open west from the M6 to Workington. A595 and A596 still open, but the information we have is they're expected to be closed soon. The M6 is down to one lane in both directions from junction 36 to Carlisle, but please remember that if you're travelling north, all routes from Gretna are currently blocked. Whatever you do folks, stay at home and stay safe.*'

The travel update made for grim listening, but to Beth it was also a boon. If they couldn't move around, neither could the Sculptor and Babes. Every minute the weather delayed that meeting was another minute that could be used to identify and track down both Babes and the Sculptor.

'Beth, pay attention to this, will you? That brain of yours may well spot something in what DS McKay has to say.'

Beth doubted that she'd spot something in McKay's report, but she listened in on the off-chance that he'd asked the right questions and got an answer that'd help them solve the case. Maybe the chat with the minister would prove to yield a decent clue about the two symbols and the relevance of the Broken Men as McKay was referring to Sinclair and Benson.

'Yous listening 'cause this is a bit complicated? According to the minister I spoke to, there is a character in the Bible called Mephibosheth who's an illegitimate son of Jonathan. When he was five years old, his father and grandfather, King Saul, died in a battle at Mount Gilboa. After hearing of their deaths Mephibosheth's nurse fled the house with him. At some point the boy was dropped or fell. After that he couldnae walk. Some years later after his accession to the throne, King David sought out someone from King Saul's family to repay the kindness he'd been shown when Saul was the king. Mephibosheth was duly brought forward and all of Saul's inheritance was restored to him and he lived the rest of his life in King David's palace in Jerusalem.'

'Correct me if I'm wrong, but that sounds like Old Testament to me.'

'You're right.' McKay gave O'Dowd a piercing look. 'You haven't heard the best bit. According to Pastor Jamieson, the Hebrew translation for Mephibosheth means "from the mouth of shame" and "from the mouth of God Bashtu". Bashtu apparently represents pride or dignity. I also asked him about the fish. Apparently it originates from Greek letters which spelled "ichthys". At first it was a symbol made up from the Greek letters and it basically looked like a wheel with eight spokes. It soon evolved into the fish which we all recognise.'

Beth sat back in her chair and let the information McKay had just shared sink into her brain in relation to James Sinclair and Pete Benson. The little research she'd done online about the fish had shown that the symbol originated from the Greek for 'fish', which the early Christians adopted into an acrostic. She'd not found anything about the broken man, but if McKay's error on the fish was anything to go by, he'd undoubtedly got some of the finer nuances of the story wrong. The more and more Beth tried to make this information fit with the attacks, the less sense it made to her. And none of McKay's information, nor any possible Biblical or religious links to the attacks, explained where Babes would fit into the narrative should the Sculptor get his hands on her.

The call she'd made earlier had relieved her like no other had ever done. Pete Benson had survived the night and his vitals were looking positive, although the doctor she spoke to had warned that Benson was by no means out of danger. Regardless, Beth was delighted to know he'd made it through the night and she was clinging to the tiny improvement in his condition as a sign he'd survive his ordeal.

O'Dowd rose from her chair and reached for her jacket. 'Paul, I want to know everything there is to know about the Sculptor's victims, both accredited and suspected. Make sure you look at any possible religious connotations. George.' A finger extended towards McKay. 'I want you to get the paperwork up to date and keep an eye on the email account. Me and Beth are off out.'

'Wait, ma'am. There's another email. It's from the Sculptor to Babes.'

'What's it say?'

Beth reached for the sheet of paper with her decoding table on it and set to work deciphering the email as the other three members of the team crowded behind her to look over her shoulder as she worked.

She normally hated having people watch over her this way, but she shared their desperation to know what the message said.

When she was finished transcribing it, the message in block capitals on her pad left no room for ambiguity.

URGENT WE MUST MEET TONIGHT OR WILL
BE TOO LATE

'She's at work. She's not responded to the first one with any great urgency, we have time to spare.'

As harsh as O'Dowd's words were, Beth agreed with their sentiment. Unless Babes did a total U-turn, time *was* on their side.

'C'mon, Beth. George, we'll not be far away. Call me the second something happens.'

Beth followed O'Dowd from the office, unsure as to where they were going, and why they were leaving the office at such an important time in the investigation.

CHAPTER SIXTY-TWO

Beth braced herself in the passenger seat of O'Dowd's 4x4 and looked back on yesterday's trip to Cockermouth as a pleasant dream compared with the nightmare of O'Dowd's drive to Pooley Bridge.

Visibility was at no more than ten feet and they were travelling on a layer of compacted snow, which meant that every time O'Dowd stamped on a pedal the 4x4 reacted with a slide. Instead of selecting a high gear and letting the vehicle pull itself across the rutted surface, O'Dowd was in a low gear, which meant that every time she buried the throttle – which was often – the 4x4 either went into a four-wheel drift, or picked up enough speed that O'Dowd would be forced to brake which in turn precipitated another skid. The DI was usually an excellent driver, but her obvious frustrations with the case had her trying to rush the journey despite the driving conditions.

The one consolation Beth had was that the 4x4 was a sturdy vehicle, and so long as they didn't end up in a ditch, O'Dowd wasn't able to build up enough speed to cause a serious injury if they crashed.

What the DI expected to see out here in the middle of a snowstorm was beyond Beth, yet she'd worked with O'Dowd long enough to know there was always a reason behind her thinking, regardless of how insane her actions might seem.

The metal framework of the bridge over the River Eamont heralded the fact they'd reached Pooley Bridge itself. A tractor pulled away from the village shop causing O'Dowd to stamp on the brakes with the same vehement force she used to berate the tractor's driver, but the DI fell silent when the tractor turned onto the narrow road they intended to follow.

It was a stroke of luck as the tractor set a pace that O'Dowd could match without any further stamps on throttle or brake.

There were few houses along the roadside, but Beth's focus was on the shadowy outline of the tractor and the increasing depth of the virgin snow in the middle of the single-track lane.

To her mind it was only a matter of time before the underside of the 4x4 started brushing then collecting, then bulldozing the unspoiled ridge. Sooner or later the 4x4 wouldn't be able to go any further. Then, providing O'Dowd didn't beach the 4x4 on the snow, they'd have to reverse until they could find a place where they could turn.

The whole exercise was a waste of time so far as Beth was concerned, as there was no way they'd see anything of worth in the swirling snow.

Ahead of them, the tractor disappeared into the distance. Driving as erratically as she was, O'Dowd couldn't match its pace on the slippery road.

The radio crackled into another travel update.

'… *severe restrictions on the A595 and 596. A66 blocked westbound by a jackknifed lorry near Keswick. M6 down to one lane throughout Cumbria. All minor roads are either blocked by stranded vehicles or snow drifts. Stay off the roads, folks.*'

A sign on their left advertised a camping site, but it was bound to be deserted. Even the hardiest campers would have packed up and headed for home in these conditions.

O'Dowd had slowed to a trundle, and Beth could hear the brushing of snow underneath the 4x4. If they didn't get to the marina soon, they wouldn't get there at all.

On their right the beech hedges gave way to a pair of long grey gates. The top bar of the gates had a crust of snow two inches high. A sign proclaimed it to be the Ullswater Yachting Marina.

Beth pulled her scarf tighter and jammed a beanie hat on her head. O'Dowd might still be dressed as if she was going to a civic function, but that didn't mean Beth had to freeze.

O'Dowd stuck a hand inside her dress and pulled out a packet of cigarettes. 'Go on then, out you get and have a look.'

The cold wasn't too bad for Beth, but until she'd stepped off the road, the ground was slippery under her feet. As she stood before the gates of the marina, Beth was drinking in the details. Snow was blowing in her face and eyes adding to the difficulty in seeing anything of note in the snowstorm.

The first thing Beth examined was the padlock on the chain wrapped around the point where the two gates met in the middle of the gateway. It looked to be fastened tight, but when she took a closer look she could see there was a large dent in the top of the brass lock. It ran parallel to where the padlock's hoop linked through the chain.

Beth had seen this type of damage to padlocks before. As secure as they might be against opportunist thieves, a few downward strikes with a hammer would do enough damage to the internal mechanism to render the lock useless.

Once she'd pulled on a pair of nitrile gloves, Beth grasped the lock between her fingers and gave a sharp downward tug. The gates bounced under her action and dislodged their snowy capping on to the ground. Undeterred, Beth yanked down three more times until the lock came free in her hand.

With the lock safely inside an evidence bag and stuffed into her pocket, Beth turned her attention to the ground behind the gates. From the point where they met, the marina side of the gates had a sweeping quarter circle brushed into the snow. It wasn't full and pronounced, but it showed in the levels of the snow. The bottom rungs of the gates were now engulfed in snow, yet a couple of days ago, when Dippen and Harrytosis were put into the lake, there was less snow so it made sense that the bottom rung of the gates had brushed the top layer of snow away when opened.

Her next move was to squat down and peer between the second and third rungs of the gate. She wasn't looking at the ground in front of her, rather her focus was on the snow beyond the gates.

It took a moment for her eyes to adjust to the glare reflected back from the torch she was using to illuminate the ground, but she found what she was looking for. Running away from the gates were two parallel indentations in the snow.

This told Beth a vehicle of some kind had driven down here and that its tracks had been buried by snowfall. She moved along the right-hand gate until she was at the hinges and climbed over the gate.

The snow made crumping noises under her feet as she followed the tracks towards Lake Ullswater. Rather than walk in the tracks herself, Beth kept two feet to their right so she was on undisturbed snow. By the time she was five feet from the gate, the snow was almost knee deep sending occasional icy presents down the top of her boots.

When she was out of sight of the gates, the depressions in the snow became jumbled until Beth realised the vehicle whose tracks she was following must have swung in and turned. When she lifted her torch from the ground and swung it around her, Beth could see the faint shapes of snow-coated boats through the snowstorm.

What she couldn't see were the gates she'd passed through to get here, another living soul, or even the lake she knew was nearby. The sense of isolation was complete, and caused Beth to give thanks that she didn't suffer from claustrophobia as whichever way she looked, the snowstorm seemed to be closing in on her. It was easy to understand why people got lost and perished in snowstorms. Without the tracks and her own footsteps as markers, Beth's only indication of direction was the ground which had been gradually sloping downwards since she'd clambered over the gates.

Beth's torch picked up the depressions in the snow where the vehicle had reversed after turning.

On and on she trudged until the snow at the edge of her vision gave way to water. Beneath her feet, the slope increased its gradient and Beth realised she was standing on the slipway used to launch the yachts from the marina.

The tracks ran right to the water's edge.

It wasn't hard for Beth to picture the scene. The Sculptor would have chosen this place for its remoteness, broken the lock and driven his van or pickup truck into the marina. He'd nosed into one of the tracks between the wintered boats and then reversed to the water's edge. Two splashes later and Dippen and Harrytosis were in Lake Ullswater. Maybe the Sculptor used an oar to push their corpses out into the lake and maybe he just left it to chance.

Either way, he'd have been able to dump their bodies in splendid isolation.

*

O'Dowd's 4x4 stank of cigarettes by the time Beth got back to it, but it was warm and at this moment in time that mattered more to Beth than the dangers of passive smoking. The DI had managed to turn the vehicle round.

'I'm guessing you've found something as you went off exploring. What is it?'

Beth pulled the evidence bag from her pocket and showed O'Dowd the padlock. 'This was smashed and put back into place to make it look as if it was fine. There were tracks in the snow which went right down to the lake.'

'Good work.'

'That's not all, ma'am. Look at this dent in the top of the padlock where it was smashed.' Beth pointed at the dent which ran along the top of the brass padlock. 'It's rounded, just like the points of the chisels we suspect were used to inflict the wounds and symbols onto the victims.'

O'Dowd pulled a face. 'Be nice if we could get a print off it.'

Beth understood O'Dowd's point. Due to the fact the padlock had been open to the elements for days after the Sculptor had touched it, there was little chance of lifting a print from the padlock. When you factored in the Sculptor's professionalism and the cold weather, it was unlikely he wouldn't be wearing gloves. Still, they'd have the padlock tested on the off-chance.

They'd also have to identify the owner of the marina and advise him they'd taken his padlock and get his prints for comparison with any they found on it.

O'Dowd buried her right foot and set off back towards Pooley Bridge in a mass of spinning wheels. Beth wanted to ask her DI to slow down, but having been responsible for a crash on a previous case that had seen O'Dowd twist an ankle and crack three ribs, she didn't want to prod that particular rattlesnake.

They were most of the way back to Pooley Bridge when a Land Rover appeared out of the snow. O'Dowd braked but her 4x4 ploughed straight towards the Land Rover.

A hard twist of the wheel saw the 4x4 take a violent swing to the left as the back end started to come round.

O'Dowd swung the wheel back right and managed to regain some control of the 4x4, but she was too late. The front left wheel was in the soft verge and was pulling the vehicle into the shallow ditch that bordered the road.

Beth braced herself for the inevitable impact, but the 4x4 didn't so much crash as slide to a halt and slowly lean over until the snow it was resting against would compress no more.

'Fuck sake.' O'Dowd levered her door open and jumped out.

Beth couldn't open her door as it was against the snowy bank, so she had to clamber over the driver's seat to exit the vehicle. When she did there was a three foot drop to the ground. Looking at the 4x4 she saw it was bottomed out and the rear right wheel was clear of the ground.

Rather than keep going, the driver of the Land Rover had parked in a position six feet from the back of O'Dowd's 4x4 and was rummaging in the back. Looking over his shoulder, Beth saw a bale of hay, a bag of cattle feed and a collie whose tongue was lolling from the side of its mouth.

The driver turned and Beth was confronted with a ruddy-faced farmer. He wore a wax jacket, wellies and a tweed cap, around his neck was a faded peach scarf. In his hands was a rusty chain.

'Thanks very much.' Beth made sure it was she who spoke first, as she didn't trust O'Dowd not to give the man a mouthful and blame him for her being in the ditch.

A nod was all the farmer gave her by way of recognition.

He looped one end of the chain over the tow bar protruding from the back of the Land Rover and attached the hook at the other end to the tie down hook beneath the 4x4's rear door.

He pointed at the driver's seat. 'When I start pulling, keep thee right hand down then thee left once it starts to come out.'

Beth had to turn away so O'Dowd didn't see her smile as the DI tried to clamber back into the 4x4. In her usual rumpled trousers, the step up in the tilted vehicle would have been a struggle for her, in the dress she didn't stand a chance.

After a minute of watching her struggle Beth tapped O'Dowd on the shoulder. 'I'll do it, ma'am.'

Beth climbed into the 4x4, moved the seat back to accommodate her long legs, twisted the key and waited for the jerk of the chain tightening.

The farmer was obviously experienced at this sort of thing as there was only the slightest yank, then the sound of the Land Rover's powerful engine revving as the 4x4 began to edge out of the ditch.

She followed his instructions and turned the wheel first right then left. It took a full two minutes to drag the 4x4 back to the road, but Beth assumed that the slow and deliberate farmer had engaged a special low gear in the Land Rover, as there was no sign of it slipping or sliding despite the icy conditions.

With the chain unhooked and back in the rear of his Land Rover, the farmer pointed at Beth. 'Thee'd better drive, lass. Thon party woman'll kill thee both.'

Without another word, the farmer went back to his vehicle. When Beth looked at O'Dowd and saw the way her hands shook as she fumbled with her lighter, she climbed into the driver's side and waited for the DI to comment.

O'Dowd didn't say a word as she got into the passenger side, but as they left Pooley Bridge she looked across at Beth. 'Party woman! Cheeky old sod. I should have done him for dangerous driving.'

Beth said nothing. O'Dowd's bluster was nothing more than a reaction to the crash. The truth of it was that the farmer had stopped his Land Rover by the time O'Dowd had swerved into the ditch to avoid hitting him.

They'd heard nothing from Unthank or McKay, but that didn't stop Beth wondering if Babes or the Sculptor had sent another email yet.

CHAPTER SIXTY-THREE

As she trailed O'Dowd to their office in Carleton Hall, Beth's ears were still ringing from the threats O'Dowd had issued about repeating the term 'party woman'. The more the DI had raged about the farmer's terminology, the harder it had been for Beth to keep her face straight.

McKay and Unthank were sombre when they entered the office. Something was amiss, but it took Beth a minute to work out that it was related to the case and not just the sourness of McKay's personality.

Unthank sprang to his feet, his voice full of dread. 'We've had another email.'

'What's it say?'

'Don't know, ma'am, DS McKay is still decoding it. It's from Babes though.'

Rather than crowd him like the others, Beth crossed to her own desk, logged into her computer and brought up the responses they'd formulated earlier.

Underneath the desk her feet were moving back and forth as she tried to muster some heat into her frozen toes. The snow which had breached her boots had long since melted and soaked her trouser legs and socks.

'Got it. It says.' McKay cleared his throat as if he was about to address an auditorium. '"Snowed in. Can't leave town."'

'Phew. This bloody weather is actually helping us.'

O'Dowd rounded on Unthank. 'What the hell do you know about the bloody weather? We've been out in it risking life and limb while you two heroes have been sat in the office.'

'Detective Inspector O'Dowd, may I remind you that as the senior officer of this team, you are responsible for the allocation of tasks? Therefore I presume that it was your decision to leave the office in such foul weather while leaving your male colleagues here. That would be commendable leadership had you not just criticised a junior officer for something which was entirely your decision.' Chief Superintendent Hilton's tone was soft but there was no mistaking the fact he'd just bollocked O'Dowd in front of her team. O'Dowd gave a muttered grumble as she retreated to the safety of her desk. 'Perhaps you'd like to update me on your progress.'

Beth sat in silence as O'Dowd did as she was bidden and got Unthank to add what he'd learned about the Sculptor's other victims.

Taken as a whole, the investigation was progressing, but other than the secret emails, they were no closer to identifying, let alone catching, the person who'd assaulted James Sinclair six days ago.

Unthank's info on the Sculptor's previous victims brought no new information to light. They'd already ascertained that all bar the hotelier were known gang members, which supported the vigilante theory to a point, but the hotelier's police record was spotless and the gang members' crimes ranged from money laundering and punishment beatings, to petty dealing and fencing stolen goods.

It was possible the hotelier wasn't on the police's radar for his crimes, but the takeover of the hotel had been too smooth to support that theory.

'Okay. We've covered what you've learned. What do you have going forward? What are your action plans?'

Beth had to strain to hear Hilton as his voice was so low. She knew from experience that the quieter he spoke, the angrier he was.

O'Dowd was the one to answer him. 'We're monitoring the email account. So far the snow has helped us as it's restricted travel and prevented a meeting between Babes and the Sculptor. We have responses already formulated for both Babes and the Sculptor should we need to join the conversation. We're looking at all four victims both individually and collectively to try and establish a link so we can identify the person who has a grudge against all of them.'

'What else?'

O'Dowd flapped a hand towards Beth. 'DC Young has suggested something, I'll let her explain, sir.'

Beth drew in a breath. O'Dowd had been very neat in the way she'd transferred the chief super's attention away from herself.

'Sir. Having read the statements of those in The Boilermaker's it's possible that Dippen and Harrytosis followed a woman from the bar. Whether they intended to rape or mug her nobody knows. However, looks like the Sculptor caught them doing whatever they were doing and dealt with them there and then.'

Hilton's eyes narrowed. 'Let's get this straight. You're saying their selection as victims is nothing more than chance? So what you're basically telling me is that there's about to be an unholy turf war in Carlisle because a pair of meatheads decided to get fresh. And to cap it all off, the hitman who's running around Cumbria is basically a good guy who's taking down criminals. Don't you think that's a little preposterous, detective?'

'I would, sir. If I could think of something else which made more sense. After doing what he did to James Sinclair, the Sculptor actively went after Pete Benson and the woman called Babes.' Beth was getting a head of steam up and as she was speaking, new ideas were taking shape in her mind. 'Apart from Dippen and Harrytosis, nobody from either the RF or the Currockers has suffered anything worse than a shaving cut. You said yourself that you're expecting a turf war, except it hasn't happened because neither of them know what's going on. One hit on either party would be enough to start that war, yet the Sculptor hasn't done that. So far as we can tell, he's now focussed on Babes and nobody else, which suggests to me that's his real purpose in Cumbria. The thing with Dippen and Harrytosis was pure chance.'

'Hmmm. When you put it like that.' Hilton rested a bum cheek on Unthank's desk. 'What would be your next step?'

'We need to find this mystery woman from The Boilermaker's. She might have seen the Sculptor.'

'My thoughts exactly.' He looked at his watch then flicked a glance at O'Dowd then McKay. 'I'm calling a press conference for three. DC Young will accompany the press officer and myself in a public call for this woman to come forward. Since you're dressed for it, DI O'Dowd, take DS McKay and go to The Boilermaker's. Buy as many rounds of drinks as it takes to get an accurate description of the woman to me. Your deadline is five to three. DC Unthank, you're to keep tabs on that email account.'

Hilton turned on his heel and strode out leaving them all looking at each other.

CHAPTER SIXTY-FOUR

The spreadsheet in front of Beth was making little sense. Every box had an entry which related to a known fact, but while they were collectively speaking to her, all she could hear was a chatter rather than a distinct voice.

No matter which way Beth looked for connections or links, there was nothing which cowered in the bushes, let alone jumped out at her.

'There's been another message.' Unthank's voice was underpinned with excitement.

'What does it say?'

Unthank handed her a printout. 'You tell me. You'll be quicker at deciphering it than I will.'

Beth set to work, and in less than a minute she'd transcribed the message.

ME TOO MEET TOMORROW INSTEAD

This was good news, as not only was Babes trapped by the weather, the Sculptor was too.

Beth returned her focus on the spreadsheet, determined to make the most of the extra time that had been bought by the weather.

The more she looked at the spreadsheets, the less she was seeing, so Beth got to her feet. As a rule when she became screen blind like this, she'd walk the perimeter of the building and gather her thoughts, but she didn't plan to wade one more step through snow than she had to, so instead of going outside, she paced the length of the corridor. Five times north and five times south she went.

Beth was passing the FMIT's office on her sixth walk north when something clicked in her brain. She didn't like what she was thinking, but it made a lot of sense.

To find out if she was right, she'd have to speak to Hilton, but she didn't expect him to have the answers. For those, even he might have to go up the chain of command.

She went upstairs and knocked on the chief super's door.

'Come in.'

It was hard to believe the soft-spoken chief super's voice carried through the solid door, but it was definitely him.

'What is it, DC Young?'

As Hilton sat at his desk, one of his martial-arts trophies on the cabinet behind him seemed to sprout from the top of his head.

'The case, sir. I think I've made sense of the connection.'

Hilton sat back in his chair as Beth explained her theory. When she was finished he nodded once as he reached for the telephone on his desk.

'I like your thinking. When I have confirmation of whether you're right or wrong, I'll be in touch. If you don't hear from me first, be here at quarter to three to prepare for the press conference.'

Beth recognised she was being dismissed and left the office. If she was right, they'd be able to identify Babes with ease and protect her. If wrong, it was yet one more theory up in smoke.

CHAPTER SIXTY-FIVE

As instructed earlier, Beth returned to the chief super's office at quarter to three. The press officer was already there. A smart man, Beth had never found herself able to trust him, as he had a way of putting across a different version of events than was actually true. She knew it was the nature of his job, but she'd spent many hours interviewing hardened criminals who could learn a thing or two from him about obfuscation.

Because she hadn't heard from the chief super, Beth made sure her greeting was also a question. 'Sir?'

A minute shake of the head told her that he had no news and that he didn't want to discuss it in front of the press officer.

When the chief super's phone rang, the press officer gave Beth a rundown of what he considered appropriate phrases and what conduct he expected from her at the press conference.

Beth only half listened to the press officer, her focus was on Hilton's side of the telephone conversation.

From what she could gather, he was talking to O'Dowd and getting a description of the woman who'd been in The Boiler-maker's.

He hung up the phone and looked at Beth rather than the press officer. 'The woman we're looking for is approximately mid- to late thirties, of medium build but she's quite tall. She is apparently quite, shall we say, buxom? A fact that was apparently remarked on by the majority of the men who noticed her.'

'We can't say buxom.' The press officer wagged his finger until Hilton caught his eye.

'I didn't for one second think we could. Though if you'd prefer, I could use some of the terminology DI O'Dowd passed on from the patrons of The Boilermaker's.'

'What was she wearing, sir?'

'A pair of black jeans and a blouse.'

'What colour was the blouse?'

'According to the witness statements, it was several different colours. Some said green, others said blue and some said pink, yellow or red.'

Beth got the underlying subtext. Eyewitnesses were notorious for their unreliability. No two ever gave the same version of events and when it came to describing a woman, a bunch of half-drunk men would only focus on the parts of the woman they were interested in. The fact there had been comments on the woman's bust size showed where their attentions had been aimed.

'What about her hair: long, short, straight or wavy; colour?'

'It was tied up according to most of them. Colours ranged from blonde to light brown.'

'That's good.'

'I don't suppose they got an eye colour, glasses, anything remarkable about her facial features.'

'I think you're overestimating the clientele of The Boilermaker's.' Hilton gave a weary sigh as he looked at Beth. 'From what I can tell, it's a miracle any of them noticed she had a head.'

'Well, at least we have something to go on.' The press officer seemed chipper to Beth. It was almost as if he was excited about the forthcoming press conference.

Personally, she was dreading it, as she expected that as soon as their plea for the woman to come forward was given, the press would use the opportunity to put their own questions forward. It was an unspoken *quid pro quo*, that in order to get help with the case, the press would demand a few answers. When it came to questions about Pete Benson, Beth was praying she could keep the guilt she felt from showing on her face.

When Beth followed Hilton and the press officer into the room they used for public briefings, she was surprised to see there were only four members of the press there. However, as soon as she thought about it, she realised that not only would reporters have struggled to get here, the vast majority of them would be out covering the chaos brought about by the snowstorm.

As expected there was a cameraman from *Border News*, and a reporter for the *Cumberland News*. Unthank's girlfriend, Teri Veitch, sat at the front with perfect hair and make-up as the representative for the *Evening News and Star*. The fourth person wasn't anyone she recognised, but she guessed he was a freelancer who happened to be in the area and had been sent by either one of the national papers, or perhaps the *Westmorland Gazette* which covered the more southerly reaches of Cumbria.

Hilton took a seat behind the table and waited as the various Dictaphones laid on the table were switched on. 'Thank you for coming out on this horrible day. Myself, Mr Kingston and DC Young are happy to take questions, but first we have an appeal we'd like your help with.' Hilton looked directly at the *Border News* camera. 'We are appealing to a particular member of the public. A lady who was in The Boilermaker's pub at the bottom of Botchergate on Monday evening. We believe this lady was by herself and that when she left she may have been accosted by the two men whose bodies were retrieved from Lake Ullswater. We urge this lady to come forward to help us with our enquiries. The lady we are looking for was described as quite tall, of average build and had fairly light-coloured hair that was worn up.'

The unknown reporter's hand shot up. 'What leads you to think this lady was accosted?'

Kingston leaned forward so he was nearer the Dictaphones. 'We're not at liberty to disclose that information at this time.'

'Were the two men Harry Anderson and Tommy Long?' Teri Veitch.

'Yes they were.'

A look of understanding crossed Veitch's face. 'Do you believe the lady in question can help you identify their killer?'

'That's a conclusion you'll have to draw for yourself.' Kingston again.

'Does your appeal for this lady to come forward signify your lack of success in catching the killer, or is it a symptom of a wider malaise in the Cumbrian Police force, whereby you're happy to let the public do your work for you?' The unknown reporter sat back with a smug expression as he waited for an answer. When it came, it was from Hilton rather than the press officer.

'That is absolutely incorrect. Despite budgetary constraints, Cumbria Constabulary provides a cost-effective service and does all it can to keep the residents and visitors to this wonderful county safe. Yes, we rely on witnesses, but all police forces do that, as much today as they have always done. I have every faith that our Force Major Investigation Team will get a timely result in what is proving to be a most trying case.'

'Budgetary constraints, cost-effective service. Tell me, Chief Superintendent, are you a policeman or a bean counter?'

Beth laid a hand on Hilton's arms before the hues in his face destroyed the colour filter of *Border News*'s video camera. 'I'd like to answer that question if I may, sir.' Beth looked directly at the unknown reporter who was putting them to the sword. 'We have a case with four disparate victims. There are no ties linking more than any two of them. None of the lines of enquiry we have pursued has given us a credible suspect, because the person behind the attacks and killings is a very clever individual. However, we're not called the Major Investigation Team for nothing. Chief Superintendent Hilton has given us his backing. Resources have been allocated and we are making headway. This is by no means an excuse, more a statement of fact.

'I travelled with a colleague to Cockermouth yesterday. The journey there took twice as long as normal, and the one back even longer due to the inclement weather conditions. I'm sure you feel the world would probably be a safer place if we could go back to the days when every village had its own bobby, and there were bobbies on every street corner. While modern policing might not be quite as visible, I can assure you that we stand a far better chance of catching a heinous serial killer than your traditional bobby would ever have, regardless of how good they were as individuals.' Beth felt the press officer's foot tapping against the side of her boot but she didn't care about him trying to shut her up. 'Personally, I've had six hours' sleep in the last three days, but rather than complain about budgets and resources, I'm doing everything I can to catch this heinous killer along with the rest of the FMIT. We're asking you for a little help. If you choose not to help us, you're every bit as neglectful of the police force as the politicians who keep cutting our budgets.'

Kingston reached for the Dictaphones and started handing them back to their owners. 'That will be all, thank you. Please help us find the lady in question.'

Beth was desperate to get back to the FMIT office, but it looked as if Hilton had other ideas for her. She'd lost her temper at a press conference once before and managed to escape without reprimand, the chances of doing so again were slimmer than a flea's wing.

CHAPTER SIXTY-SIX

Beth couldn't hide her yawns as O'Dowd and McKay filed back into the office. The appeals had gone out in the press, and *Border News* had agreed to schedule their appeal in the next news bulletin and *Lookaround* plus the mini programme later that evening.

Hilton had given her a mild dressing-down over her rant at the unknown reporter, but had also praised the way she'd turned the tables on them and pointed out that the press would be failing them if they didn't share their appeal for the mystery woman to come forward.

Both O'Dowd and McKay looked pissed off and it was little wonder. They'd have been given the runaround by the clientele of The Boilermaker's and would have spent as much time analysing statements for truth as they did taking them.

O'Dowd threw a look Beth's way. 'Heard you had another ranty press conference experience. By all accounts that prick Kingston nearly had a coronary. In one respect I'd like to congratulate you. As your boss, I think I ought to warn you that sooner or later the press will get sick of your spirited rants and turn against you.'

'Ma'am.'

Beth wasn't sure how O'Dowd had already heard about the press conference seeing as how she'd been out all afternoon, but she wasn't surprised. Like any other workplace, police stations were gossip shops and there was always someone quick to spread news of a misdemeanour. Especially if they thought someone would get into trouble.

'Beth's had one of her ideas, boss. We're waiting on the chief super getting word back and verifying it.'

Beth flapped a hand at Unthank, as O'Dowd and McKay looked at her with expectation.

'You know how I thought the real targets were Sinclair, Benson and the Babes woman? Well, I couldn't get past Sinclair's fervent privacy.' Beth made sure she wasn't looking at Unthank as she spoke. 'Then when I thought about how Benson was very similar about his past and the way the three of them communicated with the coded messages by email, it made me think about what they had to hide. Next I wondered if it was a troubled past or that they'd committed some crime and were hiding out. Then I looked at it another way. What if the thing they had to hide was themselves? Both Sinclair and Benson were from London and I'd swear that picture Benson had was a young James Sinclair. They're connected, but instead of thinking they were hiding because they'd been in trouble, I starting thinking they might be hiding because they were the good guys.'

O'Dowd's fingers snapped. 'You mean you think they're protected witnesses?'

'Yes, ma'am. If they are, and we're able to identify them – which we should be able to from Sinclair's and Benson's assumed names – then we'll be able to issue Babes a Threat to Life warning and then set up a sting to catch the Sculptor.'

'How long have you been waiting to get this info?'

'A few hours. According to the chief super, the guy he spoke to at the NCA,' – the National Crime Agency, who oversaw all protected witnesses – 'said he'd have to dig through a lot of old files due to their system being renewed a few years ago and only the most recent files being added to it. Once they've done that they'll get onto the local UKPPS.'

The UKPPS was the UK Protected Persons Service which dealt with protected witnesses on a day-to-day basis. Beth stopped talking and looked at their faces as they digested her theory and the implications which came with it.

Both Sinclair and Benson had received life-changing injuries, yet their ordeals bore all the hallmarks of a punishment beating. They weren't given a quick clean death, they were made to suffer unimaginable agony. Beth believed they'd been tortured to disclose the locations of the others and it made sense that, under the Sculptor's brutal ministrations, each had shared everything they knew.

The TTL warning was what the police issued when they believed there was a threat to life. Babes's handler at the NCA would get the local UKPPS handlers to issue it for them and in all likelihood take Babes into protective custody until the Sculptor was apprehended.

That their email chain went back nearly twenty years had complicated things even further as it meant they could well have been more or less forgotten by the system and had moved on with their new lives. Apart from an annual review, their files would be all but closed, hence the fact they were no longer classed as active cases.

Now it was a question of waiting to see if the theory was correct.

'… the forecast is for the snow to stop this evening and a warmer front to arrive in the small hours of the morning. On the roads the A595, A596 and the A66 from Penrith to Workington have been reopened, but Highways England is still asking the public to only make essential journeys. This is…'

O'Dowd approached Beth's desk. 'Right you. Off you go home. There's nowt we can do until we hear from the chief super and I want you at your best, not dead on your feet.'

'I'm okay, ma'am.' Even as she was denying her tiredness, Beth had to stop speaking to yawn. 'Really.'

The look on O'Dowd's face was enough and despite her desire to stay on, Beth knew that unless she got some rest soon, as her mother would say, she'd be neither use nor ornament.

That didn't mean she wasn't going to go without a fight. 'Call me if anything happens. I don't want to miss any arrests.'

CHAPTER SIXTY-SEVEN

With a half hour to spare before Leo was due to arrive, Sandi logged in to the email account and started to compose a message. Now she'd had time to get her head around the idea, she was desperate to see Kevin again. The reason for him breaking protocol and arranging a meeting played at her mind, but she was resolute. If he wanted her back, he was too late.

Border Craic and *Deeksaboot*, as many folk called *Border News* and *Lookaround*, had been full of items about the snow that had fallen on the county; although while she thought snow made everything Christmassy, the amount that had fallen was too much and had crippled the whole area.

Sandi scoffed at the appeal for the woman who'd been in a Carlisle pub. If she'd not come forward by now, it was unlikely that she would anytime soon.

Even though the A66 was open and the forecast for tomorrow's weather looked a lot more positive than today's, Sandi made sure that when she composed her message, she chose a location that wasn't too far from home.

With that done she turned her attention back to wedding venues. She'd be forty next year and time wasn't on her side, as the risks of having a baby increased as the mother aged.

With the message sent and her research into wedding venues underway, Sandi went upstairs to grab a quick shower before Leo arrived.

CHAPTER SIXTY-EIGHT

I put down the remote control before I wring it to the point of destruction. That the police are looking for me is something of a concern.

On the one hand it is laughable how inept the cops are, but the other side of this is that complacency may have crept in to my tradecraft. Killing those no-marks from the pub and sculpting them had been fun, but it may have been more prudent to have just beaten them up and left it at that. It had just seemed like such a perfect opportunity to try those designs when a pair of bald thugs had presented themselves, and since I was up here anyway, I hadn't seen the harm in having a little 'me' time.

Tomorrow will hopefully see the end of the Cumbrian mission. Michaela has messaged with a time and location. It is a far more public place than I would have chosen, but there are always ways round that.

Once Michaela has been sculpted, and weather permitting, I'll be able to set off on the long drive home. The snow has delayed things by a day or two, but I learned patience many years ago.

After Grandmother died, I spent more time with Grandad. He wasn't a trained carpenter, but he could make all manner of things from wood. As my late teens approached, Grandad took to carving as a hobby. I watched him work, observed the different chisels he used for different parts of the animals he carved from pieces of wood. Saw how he'd outline the shape he wanted with bold cuts and then spend hours paring away until he had the carving finished.

On more than one occasion I picked up the chisels and tried to carve something. In my hands the chisels would cut too deep, or a misjudgement of the timber's grain would see vital pieces splinter off.

Grandad had watched my attempts and, as he always did, came up with a solution. A lump of sandstone the size and shape of a briefcase had been rolled from the garden into his shed and a stone chisel had been pressed into my hands along with a lump hammer and a suggestion that I try to carve a cylinder.

I had heeded Grandad's words of advice on how to cut the stone, and after a fortnight spent chipping away, the block of sandstone was transformed from a rectangular slab into a cylinder that was eight inches in diameter and four in depth. Grandad wasn't finished there though. He'd given me a different set of stone chisels and a stencil set. A week later, I had etched 'Grandmother' into the smooth top of the cylinder along with the date of her death.

It was a sentimental thing to carve, but I knew how to play him. Knew how to appear normal. The enrolment at the martial-arts classes helped me keep up the facade of being normal, but so far as I was concerned they had a far greater purpose.

Twice a week I would don a loose white suit and learn different ways to hurt people. Unencumbered by the life distractions others faced, I trained hard and would have progressed through the belts in record time, but there were so many reprimands for being overly brutal when taking on opponents that it got to a point where not even those who wore a black belt were willing to fight me. This didn't faze me. There was always a new discipline to learn. Karate became aikido which in turn became Krav Maga.

By the age of twenty-one, I was an accomplished sculptor and confident that regardless of who stepped forward, the martials-arts skills learned through blood and sweat would be more than sufficient to make sure I was the victor.

CHAPTER SIXTY-NINE

Beth lay back on her bed and tucked the bottom of the duvet beneath her feet. A large bowl of soup and a hot bath had restored heat into her fingers and toes and she wanted to keep them warm for as long as possible. Ethan had been called in to work due to the snowstorm, so she had no reason to fight the sleep that was threatening to overwhelm her.

Before climbing in to bed, she'd set out clothes for the next day, including a dry pair of boots. Her mobile was charging on her bedside table. But even though she was exhausted, her brain just wouldn't shut off. As well as the guilt she felt for what happened to Pete Benson, there were a thousand and one details about the case swirling in her mind. She felt it was unfair of O'Dowd to send her away before verification came about Sinclair and the others being in protective custody, but at the same time she knew that her time would be better spent resting than sitting on her hands.

The fact it was late on a Friday afternoon when the request for information had gone into the NCA shouldn't make a difference, but in all likelihood, there would be fewer officers around during the evening.

Beth sent a text to Unthank imploring him to keep her updated. As she pressed send she had a suspicion that he might well be getting the same text from his reporter girlfriend. It was an uncharitable thought, but she couldn't help but wonder if the reporter was using him. Even as she was thinking of their relationship, she was going over the press conference. Teri Veitch hadn't shown any deeper insight into the case than the other reporters. Granted, the unknown reporter had arrived with the agenda of making the police look incompetent and stupid, but Veitch's questions had shown no knowledge of things she shouldn't be aware of.

What had shown though, was the way that she'd been at pains not to make eye contact with Beth. This suggested there was something she was ashamed of or didn't want Beth to see in her eyes.

Beth remembered how Richie had fooled her and used her phone to go on Amazon to buy some books on body language.

Now that she had Richie in her thoughts, she spent a few minutes thinking about him and the grief he carried. How she was going to square Ethan's actions with Richie was a mystery, but she'd have to find a way.

As for what lay ahead of them in terms of bringing Dane Kenyon to justice for the accident which killed Richie's parents, and the fight which left Beth scarred was something to think about at another time.

Her phone beeped, so she looked at its screen then when she saw Unthank's name she sat upright before lying back down once she'd read it. The meeting between Babes and the Sculptor was scheduled for noon tomorrow at the Rheged Centre.

The Rheged Centre was an exhibition centre, cinema and visitor attraction which lay a mile east of Penrith. It was a far more public location than Boustead Hill, which would present challenges in terms of recognising the Sculptor; however it was close at hand, and they'd be able to have a lot of plain-clothes officers posing as visitors, which would mean that once the Sculptor was identified, they'd easily be able to close in on him.

When she snuggled into the pillow and closed her eyes, Beth was picturing a clock face with the hands at five. The alarm on her phone was set for the same time, as she wanted to be in the office bright and early.

CHAPTER SEVENTY

Heather locked the house behind her and took careful steps along her drive until she could get into her car. The last thing she'd expected on a Friday night was to be called up and asked to deliver a TTL warning to a protected witness. Thank goodness she hadn't had a second glass of wine.

What made the call even more unusual was that it was someone who'd entered the system almost twenty years ago and had suffered no perceived threats before.

The news that Michaela's two cohorts, Owen and Kevin Grantham, had already suffered grievous injury didn't sit well with Heather. Their new names of Pete Benson and James Sinclair might not have been released to the press, but when their names and fictitious dates of birth entered the system, it should have raised a flag somewhere.

She'd asked her boss if she ought to call ahead and tell Michaela to be ready with a bag packed, but he'd worried that Michaela might take flight and not be contactable when Heather got to her house, so it was decreed that Heather was only to call when she was on the outskirts of Keswick.

Heather waited for a gap in the traffic at the junction and joined the A6 heading south. From Kendal it would normally be quicker to go across the A684 to join the motorway, but in the current conditions, the only road in or out of Kendal that was open was the A6.

She drove with care and made sure she had more than enough stopping distance between her and the car in front.

At the point where the A6 joined the A591, Heather drew to a halt a good three feet from the 4x4 whose lights she'd followed.

The 4x4's brake lights eased off and it started to pull away at the same moment Heather noticed there was a wagon barrelling up behind her. There was no way it would be able to stop before it collided with her car.

Heather gunned her engine and tried to follow the 4x4, but there was a car coming along the single lane that had been cleared of snow. With nothing else to do, she turned her wheel to the left and aimed for the snowdrift. Better to get stuck than be shunted by the wagon.

As Heather's car was a small city runaround, it didn't have the power or the traction to get more than a couple of feet into the drifting snow, which meant that its rear end was still poking out onto the part of the road which the snowplough had cleared.

There was a blast from the wagon's airhorn then a bone-rattling impact which threw Heather's little car forward.

The compacted snow acted like a ramp and Heather's car shot forward and upwards before landing on the path at the roadside. Its forward momentum carried it onwards, and Heather screamed as she tried to stop the car rolling over the edge of the bank.

Her last thought as the car began to roll down the bank was that she should have phoned ahead to warn Michaela about the danger she was in.

CHAPTER SEVENTY-ONE

Beth flicked on the office kettle and booted up her computer. Once the computer was ready Beth checked the email account, but found no new messages.

Unthank had texted last night to let her know the theory about Sinclair and co. being protected witnesses was correct and that an NCA handler had been sent to bring Babes into protective custody.

Beth had given a fist pump when she'd read the text. Her elation wasn't at being right, it was about the knowledge that a potential victim had been spared. Now it was a case of getting officers in place around the meeting site and capturing the Sculptor.

In theory it should be easy enough, but there was still a lot of room for error in attempting to catch a ruthless hitman in a public place.

Rather than do nothing until the others came in, Beth busied herself with paperwork. First she compiled the reports she should have done yesterday and then she opened up her spreadsheet. She'd learned that her spreadsheets were invaluable, not just for solving cases, but for compiling evidence that would help secure a conviction. They were also a useful memory aid for when a case made it to court. Sometimes several months could pass between arrests and the subsequent trial and with a heavy workload, it was easy to get details mixed up between cases, so every officer found a way to make sure they could recall the necessary details when asked in court.

O'Dowd was the first to arrive. She was wearing what looked to be a new suit and when she turned round, there was still a sales label attached.

Beth couldn't leave her like that all day, so she got O'Dowd to stand still while she snipped the sales label off.

'Cheers. Instead of wearing a bloody dress all day again, I sent Mr O'D to Asda.' O'Dowd flapped at the voluminous suit jacket. 'We've been married twenty-two years and the useless bugger still has no idea what size I am.'

The fondness in O'Dowd's voice made liars of the critical words she used about her husband and brought a smile to Beth's lips. It was the kind of relationship she wanted with Ethan.

McKay and Unthank arrived around eight and when all members of the team were in the office, there was an air of expectant optimism. Even the perennially grumpy McKay had a grin on his face at the prospects of catching a killer.

CHAPTER SEVENTY-TWO

Beth sat at her desk listening to the chief super as he outlined his plan for the operation to catch the Sculptor. With only two drivable ways in and out of Rheged, it wouldn't be hard to corral their target. Once a positive identification had been made, the two entrances were to be blocked off with vehicles.

A slew of police officers had been drafted in from Carlisle and Kendal to attend in plain clothes. With Babes in protective custody, a female officer in her thirties would play the role of Babes.

Beth caught Hilton's eye. 'Sir, can I volunteer for the part of Babes?'

Hilton shook his head. 'Absolutely not. Unless we spent the rest of the morning dragging you through a hedge, there's no way you'd pass for late thirties.'

O'Dowd cleared her throat in a way that was designed to attract attention, but Hilton made a point of ignoring her. Without being unkind, Beth knew the chief super wasn't taking O'Dowd on because there was no way she could pass for being in her thirties either, without a comprehensive makeover.

'So. We will have six officers in the grounds posing as grounds-men, two dressed in security-guard uniforms and a further eight in plain clothes acting the part of visitors. DI O'Dowd will be with me in the manager's office which overlooks the main car park. Your stations are as follows: DC Unthank, you're to be at the fuel station at the main entrance and exit with another officer. You'll both have cars and it's up to you to block off that route of access and egress. DC Young, you'll have a car too and your position is the lane which runs along the back of Rheged to Redhills. There's a gateway there which will need to be blocked off once we have the target in our sights. DS McKay, your position is on the roof of the Rheged Centre. I want you to be monitoring all behaviour from above.' Hilton scanned the room. 'Any questions?'

'Will there be firearms officers on site?' Unthank's face was like a child's on Christmas morning.

'Yes. The six officers posing as groundsmen will all be firearms officers. There will be a seventh and they'll be with DS McKay.'

McKay lifted his head. 'What are we to do if the target gets wind of us and takes a hostage?'

'We follow procedure. One of the firearms officers is a trained negotiator, so we'll leave it to them. Let's hope that it doesn't come to that though.' Hilton pointed at the plans of the Rheged Centre. 'Fortunately the manager of the centre is a friend of my wife, so I've been able to get full cooperation without any trouble. At 11.55, she's going to go round the building and lock every door that doesn't need to be open. Also, as soon as we have the target identified, the centre itself will go into lockdown. Don't forget, the meet is due to take place in the car park, so we'll largely be able to keep the public away from the operation.' He huffed out a breath. 'Besides, the weather is still horrible, there's every chance that nobody will be around.'

Out of habit more than anything else, Beth checked the email account. When she clicked through, she saw something which made her yelp in surprise. It could only mean one thing.

'Sir. Are you sure Babes has been picked up? Because she's just sent a message to the Sculptor.'

Hilton's eyebrows lifted, but it was O'Dowd who asked the obvious question.

'I'm working on it, ma'am.' Beth didn't care if her irritation showed. O'Dowd should know she'd have already started work on the code.

Beth transcribed the message from Babes as quickly as she could. Some of the symbols were now memorised, but others had to be drawn from her decoding table. As much as she could feel the eyes of the others on her, Beth didn't rush to the point where she made a mistake.

'Got it. It says, "Looking forward to seeing you after all these years. I will be wearing a yellow coat and black jeans".'

'Drat.' Hilton fished a mobile from the handkerchief pocket of his suit and scrolled until he found the name he was looking for. As he put the phone to his ear, he left the office.

'Shit. Does that mean the operation is off?' Unthank looked to O'Dowd for an answer but all he got was a helpless shrug.

They sat in silence until Hilton returned. His face had lost a couple of shades from its usual ruddiness, but there was a purpose to his walk.

'Change of plan. Babes's handler was involved in an RTA last night on the way to bring Babes in. The handler is in Westmorland General with concussion and a broken arm, but is otherwise okay. I have an address for Babes as well as her real name. DI O'Dowd, we're to proceed as planned. DC Young, with me.'

CHAPTER SEVENTY-THREE

Sandi was second-guessing her choice of outfit. A big jacket and jeans made sense for an outdoor meeting in the current weather conditions, but she also wanted to look nice for Kevin. She hadn't seen him for nigh on twenty years, and she didn't want him to think she was now some frumpy type. Back in the days when they'd been an item she'd worn short skirts and dresses to show off her legs, crop tops to display her flat stomach and push-up bras to accentuate her bust.

While the years had added a few pounds, she hadn't let herself go and for some reason it was important to Sandi that she show this to Kevin. Instead of opting for a thick jumper over a T-shirt, Sandi chose a blouse that was that little bit too tight and therefore made her chest look bigger. She knew it was early to start putting on her make-up, but she wanted to look her best and if she started now she'd have plenty of time to get her hair just how she liked it.

Sandi was reaching for the blusher when her doorbell went. She gave a frown as she wasn't expecting any visitors and it was too soon for any of the things she'd ordered online to be delivered.

When she opened the door she was greeted by a young woman with a scar on her face. A few paces behind the woman, there was a heavyset man in a suit.

'Sandi? My name is DC Beth Young and the gentleman behind me is Chief Superintendent Hilton. We need to talk to you.'

Sandi took the little wallet that DC Young was showing her and took a proper look at it. She'd been shown what a warrant card should look like and this one looked genuine. Her mind was awhirl with possibilities, but she didn't think it was anything to do with her past. If that was the case, Heather would have been in touch. All the same, she wasn't going to take any chances.

A polished fingernail was aimed at the man. 'Does he have a warrant card?'

Hilton produced one and she saw that it looked genuine, too. Still, she wasn't prepared to invite them in until she knew what they wanted.

'What do you need to talk to me about?'

DC Young's tone was smooth when she answered. 'We need to ask you a few questions about a friend of yours called Michaela Ingles. Heather said you'd be able to help.'

Sandi had to make an effort not to let her knees give way, but she managed to stay upright.

'You'd better come in.'

The minute it took for the two coppers to follow her into the lounge wasn't enough for Sandi to recover her poise, but such was her shock at the copper using her real name that she didn't know what to do or say. The fact she'd also mentioned Heather offered a smidgeon of reassurance, but she was still worried. As her handler, Heather should have been the one on her doorstep, not a couple of strangers. Sandi didn't know a lot about police ranks or the roles of each rank, but she was sure a chief superintendent didn't make house calls on a Saturday morning unless there was a major problem.

CHAPTER SEVENTY-FOUR

Beth could see that the woman in front of her was bewildered and frightened by their presence. She knew she had to find a way to put her at ease, and the best way she could think of was to get to the point as soon as possible. All the same, with Hilton accompanying her, she'd best do everything she could to lessen the impact of what was sure to be terrible news.

As she was about to speak, Hilton stepped forward and took charge of the situation with his customary soft way of speaking. 'I'm Matthew and this is Beth. We know you're called Sandi now but you used to be Michaela. What would you rather we called you?'

'Sandi.' A look from Hilton to Beth. 'Please… please, will one of you tell me what's going on?'

'I'm very sorry to tell you this. But the two men who were put into protective custody at the same time as you have been attacked and badly injured.'

Sandi's hand flew to her mouth. 'Oh my god. How badly are they hurt?'

'Very badly.' Hilton gave a soft grimace. 'I'm afraid best-case scenario, we're talking about life-changing injuries.'

Beth sprang forward as Sandi's legs gave way. She managed to catch Sandi and lower her to the carpet. Tears were now streaming down her face and sobs juddering her body.

Offering comfort wasn't Beth's greatest strength and she knew it, but she wound an arm round Sandi's shoulder and tried a few soothing phrases. None worked.

Sandi brushed Beth away and leapt to her feet to confront Hilton. 'You've got it wrong. It can't be them. I'm meeting Kevin at noon.'

'We know. You're meeting at Rheged. It's not Kevin who's been messaging you. It's the person who attacked him.'

'If you know that, why aren't you catching him instead of coming here?' A finger with a cerise nail jabbed into Hilton's chest. 'Come on, answer me that.'

'We're here to take you into protective custody. Your handler, Heather, was on her way to do this last night, but she was involved in a car crash.' Hilton pointed at his watch. 'We can explain things to you later, but right now, we need to get cracking. Beth, over to you.'

Beth picked up on Hilton's cue and took a gentle grip of Sandi's elbow. 'Come on, Sandi. Let's get you a bag packed.'

Sandi let Beth lead her upstairs. The anger she'd shown Hilton now replaced with what appeared to be a catatonic state.

'Right, Sandi. We need to focus. You're going to need clothes for a couple of days, toiletries and any medicines you take. First off, do you have a backpack or a small suitcase?'

Sandi just pointed at the built-in wardrobes, so Beth slid them open and searched until she found a backpack. With it zipped open and placed on the bed, Beth turned to Sandi. 'Okay, T-shirts and a jumper, where do you keep them?'

Again Sandi pointed at the wardrobe, so Beth pulled two of each from a shelf and fed them into the backpack.

'Underwear? Or do you want to get that yourself?' A nod but no movement. 'Come on Sandi, time is precious.'

Rather than wait for Sandi to react, Beth zipped up the open make-up bag and put it into the backpack. Next she unplugged the straighteners and hairdryer that lay on the dressing table and slid them into a side pocket on the backpack. Whether Sandi felt like sorting her hair or make-up when she was in protective custody was a moot point. Beth was making sure that Sandi had the tools to do so if she wished.

Sandi was rooting in a chest of drawers with a blank look on her face. When she turned round and moved towards the backpack, she was holding enough underwear to last a week.

Beth said nothing. Better to have and not need.

'Well done. Toiletries and medicines now.'

'My phone.' Sandi patted her pockets. 'I have to tell Leo where I'm going.'

'Who's Leo? Your husband?

'No, my boyfr… fiancé.'

'You can't tell him where you're going. Just tell him a relative is sick and that you have to go and look after them.'

It took another ten minutes of cajoling, but Beth managed to get Sandi packed and into Hilton's car. The big Range Rover felt like a safe environment, but Beth knew that Sandi would be petrified and bewildered. Her eyes were flicking to the road as if she could see the threat coming her way.

Beth wished it'd be that easy. Catching the Sculptor was something that Monkton and countless others had failed to do. They had a shot at doing it later, but there was still a chance it'd go wrong or the Sculptor would somehow evade their trap.

Now that she was in the car with them, Sandi appeared to have reached a kind of fatalistic decision.

'Do you even know why we were in witness protection?'

Beth glanced at Hilton. Saw the permission-giving nod. 'No. That information hasn't been shared with us. We've only been told what we need to know, to bring you in to safety. And as such, we weren't given the real names of the two men you were put into protection with and we've been instructed not to let you know their current identities.'

'That figures.' Sandi gave a hearty sniff. 'Well bollocks to it all. If what you say is true, and I have no reason to doubt you, then

Owen and Kevin have been badly hurt. You've probably taken a risk coming to get me. You deserve to know the truth.'

Beside her, Beth could see Hilton's fingers grip the steering wheel that bit tighter. By rights they should tell Sandi they didn't need to know why she or the two men were protected witnesses. However, they were both police officers and that meant they spent their days searching for the truth. Sandi was about to give them her truth and neither of them were about to stop her.

Hilton gave a sigh. 'You don't have to tell us and it's probably wise that you don't, but if you choose to, I can guarantee it'll go no further. Right, Beth?'

'Absolutely.'

The selfish part of Beth's inquisitive nature crossed its fingers and hoped Sandi would keep talking.

'Twenty years ago I used to live in London. At the time I went out with a guy called Kevin Grantham. One night we were out on the town with his older brother Owen. We were on our way back, had just got some chips and this car pulled up on the other side of the road. There was a couple standing there. An older couple. They'd have been in their forties. Anyway, these three huge guys and one little guy got out of the car. One of the big guys grabbed the woman and the other two grabbed the man. The smaller guy from the car walked forward, lifted a gun and shot the man three times. The woman was thrown into the boot of the car and then they roared off.' Beth could guess the rest, but she didn't want to interrupt Sandi.

'We went to see the man who'd been shot, but he was dead. His brains had been blown out. We banged on a door and woke someone up so we could call the police.

'Owen was really good at drawing and he made sketches of the four guys. The police made arrests and we testified at the trial. It was only then that we found out the four guys were the sons of a gangster. They got fifteen years each.' A sniff and a rub of the nose. 'The police heard of a contract that had been taken out on us. The next thing we know, we're being told to say goodbye to our families and we're being taken away to start a new life. I was set up in County Durham at first and then I moved to Cumbria about five years ago when I was looking for a change of career. I thought I'd be with Kevin at first, but he didn't want to be with me. I loved him. Still do. I haven't seen my mum and dad for twenty years. We get letters through Heather once in a while, but there's no chance of me ever seeing my family again.'

'Thank you for telling us your story. You've been very brave and what you've told us has enabled us to understand more about our case.'

Beth looked over her shoulder at Sandi. She was sitting back in her seat and her face was set in a look of wistful regret.

'I wish I understood. If I'd known how my life would turn out, I would never have testified. Even now, twenty years later, I get engaged and then when my life is finally going right for once, you appear out of nowhere and whisk me away. Have you any idea how many times I've wished that we'd just kept walking?'

Neither Beth nor Hilton tried to answer. Sandi and the two brothers had paid a terrible price for being good citizens and testifying against the four gangsters. Sometimes words couldn't express the injustices of life. There was nothing either of them could say that could heal the pain or erase the years of living in fear and wishing that a different choice had been taken.

The National Crime Agency would follow up the London end of things and look for evidence linking the gangsters with the Sculptor. If the Sculptor fell for their trap, they may be able to get him to turn against those who'd hired him, but Beth doubted that a hitman would turn grass.

CHAPTER SEVENTY-FIVE

Beth listened as Hilton delivered the final briefing to the assembled troops. The firearms officers were all macho poses and grim faces. It was understandable they were tense. In an hour's time they'd be called upon to arrest a known killer. There may well be a gun battle and the Sculptor's first targets would be those who offered the biggest threat to him, ergo it would be on the firearms officers that he'd focus his aim.

None of the files on the Sculptor mentioned him using a gun, but that didn't mean he didn't have one. A gun would be the ideal thing to help him control Sandi until he could tie her up or incapacitate her in another way.

Unthank's face was full of childish enthusiasm and he kept flicking glances at the body armour the firearms officers wore or the pistols holstered on their hips. McKay and O'Dowd were paying attention to the chief super, but Beth could tell from their expressions that they'd sat through many such briefings before and were just anxious to get on with things.

That was how she felt herself. Her feet were restless and all she wanted to do was get into position and for the operation to become active.

The most nervous person in the room was the officer who'd take on the role of Sandi. She was mid-thirties, looked her age, and was in good physical shape. Hilton had offered her body armour, but she'd refused it as she was worried that if the Sculptor touched her, or observed the shape of the body armour beneath her sweater, he'd have advance warning and they'd lose the element of surprise.

Hilton was insistent on one point though, as soon as it became clear that the Sculptor had been identified, the officer was to throw herself to the ground so the firearms officer could get a clear shot if they needed one. It would also prevent the Sculptor using the officer as a shield.

Beth wanted to be more involved in proceedings, but she understood that the firearms team would have to take precedence on the actual operation. Most of all, she was hoping the sting went smoothly and the Sculptor could be caught without any officers or members of the public getting hurt.

Hilton's last instruction was that they were all to take care of themselves and that none of them were to take any unnecessary risks.

CHAPTER SEVENTY-SIX

Parked where she was, Beth couldn't see the top car park of the Rheged Centre. She had to rely on the radio reports from the other officers to get a picture of what was going on. The little road from Redhills that connected to the A592 which ran past Lake Ullswater and on to Windermere was empty save for a couple of cars and a van that were parked in an unofficial lay-by. As a matter of course she'd jotted down their licence plates to check them later, but for the moment, she didn't want to clutter her radio with chatter from Control.

Snow was banked on the verges of the road, but an area had been gritted from the access gate that led from Rheged's car park right up to the junction with the A592.

The gateway from the car park was formed by a pair of wooden gates that bisected the drystone dyke that surrounded the visitor centre.

Both gates were pegged back so the gateway was open. Beth had parked her car twenty yards up the road, but she'd left the engine running, as much to power the heater as in readiness to block off the gateway.

From the radio she could hear that everyone was in position and that 'Sandi' was due to arrive in the next two minutes.

So far none of the officers stationed around the visitor centre had found someone they suspected of being the Sculptor, but that didn't mean much. A professional hitman would be good at disguising themselves. The one advantage they had was that they knew who the Sculptor's target was.

It was also possible the Sculptor would only arrive at the last minute, or not show at all.

The radio on the passenger seat crackled and she heard Unthank's voice. 'Sandi has just driven past the filling station.'

As alert as she was, Beth felt herself tense up even further. The next few minutes would be crucial.

'Sandi in sight. No suspicious males in the top car park. Stay alert.' Hilton's last two words were unnecessary; if the rest of the team were as keyed up as Beth, staying calm would be a more appropriate piece of advice.

It was now a case of being patient and waiting for the Sculptor to make his move.

CHAPTER SEVENTY-SEVEN

I walk out of the visitor centre and head towards the top car park with my eyes scanning for a yellow coat. There are a couple of cars parked, but the area is largely empty. December isn't a time when there are lots of tourists around, and yesterday's heavy snow seems to have deterred people from coming to the shops in the visitor centre.

After arriving a full two hours early to scout the location properly, I had browsed the shops and bought a few jars of various preserves and a few other knick-knacks. The purchases weren't made solely for my return to London – although I have always been a sucker for chutneys – but, by carrying a bag that was branded with one of Rheged's shops, it is easier for me to blend in.

Not seeing a yellow coat, I scan the area once again. A hatchback is disgorging an arguing couple. I can't help but smile at the man's insistence that his parents should come for Christmas dinner, and the woman's threat that if he invites them, she'll be at her parents'. Thankfully I have none of that nonsense to deal with.

It is normal everyday life, but my instincts are telling me there is something amiss. There are four large men in coveralls shovelling away at the snow and slush which still covers the car park.

Every one of my senses begin screaming that something is wrong. I work out what it is in a flash. The four shovellers

aren't paying the right kind of attention to their jobs. Instead
of buckling down and watching what they are doing, their
heads are rotating as if they are looking for something, or
someone. One is flicking shovelfuls of snow forward without
looking, only for the snow to land on a pathway that
someone has already cleared.

At once I understand that they aren't genuine workers,
they are undercover cops posing as workers. The car park has
been gritted, so there is no need for the men to be shovelling.

This must be a trap. The police must have connected the
beatings of Kevin and Owen Grantham and set up a sting
operation for when I'm due to meet Michaela.

Rather than show any panicked reaction, I carry on walking
with the same steady gait. My name isn't on any police database
and there's not one copper alive who knows what I look like.

A woman in a yellow coat climbs out of a blue Mini.
Like the men shovelling, her eyes are flicking everywhere.

I walk right past Michaela without giving the woman a
second look. It won't really be Michaela, it will be a copper
posing as her in order to draw me out.

There is no way I'm going to fall into the police's trap.
Step by step the exit gate to the little road behind the visitor
centre gets nearer. I don't look back, don't try and spot any
pursuers. I hear no footsteps behind me just the crump of
snow beneath my boots.

I walk through the gateway onto the narrow road and
turn right. In the little lay-by where I've parked, a car is sat
with its engine running. As I near the car, the figure behind
the wheel comes into focus.

It's the copper who'd been on the news. I'd seen her
making an appeal for the woman who'd been in the pub the
night that Squint and Bad Breath had become tableaux for
the designs I wanted to carve.

So far as I'm concerned, the copper in the car is far more than just the public face of the investigation, she is the one who's cost me half a million quid, as there is no way that I will be able to trace Michaela after this. She'll be moved on and given another new identity.

Yes, I can climb into the van and head back south to the anonymity of London, but the contract hasn't been completed. For the first time, there is a stain on my reputation. I make a snap decision; the scar-faced copper will have to pay.

I feed both hands into my jacket's pockets. The left fastens around a packet of cigarettes, the right grasps a small blunt chisel.

With the copper focussed on the gateway, I take a brief moment to look around for witnesses.

The narrow road is deserted.

I feed a cigarette between my lips and knock on the driver's window then mime the flicking of a cigarette lighter.

The window buzzes down and the copper looks my way.

'Sorry to bother you, but do you have a light?'

'I don't smoke. Sorry.' The copper's eyes turn back towards the car's centre console. 'Hang on. I can use the car's—'

The copper freezes as she's reaching for the lighter. It's like she's just had an epiphany. I guess she's realised that I'm her quarry.

Before she can react my right hand snakes through the open window and crashes the hammer-gnarled end of the chisel into the copper's temple.

I've judged the strength of the blow to perfection. The copper slumps forward with a moan, but she is only groggy rather than knocked out. I want her to be awake to suffer her fate.

Considering the reputational damage and financial cost of failing to complete the contract, the very least the copper can do is to let me see the fear in her eyes when she realises she is going to die.

CHAPTER SEVENTY-EIGHT

Beth tried shaking her head to clear it, but rather than bring clarity, the shaking did nothing but exacerbate the pain radiating from her temple and blur her vision again. Even before trying to clear her head, she'd tried to move her arms, but they were pinned behind her.

She was aware of motion. There was the sound of an engine and the occasional jolt as the vehicle hit a pothole.

Beth remembered the woman who'd asked her for a light, but there was nothing after that. She didn't know what had happened, but when she opened her eyes, the woman was driving her car. Beth guessed she had taken the handcuffs from her jacket pocket.

In this position, there was little Beth could do. She couldn't open the door or grab the wheel. She couldn't even haul on the handbrake to slow the car down. All she had was her mouth.

'You're making a big mistake. I'm a police officer. If you harm me in any way, my colleagues will stop at nothing to catch you. I don't know who you are, but if you let me go right now, things will go far better for you.'

'Oh shut up, you stupid cow. You know exactly who I am. I'm the Sculptor. I'm the one you've been looking for. The woman in the pub you're searching for. Me. You and your colleagues, as you call them, have cost me an awful lot of money. As the representative of that team, you're the one who's going to pay the price.' The car drew to a halt alongside a drystone wall. 'Brace yourself, it's time to die.'

The Sculptor got out of the car.

As the Sculptor made her way round to the passenger side, Beth thrashed against the handcuffs pinning her arms behind her back. Whichever way she moved, all she did was bruise herself as she crashed off the door or dashboard.

In a futile attempt to escape through the open driver's door, Beth flung herself that way and used her legs to propel her onwards.

She heard the car's passenger door open and felt a pair of hands grabbing at the handcuffs and dragging her out.

CHAPTER SEVENTY-NINE

As much as I want to get my toolkit and spend hours dismantling the copper's bones, I'm all too aware that I'll only have a limited window to deal with her.

Besides, what she said was true. If I am identified as having killed a copper, the hunt for me will reach new levels. It's not what I want, but I'll have to kill the copper another way. A way that means there's no proof I killed her. I'll still be able to have some fun killing her, but there'll be none of my trademark chisel wounds. They'll want to connect it with the Sculptor, but I'll make sure there will be no evidence they can use against me.

By hauling up on the handcuffs, I'm able to control where the copper goes. I direct her to the drystone wall. Twenty yards beyond the wall is a river. It'll do my dirty work for me and then wash away the evidence.

The copper's gut hits the wall, so I raise the handcuffs until the copper is leaning over it. After that I use both hands to grab her legs and lift.

By the time she's rolling onto her front, I'm across the wall myself and have two booted feet ready to subdue any attempt to fight that the copper makes. I have to give the copper credit, she lies motionless as I lift the handcuffs until there is a terrific strain on her shoulders, but in the end the pain stops her from resisting my efforts to draw her back to her feet.

I sidestep her mule kick with ease, but rather than let the defiant act go unpunished, I lash a kick forward of my own. My target is her coccyx and I catch it perfectly. The bone will be broken and is sure to cause a lot of discomfort, but it being broken won't impede the copper's movement to the point where she can't walk.

She is making all kinds of threats about her colleagues and a few pleas for her life, but I'd stopped listening as soon as I'd said my piece in the car.

The best part of the whole experience was seeing the shock in her eyes when I unmasked myself as the Sculptor. I know that cops and gangsters alike all think the Sculptor is a man and I've always been happy to have this misogyny work for me. It means that I can walk right through a trap like the one laid for me today and not get a second glance.

Had the real Michaela turned up, I'd have approached her and played the part of Kevin's wife, to win the woman's confidence. Then it would have been simple to overpower the woman and spirit her away. I've dressed in a loose knee-length skirt and ankle boots, to make me seem less of a threat.

I have six skirts like the one I am wearing. Coupled with thick tights, they are far more suited to martial arts than a pair of jeans or trousers, as they allow so much more move-ment. A couple of rolls on the waistband to shorten the skirt and my legs become a distraction for targets, which allows me to get close to them. At other times, I'll use my cleavage as a focal point.

It never fails to amuse me how many supposedly alert men lower their guard when confronted with a pair of toned legs or a heaving bosom. That men leer at me isn't something which bothers me. On the contrary, it means the men are susceptible, weak creatures. Every last one of them, Grandad included, are inferior beings. Like my chisels, hammers and buffs, I consider my body as nothing more than a tool to be used. While I take pride in my fitness, I only maintain it so I can carry on sculpting and attack or defend myself when required. As much as I enjoy carving shapes from stone, for me there is far greater satisfaction in breaking bones with perfect weighted strikes.

There are the remains of a fence at the river bank, but the fence lies flat, matted with flood-deposited debris.

I force the copper over it and as soon as her boots hit the gravel by the tumultuous river, I give her a hard kick to the back of the leg.

While I can't set about her with my chisels before killing her, if I'm going to keep this kill separate, there is no reason why I can't have a little fun.

As she yelps in pain and anger, I swing a left hook that crashes into her ear and sends her staggering. I may only have five minutes or so with her, but I'm determined that not only am I going to enjoy them, I'm going to make full use of every second.

CHAPTER EIGHTY

Beth took the kicks and punches with as much fortitude as she could. The outraged squeals and curses were more for effect than anything.

As scared as she was to be in the Sculptor's clutches, she knew that if she gave in to fear, she was doomed to an excruciating death. The only chance she had was to fight back.

With her arms bound behind her back, only her legs and head could be used as weapons.

Due to the handicaps she was facing, Beth's plan was a simple one. Somehow she had to withstand the Sculptor's blows and get close enough to deliver a headbutt that would drop the Sculptor to her knees. After that, it would be a case of kicking out at the Sculptor's head until she was knocked out. Only then would Beth be able to try and get help.

Another kick came in, this one hit Beth's right thigh hard enough to numb the muscle.

Beth didn't go down, but her right leg wasn't fit to bear much of her weight.

A fist or a boot slammed into her kidneys; Beth didn't know which and didn't much care as all of a sudden she was bent over trying not to retch. She saw a pair of boots appear on the stones beneath her head and then a knee was arcing upwards.

Beth managed to turn her head to one side before the knee connected, but it still had enough force to rattle her jaw and leave her reeling. The uneven gravel made keeping her footing awkward. The fact it was layered in slushy snow, just added to the problem.

She pulled herself upright and looked in the Sculptor's eyes. They were a pair of empty abysses, devoid of emotion and light. Beth wasn't looking for humanity though, nor did she expect to see pity or empathy. What she wanted, needed, to see was anger.

So long as the Sculptor was calm and collected, she'd be able to pick Beth off at will. Therefore Beth's only chance of survival was to force the Sculptor to make a mistake.

'You can't be the Sculptor. If you were, I'd be dead by now. You're nothing more than a pale imitation of a real killer. You're oh-so-tough when I've got my hands held behind my back. Bet you wouldn't be so tough if I didn't.'

Beth's words bounced off the Sculptor as she cocked a fist. 'I've told you to shut up once. Looks like I'm going to have to shut you up myself.'

A fist shot towards Beth. She dodged left as the punch came up short, only to feel her nose crumple beneath a vicious right hook.

The nose-breaking punch had snapped Beth's head upwards. As soon as she'd corrected her backwards momentum, she focussed on the approaching Sculptor and threw her head forward. She didn't make the contact she wanted as the Sculptor was still on her feet, so she advanced ready to repeat the blow.

A punch to the stomach all but lifted Beth off her feet. She doubled over and fell retching to her knees.

Nothing came out, but the Sculptor's ankle boots came into Beth's view. She looked up at the killer and saw something that was akin to a snake coiling ready to strike.

A kick that exploded into her left thigh was followed up with a kick to her left bicep. The muscles screamed and numbed together.

A second pair of blows hit Beth's right limbs.

'Time for me to say game over.'

Beth never saw the kick that hit her solar plexus. One minute she was breathing, the next she was gasping. She was aware of the Sculptor bent over her, but could do nothing to combat whatever the woman planned. Even when the handcuffs were released, there was a powerlessness to her limbs that made her attempts at movement irrelevant.

Beth yelped in pain as the Sculptor grabbed her arms and dragged her. She knew she was being moved closer to where the river was flowing as she could hear the sound of its waters increasing.

Was that the Sculptor's plan? To dump her in the river so she'd drown?

Beth tried moving, but the only muscle which obeyed her brain was her neck. She felt her head and shoulders buffeted by icy water. The water was pushing against her, chilling her limbs and trying to climb up and into Beth's eyes and nose.

Beth craned her neck to keep her mouth above the river's dirty brown water. She could see the Sculptor retreating to the bank where she was bending over something.

The Sculptor reappeared as a branch smacked into the side of Beth's head on its way downstream.

She was returning towards Beth and she was dragging something – a huge piece of driftwood.

Is she going to dump that on my head to hold me under?

Beth tried to will her limbs to work, but the blows delivered by the Sculptor had played havoc with her nervous system and none of them obeyed her commands.

The Sculptor laid one end of the driftwood by Beth's left side and then moved round to lift the other side. For a moment the Sculptor held her end of the driftwood above Beth's stomach and then she dropped it.

Beth's stomach convulsed at the sudden impact and her shoulders reared out of the water before the weight of the driftwood pushed her back down. Her head went underwater for a brief moment and hit one of the rocks littering the riverbed but she craned her neck up once again.

The Sculptor stood on the stony riverbank looking down on her. 'This river has only just started flooding. You'll drown in the next few minutes. Then the floodwaters will carry your body away with this log. Your colleagues may blame me for your death, but there won't be any proof. If your body is ever found, any bruises I've given you will be blamed on the river. Believe me, this isn't how I want to kill you. I'd much rather spend hours sculpting you. I want to hear you scream in agony, to hear you plead for your life and then when the pain gets too much, I want to hear you begging for me to put you out of your misery and kill you. I'd love to see the fear in your eyes as you anticipate each new injury and the pain that comes with it. Sadly I don't have time for that, so I'm going to have to content myself with the knowledge your last few minutes alive will be spent fighting to keep your head above rising floodwaters. You'll manage for a short while and then your muscles will start to cramp. Your neck and back will ache in ways you can't imagine and when you try to ease that pain, your head will go under. You'll cough and splutter and then it'll be those aching muscles again. You won't be able to keep your head above the water as long the second time, as the pain increases when you get colder and colder. In about ten minutes, you'll give up, maybe say a prayer, or think of your loved ones before accepting your fate and allowing the river to fill your lungs.'

As the Sculptor stared into her eyes, Beth hoped she was showing the hate in her heart rather than the fear in her gut. The Sculptor's words were delivered in a tone that bordered on seductive such was the woman's pleasure in detailing Beth's fate.

One by one, the Sculptor threw Beth's phone, car keys and police radio into the river. 'You'll not need those again. Happy death day.' With that final three-word sentence accompanied by a malicious smirk, Beth watched as the Sculptor turned away and left her to die.

CHAPTER EIGHTY-ONE

Beth used every muscle that would work as she tried to sit up and roll the piece of driftwood down her body.

All she achieved was to lift her head and shoulders out of the icy brown torrent for a few seconds. Even as she eased backwards, she could feel the effort to keep her mouth above the water had increased due to the rising floodwaters. The edge of the river, where she was, was shallow at the moment, but would flood along with the stony beach where she'd fought the Sculptor as the waters rose.

While the river wasn't the biggest, it was fast flowing and littered with large boulders around which the waters flowed in a swirling maelstrom. The banks at either side were steep enough to contain more than enough water to drown her as all the melting snow swelled the river.

The cold of the water was another problem: it was sapping her strength. The Sculptor's vision of what would happen to her felt accurate to Beth, as she wrestled with not just the physical problem, but the mental one.

Her limbs weren't working and she was trapped. There had to be a way out of this; she just had to find it.

A sense of rage colder than the water crashing into her engulfed Beth and she screamed obscenities as she gave way to the anger and squirmed her torso as much as she could.

For all her squirming, Beth didn't move herself out of the water. If anything, she seemed to be digging herself in deeper.

As she realised this, the kernel of an idea began to form in her mind. For it to work though, she'd need working arms and legs.

To try and restore movement in her limbs, she tried to make fists with both her hands and her feet.

Due to the cold, she couldn't feel it making any difference, but she tried ten times before she gave another squirm.

This time when she squirmed Beth felt something akin to movement in her limbs. She squirmed a third time and managed to pull her right arm free. The next squirming wriggle dug her deeper into the gravel bed as the rising water washed away the small pieces of grit she was loosening from the riverbed.

The more she was squirming into the river, the harder it became to keep her head above the water.

Beth propped herself up on her right arm and concentrated her focus on getting her left arm to obey her commands. Her supporting arm gave way and her head crashed off a stone in the riverbed, but her head didn't sink as far into the water as before.

She worked out that she'd moved far enough into the river for her head to be close to a large stone that was only partially submerged.

In a slow movement, Beth lowered her head until it was resting on the stone. Dirty brown water buffeted the side of her head and, as prophesised, her neck muscles screamed in protest at the strain she was putting on them, but she held the position as long as she could to ease the strain on her back.

Her left hand was making sweeping movements and she managed to summon enough control of the arm to pull it out from under the driftwood.

She used the left arm as a prop to give her neck a brief rest and then after taking a deep breath, pressed both hands against the piece of driftwood and started to wriggle and squirm her way further into the river.

When she had to give up her efforts and rest, the submerged stone was now below the back of her neck.

Beth could feel movement in her toes and she guessed that her legs would probably work, but with the next squirm, she'd have to drag herself far enough that the driftwood was above her thighs rather than above her waist. Once that was done, she'd be able to sit up and draw her legs out from under the driftwood.

Pieces of flotsam bumped into Beth's head as she steeled herself for the last huge effort she'd need to free herself from the driftwood.

'Come on, Beth, you can do it!' The shout of self-encouragement was followed by a thrashing squirm as she planted her hands on the riverbed and drew herself further into its depths.

The depths didn't matter. The last movement had freed more of her waist, and moved her enough that the driftwood was now just above her knees. Beth adopted a sitting position and by planting her hands on the riverbed and lifting her bum, she was able to draw her legs out from under the driftwood and into the river.

She rolled into a crawling position and worked her way out of the river on hands and knees.

As soon as she was clear of the water, Beth tried to stand. Her legs were shaky and while she didn't trust them to move with any great athletic ability, they were once again obeying her commands.

Now that she was free from immediate danger, she felt herself beginning to shiver and shake as waves of adrenaline crashing from her body joined forces with the bitterly cold air on her river-soaked body.

Beth went up the gravel patch and looked back the way the Sculptor had brought her.

Her car was there, but as her car keys, radio and phone had been tossed into the river, there was no point in Beth going to the car. She looked beyond it and saw nothing but empty fields.

She turned and looked across the river. In the distance, the roofs of some farm sheds stood uniform against the skyline.

Beth didn't waste any time, she plucked a branch from a pile of debris that had snagged on the collapsed fence and set off back to the river as fast as her aching legs would take her.

Rather than look for smooth even water, Beth aimed for the turbulent area. Smooth water indicated depth whereas rippled cascading areas were shallower.

When Beth got to the water's edge, she didn't pause or hesitate. She was already soaking wet and chilled to the bone. All that was on her mind was getting to a phone and raising the alarm.

Step by step she waded into the turbulent water. The branch in her hand used as a depth probe as the water swirled round her ankles, then calves and then her knees.

She prodded the stick into the swirling brown meltwaters of the river and kept progressing forward until the water was halfway up her thighs. By now the rampaging torrent was pushing against her legs with enough force to topple her and she had to brace herself against it.

Another step. This time the water reached the top of her thighs. The current pushed harder and Beth knew that if the water got any deeper, she wouldn't be able to fight its irresistible force any longer.

A glance upstream told her that a small bush was being washed her way. If it hit her, it would finish the job the current started and then she'd be swept away and drowned by the icy waters, just as the Sculptor had planned.

The probe found the water a fraction deeper, so Beth leaned forward and tried further away. It was shallower.

She took a leap of faith that the last of her strength would see her to the other bank and forged ahead.

The water was deeper than expected and it came up to her waist and she had to half walk and half swim her way across until her feet were well enough planted on the riverbed for her to stand firm against the current.

The river tried its best to sweep her away, but with every step forward she was escaping its clutches.

As soon as she was able, she broke into a slow trot and headed for the farm sheds. Her breaths were ragged and her gait was nothing like the assured strides she took on her morning runs around Penrith, but she was covering the ground as quick as she could and that's all that mattered. Her various injuries hit her with spikes of agony as she trotted towards the farm, but she pushed through the pain barrier. To Beth, getting word of the Sculptor out was more important than her comfort.

Upon her approach to the farm, she looked for a farmer to wave down. A dairyman or herdsman would do, so long as they had a mobile phone she could use to alert O'Dowd.

There was nobody around. Not even the sound of a tractor came her way as a focal point for her stumbling trot.

Beth spied a farmhouse and made her way towards it. It had no lights on and there weren't any cars parked by the door. She banged on the door and when that failed to get a response, she gripped the door handle.

She gave out a sigh of relief when it opened without protest. She'd been prepared to smash a window if necessary, but this was better, and quicker, than smashing her way in.

When Beth entered the kitchen, she spied a cordless telephone sitting on its cradle. Three strides got her to the phone and she had it in her hand and was dialling O'Dowd's number within seconds.

CHAPTER EIGHTY-TWO

I make the best time I can along the country lane where I'd brought the copper. The wind is cold but I have the memory of terror-filled eyes to warm me. In a perfect world, I'd have been able to sit and watch the river rise until it drowned her, but I've already taken a huge chance when common sense dictated that I get back to my van and drive away before the other cops shut down the whole area.

I don't remember it being this far when I'd driven the copper's car, but it makes no difference. She will either be drowned by now, or she'll drown in the next few minutes. As she is the only person who knows my identity, I should be able to waltz past the cops as they wait for the man they think I am, climb into my van and set off south.

The headbutt thrown by the copper has raised a large bump on my forehead, but I've pulled my hair forward and, provided a gust of wind doesn't blow my hair backwards, the injury is covered.

After ten minutes of walking, I've left the rough track and am on the narrow road that runs behind the Rheged Centre. The quarter mile of straight road ahead gives me plenty of chance to scout the area around my van and assess any potential threats.

I see none.

A hundred yards away I begin to get tingles in my limbic brain again as my sixth sense does its thing.

Still there are no obvious threats. Whether there's another trap waiting to spring on me or not, I need to get my van and its contents away from here.

Fifty yards from the van, I breathe out a curse and a sigh in the same breath. I had known something was wrong, I just hadn't been able to identify it; I can now. The front driver's side tyre is flat.

It will be a nuisance to change it, but that's all it will be.

As I open the back of the van to get the spare wheel and jack I hear the whisper of tyres on slush get eclipsed by a roaring engine.

A car slides to a halt by the van as I turn ready to run.

'Freeze. Armed police.'

The yelled instructions come from the car and when I look there is a copper pointing a pistol at me from the back seat, while two others are leaping from the passenger side and aiming pistols my way.

I have two choices. Stay calm and tough it out, or run and hope for the best.

Running will prove guilt and destroy any chance I have of talking my way out of this. Staying calm and obeying their instructions at once and without hesitation will leave them having to prove my guilt.

The copper will have drowned by now. By the time anyone looks for her and finds her car where I left it, the river will have washed her away.

'Don't shoot.' I lift my hands high above my head. The burden of proof is theirs. With the copper washed away I predict I'll be back in London by this time tomorrow.

CHAPTER EIGHTY-THREE

Beth crossed her legs and tried not to feel worried. After everything else she'd gone through today, meeting Ethan's parents ought to be a walk in the park. However, she loved him and he loved her, therefore it was important she made the right impression. Back when she'd been in uniform, she'd attended countless houses where arguments between in-laws had developed into full-on fights. While she was sure Ethan's family, like her own, were better than the brawling drunks, she still didn't want there to be any animosity.

She'd had a crisis of confidence a half hour ago and had called a friend for advice on what to wear. The friend had calmed her down and then offered her take on things. It was advice Beth was now beginning to regret taking. The skirt she'd chosen to wear looked smart, but even though she had on her thickest tights, her legs and feet still felt as if they were encased in ice. Her nose felt the size of a balloon and while she'd got the full use of her limbs back, every part of her body was sore and tender whenever she moved, and there was also the agony of sitting on a broken coccyx. Four times she'd shampooed her hair before she was confident the last remnants of the river were washed out.

Ethan dropped a hand from the steering wheel and gripped the fingers Beth was drumming against her knee. 'Relax, they're excited to meet you.'

'That's nice.' A thought struck Beth. Ethan was full of enthusiasm for the things he cared about. Had he oversold her? 'You haven't made me out to be something I'm not, have you? Please tell me you haven't told them I'm some super copper who's on the fast-track and that I'll be chief constable by the time I'm thirty-five.'

'Not at all. I told them that you were a DC, but that you were likely to be sacked at any time when your bosses found out about all the different pieces of evidence you've planted, or the kilo of heroin you stole. When I was round earlier, Mum was hiding all the silver and locking her jewellery away.'

Beth gave Ethan's leg a gentle backhand. 'As a comedian, you have a long career as a paramedic ahead of you.'

Ethan was still laughing as he drew up outside a large house. There was a tree in the garden decorated with flashing lights and a wire-framed reindeer whose blue-white lights gave an ethereal touch to the evening air.

As they walked up the path, Ethan squeezed Beth's hand. 'Don't worry, they'll love you. It's you liking them that may be the problem.'

Even as she denied Ethan's claim, Beth understood the underlying truth to his words. It was one thing them liking her, but if she had to force herself to spend time in their company, it could only be a bad thing for their long-term relationship.

Ethan opened the door and walked into the house. When he was hanging up their coats, footsteps warned of someone approaching. It was both his parents.

Ethan's father looked to be a kindly man. Mid-fifties with a trim figure, he had a clipped goatee and the first traces of male pattern baldness.

But it was Ethan's mother who made Beth feel like turning and running for the door. She knew her. In fact, she'd faced her twice in interview rooms and once in court. Those three encounters were etched onto her memory as battles she'd lost.

Deborah Allison attacked police testimony the way a terrier savaged a rat. She'd shake until she got to a truth that suited her defence of a client. While a formidable opponent, she'd never

318
                    GRAHAM SMITH

resorted to the bullying or abusive tactics some of her colleagues employed. Her style was to tie people up in knots of their own making before tightening the noose of truth.

Beth guessed that as Ethan's surname was Fawcett, his mother must have retained her surname when she married.

'Oh, look at you, standing there all nonplussed.' Deborah gave Ethan a sideways glance. 'I told you she'd be surprised to meet me.' A hand grasped Beth's wrist. 'Don't you worry, my dear, I was just having a little fun by asking Ethan not to tell you I was his mother. For what it's worth, whenever I met you professionally, I always knew I'd have a tough fight on my hands.'

Beth wanted to throw a glare at Ethan, but now wasn't the time for angry looks.

CHAPTER EIGHTY-FOUR

Last night's meeting with Ethan's parents had left Beth's head a little thicker than she was comfortable with, but after the initial shock of meeting his mother, the evening had settled down into a friendly encounter filled with laughter and stories that made Ethan blush at the recounting of his childhood antics. Beth felt closer to him than ever and by the time she'd left his parents' house, she was confident that she'd enjoy a pleasant future relationship with them.

As for today, Beth was looking forward to entering the interview suite and seeing the Sculptor again. The moment when the woman looked at her and realised that Beth had survived her ordeal at the river was something she couldn't wait to witness.

After phoning O'Dowd, Beth had looked around the farmhouse's kitchen until she found a towel. She'd dried herself as much as she could and had stood beside the Aga to try and warm her body; her own shirt and jumper replaced with a cable-knit sweater that was folded over a chair.

O'Dowd had had Unthank trace the number Beth had called from and then collect her. Beth had left the farmhouse without seeing a soul, but she'd left a note for the farmer apologising for letting herself in the farmhouse and dripping all over the floor. She planned to return the borrowed sweater along with a good bottle of whisky for the farmer, but right now her every focus was on the interview with the Sculptor. Unthank had dropped her at home and waited while she changed into warm and dry clothes, then when she'd found the spare keys for her car at the back of a drawer, he'd taken her to collect it. O'Dowd had insisted that Beth was checked over by the police doctor and other than cuts and bruises and the broken coccyx, she had been given a clean bill of health. The doctor was amazed Beth had avoided hypothermia, but had credited it to a high metabolism and the fact that Beth had kept herself in constant motion, thereby generating body heat, until she got to the warmth of the farmhouse.

This first interview would be about establishing some basic facts and rattling the Sculptor. After that, subsequent interviews would hopefully break her, although Beth didn't fancy their chances of getting a confession from the woman.

She'd be too streetwise to confess; she'd leave it for them to prove her guilt. A plea bargain may be made if she wanted to lessen her sentence, but unless the Sculptor pointed the finger at enough gangsters to fill an entire prison wing, it was unlikely that she'd ever taste freedom again.

Beth would have preferred to be facing a solicitor less capable at their job than Ian Potter. He'd travelled up from London last night and everything about him spoke of a hotshot lawyer who pulled as many punches as a heavyweight champion.

O'Dowd led the way in, but Beth made sure she was on the DI's heel so she could fully gauge the Sculptor's reaction to her presence.

The door to the interview suite opened and the Sculptor sent a bored glance their way. It turned into a wide-eyed stare before the Sculptor recovered her poise and put an implacable expression on her face again. Her eyes didn't leave Beth once.

'You look surprised to see DC Young. I wonder why that is.' O'Dowd's barb didn't get a reaction from the Sculptor, but it did earn her a couple of tuts from Potter.

O'Dowd went through the formality of naming those present. The Sculptor's real name was Alex Brockett. Beth could feel herself smiling as she looked at the Sculptor. The aches and pains were all a thing of the past. Sure they hurt when her brain wasn't focussed, but right now, they were the last thing on Beth's mind.

To keep the pressure of her 'resurrection' on, it had been decreed that Beth should be the one to lead the first interview with O'Dowd picking up any points she missed.

'So, we meet again. Bet you weren't expecting to see me again, were you, Alex?' The use of a first name implied intimacy, but Beth knew it'd infuriate the woman on the other side of the table. 'I take it that you've realised how much trouble you're in. First off, there was an iPad in your van which the good folks at Digital Forensics are having a very thorough look at. By the way, see with that, you're kidding yourself if you think they can't track your web searches just because you used private browsing, so if you've been looking at our victim's email accounts, we are going to find that out. What do you think of that?'

'No comment.'

'Fair enough. I didn't expect you to say much. I have plenty to say though. First off I'll say that your van has been thoroughly searched and we have found a full set of masonry chisels.'

'That is hardly surprising, my client is a sculptor.'

'I know. She told me that when she was trying to kill me.'

Potter screwed his face in distaste, but Beth wasn't sure whether it was her dramatics or his client's crimes that were affecting him.

'A woman matching the description of your client was also seen in the same place where a pair of local men spent their last night on earth. Both men were fished out of Lake Ullswater the next morning with designs carved into their skulls. I feel it's only fair at this point to inform you that the search of your client's van also found two thick leather pads. These pads had designs drawn on them. And yes, before you ask, the designs match the ones carved into the two men's heads. They're being analysed for particles of skin from the two victims as we speak. Perhaps your client would like to comment on this development.'

Potter looked at his client.

'I found their bodies in a lane. Because I was bored, I thought I'd borrow their corpses and try my hand at something new. I was pleased with the way those designs worked out.'

Whether or not the Sculptor was lying about finding their bodies, the dispassionate way she was suggesting that she'd taken their corpses for her own amusement sent chilling spikes through Beth that were far colder than the river had been. 'The symbols. They have religious connotations. What was that about?'

A smile touched the corners of the Sculptor's mouth. 'You may think I was sending a cryptic message to someone. Then again, maybe I was just seeing what I could achieve. You know, testing my skill as a sculptor. You think you're oh-so-clever, you work it out.'

'Our final thing is that your client abducted me and tried to kill me yesterday. This happened where the person who assaulted Kevin and Owen Grantham was due to meet Kevin's ex-girlfriend, Michaela. During the course of the abduction, your client confessed everything while she planned to kill me. The confession may well be useless in a court of law as it's my word against hers. That quite frankly is irrelevant. We have enough evidence so far to charge her for the murders of the two men in Carlisle, and it's only a matter of time before we prove the other attacks were her doing as well. From our search of your client's van we already have a sheet of paper which has the same codes that Kevin, Owen and Michaela used to contact each other.' Beth put her elbows on the table and leaned forward in front of the Sculptor. 'Anything to say?'

'No comment.'

'I thought that might be the case. Just so you're aware, your client's fingerprints and DNA are being run through the system just now. Matches for them are popping up in all kinds of interesting places. We're liaising with a DI Monkton from the Met; he's rather keen to speak to your client when we're finished with her. Just now though, he's speaking to the people who were jailed based on the testimony given by Michaela Ingles, and Owen and Kevin Grantham. Can you just imagine how helpful it'd be to our case if he can find a link between your client and them? All it takes is one bank transfer, text or message. Oh, and for the record, Snapchat isn't as secure as people think it is. Digital Forensics can retrieve every message your client ever sent on Snapchat.'

All the time she was talking, Beth was looking at Alex. The woman's expression didn't change, it was dead to the world. She was bound to know that she'd spend the rest of her life in prison. That instead of the freedoms she'd previously enjoyed, her life would become regimented. There would be communal showers, set meal times, little exercise and crushing boredom. Yes, she might be tough enough to prosper in the jail, but unless she joined one of the gangs, she'd always be vulnerable. For someone who operated as a loner, being forced into the close proximity of dozens of other humans would become a purgatory. There was no secrecy in prison. No space for someone who didn't want to engage. Loners were singled out by the bullies as they made for easier targets. Maybe there wouldn't be a lot of physical attacks, as Alex could look after herself, but she'd be the butt of snide comments and tiny snubs until her temper or sanity broke.

'You do realise you're going to go down for a long time, don't you? That unless you start talking, and I mean *really* talking about all the people who've paid you to kill, then you're going to die in prison.'

'I'm going to die in prison, am I?' A shrug. 'Do you think you're scaring me? Do you think I'm worried about dying in prison? You suspect me of being a serial killer. A hitwoman for hire. Ask yourself these questions: If I am what you suspect me to be, do you think I fear prison or death? Does someone who kills for a living expect to live a long life, or do they expect that one day they'll become a target because they know too much, or they've killed the wrong person? You've got your evidence, compiled your case and I'm sure that by the time I go to court you'll have a watertight case against me. All I'll say is, in a few years' time, when you're lying awake beside a fat snoring husband, I'll be plotting on ways to get myself out, planning how I'll escape from prison. I'll be scheming on the different things I'll have to do to track you down, but most of all, I'll be dreaming pleasant dreams of how I'm going to sculpt your loved ones. The fat husband, any kids you have. Your parents if they're still alive. I'll do them all and then... then I'll come for you. You won't die. You'll scream and you'll beg and plead for death, but you won't die.'

'Interview suspended, five thirteen.' O'Dowd gave Potter an emphatic look. 'You need to have a word with your client; she's just made a direct threat to a police officer. She's going to go down for a long time. Be easier for all concerned if she cooperates, don't you think?'

'Bye bye, DC Young, sleep tight.'

Beth kept her head high as she walked out of the interview room. She refused to give Alex the satisfaction of getting a reaction. Threats were part and parcel of the job, and the worst thing you could do as a police officer was show a criminal that they'd got under your skin.

All the same, there had been a surety in the way Alex had described what would happen that unnerved Beth.

CHAPTER EIGHTY-FIVE

Beth clutched the envelope in her hand and looked at the house whose drive she'd parked in. There was only the merest hint at showing a festive spirit and even that was clad in the last slushy remains of the snow.

The man who answered the door was one she knew, but not one she recognised. Frank Thompson had only been off work a few days, but he'd let himself go to seed.

'What do you want?' His voice was whisky hoarse and there was a stench of despair about him.

'I came to give you this.' Beth handed over the large envelope and watched as Thompson opened it.

'An application form for the Cumbrian Run? What use is that to me?'

'I'm doing it. Thought I could raise some money for Alzheimer's Research UK. Thought you might like to raise a few quid too. There's three forms in there, in case your daughters want to join in as well.'

'I will.' A teenage girl who looked like Thompson pushed her way to where she could see Beth. 'Come on, Dad. Let's do it. Let's raise some money to help people… people like Mum.'

Thompson pointed to his bulging gut. 'Look at the shape of me. I'll never run a half marathon.'

'Dad!' Thompson received a violent shove on his shoulder. 'It's not about running the whole way. It's about remembering Mum and raising some money for a good cause.'

Beth saw Thompson looking at her. 'Do it, Frank, kick the booze, get yourself into a training routine and raise some money in memory of your Julie.'

Thompson's jaw tightened with resolve and when he gave a jolting nod the spark that had been missing from his eyes was flickering back to life.

The daughter mouthed 'thank you' at Beth as she closed the door.

*

With the pleasant part of her Sunday morning over with, Beth got back into her car and prepared to visit both Kevin and Owen Grantham. When they had recovered enough from their various surgeries to have a distressing conversation, they'd be told of the investigation into the attacks on them and the subsequent arrests.

It would be scant consolation to the men whose bodies were systematically broken, but perhaps they'd be able to find some comfort in knowing their attacker and the persons who'd hired her were being punished.

Once she was finished at the hospital, she planned to go and visit Richie. The business with Ethan still needed to be smoothed over, and there was the campaign against Dane Kenyon to consider.

The case had shown Beth that, however cold revenge was when served, it never brought about the right resolution. If she was going to punish Kenyon for his actions on the night she got bottled, she would have to find a punishment that befitted her status as an upholder of the law. Ethan's brand of vigilante justice was out, as was fitting up Kenyon in some way. However she brought him to justice, it would have to meet her own moral code.

A LETTER FROM GRAHAM

Thank you so much for choosing to join Beth and me for her third outing. I do hope that you enjoyed the story and that you'll want to keep yourself up to date with all my latest releases. If you do there's a link below and don't worry, your email address will never be shared and you can unsubscribe at any time.

www.bookouture.com/graham-smith

Now that you, the reader, have read the whole of this novel, I can explain my thought processes when I set out to write it. First on my list of things to achieve was that after writing *A Body in the Lakes* – in which there was a lot of violence against women – other than Beth, no female would be harmed in this novel. As for Beth, if she didn't want to get beaten up and left to drown in rising floodwaters, well, she shouldn't have been born in my mind.

The second point I wanted to do was show Beth's puzzle-solving skills. That's where the codes came in. They gave me a perfect vehicle to test Beth and because I made the codes up, it wasn't too complicated for me to set the puzzle and have Beth solve it.

My third goal with *Fear in the Lakes* was that I wanted to progress Beth's personal story by having her actually meet and speak with 'Neck Kisses'. While it may sound trite, his story only came to me when I was writing the scene where they had their 'date'. I loved the idea of having him as a bigger victim of circumstance than Beth, and hopefully it worked not just as a twist, but also an emotional driver to Beth's quest to get justice for the scar on her face.

As always, my final point was that I should write the best novel I possibly could and that it would entertain my readers, for without readers, I'm nothing but a stenographer for the voices in my head.

If you've loved *Fear in the Lakes* and are kind enough to leave a review, I'd be delighted to read it.

I love to hear from my readers and you can get in touch via my Facebook page, through Twitter, Goodreads or my website. We've even got some handy links below.

Thanks, Graham

grahamnsmithauthor

@grahamsmith1972

www.grahamsmithauthor.com

ACKNOWLEDGEMENTS

First thanks go, as always, to my family and friends for their continued support of me and my writing.

Next up is Isobel Akenhead who, as my editor, has shown incredible belief in me and has massively improved not just this book, but my writing in general with her insightful observations and perceptive suggestions. With their publicity and marketing skills, Kim and Noelle work wonders on a daily basis and their hard work is probably the reason that you, the reader, is reading this now.

Pastor Sandy Jamieson and Maggie Everett both deserve thanks for their patient answering of my questions. Any mistakes are my own, not theirs.

My team of beta readers are the first to read my manuscripts and their advice and notes have improved my stories and helped me polish manuscripts before submitting them. They're all stars who shine wisdom onto words.

The whole crime-writing community is a hugely supportive network and none more so than the Crime and Publishment gang. Each and every one of them has cajoled, listened and offered advice to me and their peers with a selflessness that belies a true generosity of spirit. The blogging community also deserve a special mention for their tireless work enthusing about my writing and that of a thousand other authors.

Last but by no means least, I'd like to thank my readers, without you, I'm nothing more than a stenographer for the voices in my head.